Forever Secret

Forever Bluegrass Series #5

Kathleen Brooks

Prologue

Nash Dagher moved silently through the night. His footfalls were unheard. His breathing was steady and soundless. The knife in his hand would ensure no sound was made as he took the life of his last target — a target he'd been tracking for over two years. With the slice of his knife, he'd finally be able to come out of the shadows.

For two years, Nash had been embedded within a group called Red Shadow. Unlike many gangs and mafias, they had no affiliation to a particular country. Membership was open to all who believed in the old traditional ways of crime — drugs, sex, extortion, and *dispute resolution*. Cyber crime was seen as weak. It was viewed as a coward's gang since it wasn't done face to face. Although beating people to death was approved of. The victims knew who was killing them and would die knowing Red Shadow was taking everything from them — their money, their art, their drugs, and even their women.

The king of Rahmi, the small island country close to the Persian Gulf that has been ruled by the Ali Rahman family for as long as history has been recorded, specifically assigned Nash to get to the bottom of missing Rahmi women and children and the flood of illegal drugs coming into the country. In return for successfully completing the mission, Nash would become Head of Security for the entire Rahmi royal family.

Only one person stood between Nash and the career of his dreams. The man who called himself Poseidon was asleep inside the Red Shadow compound, a floating compound filled with security guards. Poseidon used his massive yacht as his home base and to easily visit all the countries where he had groups of men working. Plus, it made for quick escapes. Nash was only on board now after two years of working his way up the ranks of the organization.

He'd purposefully put himself in the position to be recruited and had developed a fake background filled with murder for hire, blackmail, and prostitution rings to tip the scales in his favor. It had worked. He'd been brought into the organization after he'd been watched for two weeks. Nash had gone through a hazing period before he was initiated and swore his oath to the Red Shadow, and more specifically to Poseidon. For two years, he'd lived in hell. Nash would never be able to wash his soul clean from the killings he'd assisted with, the drugs he'd smuggled, the little children . . . He'd helped as many as he could, but he felt anguish for every death he couldn't prevent.

But the nightmare's end was finally in sight.

He'd proven his loyalty and now he was stationed on the yacht as personal protection for Poseidon himself. For five weeks he'd traveled with, ate with, listened to, and observed every step each person on the yacht made. Tonight his mission was to take out Poseidon. But he was going to do so much more. Red Shadow would be nonexistent by sunrise.

Nash paused in the kitchen and slipped silently into the pantry. He closed his eyes and listened as the patrol passed. Nash set the bomb by the flour before heading down the luxurious hallway, up the staff stairs, and pressing himself to the wall behind the stairwell door. He heard the soft footfall of the patrol. Nash made his move as soon as the patrol was out of the hallway. He set another bomb knowing he would be on camera. The whole yacht was under surveillance. But he knew from 2:00 to 2:10 in the morning, the person in charge of watching the cameras would sneak out for a smoke on the lower deck. All he needed was thirty more seconds, then nothing else would matter. Not Poseidon, not surveillance, none of it. As soon as Poseidon was dead, Nash would leap overboard and press the button blowing up the yacht. It would be a bit of a swim to shore, but his physical training would allow him to do it.

Nash had learned that Poseidon never locked his door. He was too arrogant to do so. He believed he was untouchable. He was about to learn he was wrong. Nash opened the door and entered the massive room as he soundlessly shut the door

hind him. Nash didn't need light to know where
he was. He'd been on the boat long enough and had
done enough patrols that he could make his way
blindfolded.

In the middle of the room was a king-sized bed
with Poseidon sound asleep nearest the wide
windows overlooking the French Riviera's coastline.
You would think that someone as evil as Poseidon
would look a certain way, but it wasn't the case.
Poseidon wasn't a typical mobster. He was
unassuming and ever so charismatic. In criminal
profiling, he resembled some of the serial killers and
cult leaders more so than gang leaders and
mobsters. And he certainly liked to be worshiped
like cult leaders did.

Nash stopped at the side of the bed and looked
down at Poseidon. His eyes were closed. His skinny
chest rose and fell rhythmically as he was propped
up on his plethora of pillows. Thousands of women
and children had been forced into slavery and worse
because of this man. He'd made billions from
murder, drugs, sex, and more. Yet he slept as
peacefully as a kindergarten teacher.

Nash pressed the blade to Poseidon's throat. At
the first teasing nick, Poseidon's brown eyes flew
open. "Shhh," Nash warned as he dug the blade in a
little further. Poseidon hissed but nodded his
understanding.

"I'm an agent of Rahmi. After tonight, you will
no longer be a threat to our women and children.
Drugs will be cut off in our communities since I now

know all your dealers. I want you to know that after tonight, Red Shadow will disappear just as you will, never to be seen or heard from again. Operatives are moving into position and taking down your network now. All over the world, at this time, your organization is being dismantled," Nash told Poseidon whose eyes widened.

"You were an agent?" Poseidon whispered with surprise. "You fooled us all. Bravo. I always knew someone would come for me in the night. So tell me, who are you?"

Nash thought about not answering, but in ten more seconds it wouldn't matter. "Nash Dagher of the Ali Rahman guard."

"You don't talk as if you've lived in Rahmi your whole life. That's what threw me," Poseidon puzzled.

"I was trained by Ahmed Mueez and Nabi Ulmalhamash Mosteghanemi in Keeneston, Kentucky," Nash said with pride. Ahmed was a legend and now Nash had lived up to his training.

Poseidon smirked and Nash made his final cut. The smirk fell from Poseidon's lips as he gasped for air and pulled Nash toward him. Poseidon's lips moved against Nash's ear as he whispered his final words. And in the seconds before Poseidon slipped into darkness and then death, Nash's whole world stopped.

Chapter One

N ash sat in the dark and took a sip of bourbon. It made him feel as if he were home. To be perfectly honest, he still didn't know where home was: Keeneston or Rahmi? One thing he knew, it had been twelve hours since he swam through the ocean and onto Pampelonne Beach along the French Riviera.

No one noticed the dark shadow of a man slipping onto the beach as people rushed toward the water to stare at the massive yacht engulfed in flames and sinking fast. He had thought to notify King Dirar of his actions, but the king would want him to return to Rahmi. Nash thought about notifying Ahmed, but he'd want him to return to Keeneston. And right now, there was something infinitely more important than receiving his next set of orders.

The door's lock slid open. As the door opened, the light from the hallway illuminated her. Nash smiled as she pulled a gun.

"Hello, Soph."

Nash slowly reached for the lamp next to his

chair. The soft light brought Sophie Davies into sight for the first time in two years. Nash clutched the crystal tumbler of bourbon to prevent himself from going to her.

"Nice gun. You make it?" Nash asked casually before taking a sip of the bourbon. He saw her face flush with anger and annoyance. Nash waited as Sophie decided whether or not to shoot him. Right now he figured it was a fifty-fifty chance. If she did shoot him, it would be deserved.

"I'm shooting a body part off in ten seconds. Your pick what you want to lose," Sophie said with steel in her voice.

"My toe?" Nash tried to say with a shrug.

"Something more valuable than a toe," Sophie smirked as she pulled the trigger.

There wasn't a sound. There was no indication the gun had fired except for the plume of stuffing that had exploded from the seat cushion one inch in front of his balls.

"I take it you're still mad at me for leaving," Nash said before taking another sip of bourbon.

"It's gotten better. If this had been six months ago, then you'd be a eunuch," Sophie smiled innocently.

Nash set the bourbon down and stood up. He dusted the white fuzz from the front of his jeans and held out his hand. He and Sophie had always been able to communicate without speaking. He was glad to see it hadn't changed. Sophie handed over the weapon. Nash examined it with a mixture of pride and awe.

"This is magnificent. Tell me about this gun that Sophie *Blake* is presenting at the conference tomorrow."

Sophie looked annoyed at having been found out, but she didn't ask how he had found that she went by her mother's maiden name professionally. "Pull the trigger," she ordered.

Nash held up the gun. It was so light and compact. He placed his finger on the trigger and aimed at the chair Sophie had already shot. He gently pulled his finger back and nothing. "Fingerprint protected," he muttered as he slowly examined it. "Is this a plastic?"

"Of a sort. It's what makes it so light. The gun also unlocks by voice command as a second backup. And I've designed a new bullet. They all work together to make the gun completely silent," Sophie explained as she took the gun back. "Now, what are you doing here, Nash?"

"I'm proud of you, Sophie," Nash said sincerely. He always had admired her for her brains and her body. It was difficult to resist such a combination.

Sophie tossed her heels on the floor in the direction of the bedroom and poured her own glass of bourbon as she waited for Nash to continue. It was going to be hard to explain, and Nash didn't know if Sophie would even listen to him. Not that he was going to give her a choice.

"I finished my mission for the king," Nash started to explain.

Sophie lifted her glass in a salute. "Hope it was worth it."

"It was. Sophie, I took down Red Shadow. I killed Poseidon not even one day ago," Nash told her, trying to hide the pain in his voice. Not pain for Poseidon or the organization, but pain for the victims he'd tried to help along the way and couldn't.

"That was you? The boat explosion? Seems so extravagant for you. I figured you'd just slit his throat."

Nash smirked into his glass. No matter how much they fought it, they knew each other better than any two people could. "I did that, too." The smirk left his face. "It's why I'm here. Have you heard of Ares?"

"Of course. He was Poseidon's apprentice before going out on his own and becoming Poseidon's main rival. He was tired of going old school and brought in hackers and corporate spies to use for extortion and theft. Our company has levels upon levels of security to get in and out of our labs to prevent spies from stealing any weapon plans for just that reason," Sophie explained.

"Poseidon was evil, but he lived by a code of honor," Nash told her. "He believed in facing your enemies. I woke him before I killed him so he knew who had brought him down."

Sophie snorted. "Sounds more like an ego trip."

Nash shrugged a shoulder. "That might have been part of it, but it was mostly revenge for all the things he'd done. I told him who I was, where I was from, and then I killed him. But Poseidon had one last mission for me. Poseidon whispered something to me before he died. He told me he'd learned Ares was after someone from Keeneston—a pretty weapons developer."

Nash watched as Sophie froze. "No one knows I'm from Keeneston. It's why I used my mother's maiden name."

"Well, Ares found out. You have something he wants, and he's coming for you," Nash warned.

Sophie tossed back her drink and set the glass on the table. "You've warned me. You can go now."

Nash shook his head. "Sorry, Sophie. You're not getting your way this time. I'm not leaving your side until Ares is caught."

Sophie snorted. "I can take care of myself. You know that better than anyone. I was the one who trained with you everyday."

"I know you can take care of yourself, but you shouldn't have to do it alone," Nash said, no longer hiding the anger in his voice. Old wounds he had thought had healed ripped open.

"You're the one who left," Sophie accused as two years of silence boiled over.

"You're the one who pushed me away," Nash shot back. He took a deep breath. "And I'm not going to let you push me away now. Not when your life is in danger. Now tell me, what do you know that Ares would want?"

KATHLEEN BROOKS

Sophie stared at Nash with a mix of emotions. Two
years and he hadn't picked up the phone. Two years
and he hadn't sent a note, an email, or even a
freaking carrier pigeon. And now he waltzes into
her life and tries to take over. Nope, not going to
happen. Swallowing her emotions with another shot
of bourbon, Sophie faced the one man who could get
under her armor.

"I'm not telling you anything. It's all classified.
You, more than anyone else, should understand
that. Now, get out." Sophie padded over to the door
and yanked it open. "And don't ever break into my
room again or it won't be the chair I shoot."

Sophie held her breath as Nash stood his
ground. He was a lot different now that they were
thirty-one years old. She had first met him when
they were both twenty-one. She remembered it
clearly. He had only been a couple inches taller than
her five-foot stature and had probably weighed less
than she did. Nash had made his appearance in
Keeneston at Nabi and Grace's wedding. She
remembered the moment she saw him. He had been
smiling. His eagerness to learn etched on every inch
of his face. When Nabi escorted his bride to the
dance floor, Nash had turned his deep brown eyes
her way, smiled, and dipped his head as a way to
say hello. Ever since that glance, Sophie had had a
thing for him.

Nabi headed up the Kentucky security for the
Rahmi royals, Prince and Princess Mo and Dani Ali
Rahman and their three children, Zain, Gabe, and

Ariana. Nabi had taken over for Ahmed when he retired from security work and went into the horse racing business with Mo. The King had sent Nash to begin his training with the idea to take over for Nabi once he retired.

With the help of the Rose sisters and the town's casseroles and cakes, Nash had put on weight while Nabi and Ahmed had turned it into muscle. He worked out constantly, both physically and mentally. He grew four inches over the next year and completely transformed. Every summer and every break from graduate school, Sophie had worked out with Nash. They ran together, they sparred together, they shot together . . . all the while talking about the world, politics, weapons, and the black market. It was their talks that gave Sophie the idea for her first weapon. She developed the idea and sold it to the Department of Defense.

During her last year of graduate school, a private company named BLC Technologies approached her. BLC Tech held a huge government contract for military defense, but they also offered her the ability to build her own weapons as long as they were presented to the government for a right of first refusal. That's why she was currently in London. The gun she had developed had been passed on by the military and she was presenting it at the conference along with the company's other new products. She knew exactly what Ares was after, and it wasn't her gun. It was something much, much bigger.

"Out," she repeated to Nash. It wasn't the first time he'd be walking out of her life. Two years ago — well, she wasn't going to think about that.

"Sophie, I thought that out of everyone, you would be the one person who could separate your private life from your professional one. You need security. Let me help, even if you aren't going to tell me what Ares is after," Nash said, and Sophie had a moment of doubt. There wasn't anyone better than Nash, even Ahmed had said so. But this time she couldn't. Not when being near him caused so much pain.

"No. You gave up having a say in my life when you left without an explanation. Goodbye, Nash," Sophie said stoically, all the while a hurricane of emotions raged inside.

Nash shook his head sadly. He stepped so close she could smell him. Memories flooded her mind as the hurricane battered her resolve. "Don't forget. I wasn't the only one who left." Nash leaned forward and Sophie held her breath. She felt his warm lips on her cheek. Her eyelids fell shut on their own accord. His kiss was soft and held the anguish she felt inside.

When Sophie opened her eyes, Nash was gone.

Chapter Two

Sophie stared at the ceiling of her hotel room. She didn't need to know what time it was. She'd been staring at the ceiling since the darkness of the night gave way to the first rays of sunlight. Damn Nash for wanting to play her knight in shining armor. There had been so many things she had wanted to tell him when she finally saw him again, but they had all slipped from her mind and now she was kicking herself for it.

The speeches she'd practiced alone in the shower were all for naught now that he'd come and gone again. Though, it was her fault. She'd forced him to leave and that was why she knew the sun had risen thirty-two minutes before. Sophie had made a mistake in telling him to leave. They had a past that needed to be cleared once and for all, and she blew her chance to have that happen.

Her alarm started beeping, and she heaved out an angry groan as she turned it off. She hadn't slept in over twenty-four hours and now she had a full day at the conference. It was not going to be a good day.

Sophie shoved off the covers, took a scalding hot shower, and applied so much concealer under her eyes that she made a mental note to go out and get more during the lunch break. She had business meetings all morning, a free lunch, then she presented her gun to a select group of clientele. After that, she had a dinner meeting a couple blocks away from the hotel. Then, finally, she might get a chance to sleep. She just hoped thoughts of Nash didn't keep her awake again.

The morning meeting went as well as Sophie could have hoped for. Her concealer, on the other hand, was not holding up so well. Grabbing an apple from the table at the convention center, Sophie hurried to the drugstore a block away and reapplied many coats of the makeup.

Looking at her watch, Sophie decided she didn't have enough time to make it back to the hotel for a quick nap. When her phone rang and her boss asked to meet, she was glad she hadn't headed back to the hotel as she had wanted. Instead she pulled up her big girl panties and headed back to the convention center — exhaustion be damned.

She had just walked in the door when she saw her boss, Sam McMillan, his secretary, Amy Woodly, and a few board members seated together in the lobby. A horde of people circled like vultures to try to get into their group. Some would be vying for jobs, some would be trying to sell their product, and some just wanted to network.

Sophie plastered on a smile as Sam hailed her over. "Ms. Blake, I want to introduce you to Ethan Storme, president of Storme Company."

Sophie shook hands with the handsome man in his early sixties. He reminded her a great deal of her father, Cade Davies, who was around the same age. Her father was former Special Forces. Even though he had moved back to Keeneston to coach high school football and teach biology didn't mean he left behind the Special Forces lifestyle. Needless to say, dating had been very hard for Sophie since her father intimidated all her prospects. Even her mother, Annie, like to clean her weapons when guys came to pick her up.

Ethan's hair had started to turn gray. It mixed with the black in a way that looked sexy. The appreciative way his blue eyes took her in would have done something for her if Sophie had a thing for older men. However, she could only think about Nash. And when she thought of Nash and looked at any other guy, there simply was no comparison.

Sophie held out her hand and the two shook. "It's nice to meet you, Mr. Storme. I've heard Storme Company has some great new products coming out. Another year on top of the gun manufacturing charts will surely follow."

Ethan didn't let go of her hand as he stepped closer. "And I hear you have something I want."

Sophie didn't pull her hand away. It was all par for the course of being a woman in a male-dominated field. However, it didn't mean she put up with it either. She just knew how to play the game. "Didn't your mother tell you that you can't always get what you want?"

Ethan dropped her hand and shoved his own into the pocket of his very expensive suit. "What I want is a chance to examine your new product before others get a chance."

"I announce in an hour. I'll be swarmed immediately. What's in it for me?" Sophie asked as she watched her boss freaking out behind Ethan's wide shoulders.

"If I like it, I'll raise the highest offer by ten percent on the spot to bring it into Storme Company production."

"Raise it twenty percent, I keep my patent rights, and I get a five percent royalty on every one sold," Sophie demanded.

"And why should I do that?" Ethan countered.

"Because my product is that good. It has technology that makes it safer, quicker, and quieter. No more worries of a child accidently shooting someone, or of smart technology taking too long to work. It's so good that it'll be wanted by everyone from housewives to police officers, and that's worth every cent," Sophie said with the confidence the product deserved.

"Okay, but only if I like it. Meet me at the range the conference has reserved at ten tonight. I have a dinner that I have to attend first. Bring your offers." There went Sophie's plan to get to bed early, but she'd take it for a deal like this. Her job at BLC was salaried. However, if she developed new weapons that sold privately like this might, she and BLC split the proceeds fifty-fifty. This deal would make her enough money to retire if she wanted.

Sophie smiled and shook Ethan's hand. Tonight her whole life would change.

Sophie stood behind Ethan with her arms crossed over her chest and a smile on her face. The way Ethan had fired the gun and then look surprised told her all she needed to know. She could wrap up her top-secret project and move back to Keeneston forever. No more traveling the world. No more lying to her friends and family about where she was. No more being in the lab and having no idea how many days had passed. The feeling was almost overwhelming. Sophie had the chance to start over completely with the freedom of doing whatever made her happy. Maybe she'd teach science at the high school. She could start her own lab like her cousin Piper did. She could paint, write a book, join the sheriff's department, get married, start a family, have a full conversation with someone, and not have to lie about what she did for a living.

"Ms. Blake, you have a deal," Ethan said as he pulled the clip from the gun and handed it back to her.

Pride filled Sophie as she set the gun onto the table and reached into her bag. "Then here's my contract. Have your attorney look it over. You have forty-eight hours until it goes up on the open market. But for the record, I'm glad it's you who bought it."

Ethan grinned and his eyes roamed downward. "How about a nightcap to celebrate?'

"I never mix business and pleasure. And it would be entirely too pleasurable to be business," Sophie winked. She had no trouble stroking his ego now. He had just fulfilled all her dreams.

Ethan chuckled with appreciation. "Fine. I have to get my attorneys on this anyway. I want this deal locked up by morning. Do you need a lift back to your hotel?"

Sophie shook her head. "That's all right. It's not far, and it's a nice night. I'm going to put this away and head out soon."

Ethan held her eyes. "It's been a real pleasure doing business. Goodnight, Ms. Blake."

"Goodnight, Mr. Storme."

Sophie watched as Ethan slid the contract into his briefcase and left the underground shooting range. Sophie quickly and efficiently cleaned the gun just the way her mother had taught her. She connected it to her laptop and wiped the memory clean of Ethan's biometrics before putting hers back on it using the administrator's software she helped develop.

Sophie looked at her watch. It was 11:00 at night in London, but her internal clock was still on Keeneston time. Excitement filled her. As soon as she finalized the plans on her top-secret work and handed over the project to the government, she would be going home to Keeneston. She pulled out her phone. She couldn't tell anyone yet, but she wanted a feel of home.

Sophie slid the gun into the holster at her hip and buttoned her suit jacket over it as the phone rang on the other end. She grabbed her coat and put it on while holding the phone to her ear.

"Sophie! Is everything okay?"

Sophie smiled as she headed out of the shooting range. "Hi, Mom. Everything's great. I just thought I would call to see what I missed after I left the wedding reception."

Annie Blake Davies was an unconventional mother. Raised on self-defense, girl power, and able to identify every kind of gun made, Sophie had an amazing upbringing that inspired her career in weapon development. Her parents had met when Annie was an undercover DEA agent. After they fell in love, her mom quit the DEA and became a sheriff's deputy in Keeneston.

Her mother snorted in disbelief but knew better than to ask. "Riley and Matt are so perfect together," she said of Sophie's cousin and the soon-to-be new sheriff of Keeneston. "The wedding reception went well into the early morning. The Rose sisters spiked the punch. I swear, they're almost a hundred, and they still pull that juvenile act. Poor Pam Gilbert didn't realize it and your Aunt Morgan had to pull her sister off a tabletop. Pam was trying to unbutton her dress as she was dancing. And your brothers . . ."

Sophie laughed as she walked down the sidewalk along one side of Hyde Park, heading toward her hotel. Her two much younger brothers, twenty-two-year-old Colton and twenty-one-year-old Landon, were a bit wild. Okay, that was a huge understatement. They were the scourges of Keeneston.

"Well, they got into the punch and —"

Sophie didn't hear anything else. Tires slid on the road as someone slammed on the brakes. A sprint van jumped the curb in front of her, the side door opening as men appeared and reached for her. Sophie let out a scream and took off running into the park. Panic coursed through her as three men leapt out of the van. She heard the tires squealing as the van was thrown into reverse.

"SOPHIE!" her mother yelled with fear only a mother could have for her child.

"I'm passing the Achilles statue in Hyde Park!" Sophie yelled as she kicked off her heels and sprinted past the large statue while clinging to her phone. If she knew her mom, backup would be dropping in at any moment.

Sophie was a quarter of a mile from the hotel. She ran regularly, and now without her heels on, she knew she could make it. The dangerous part was having to cross Park Lane without the sprint van seeing her. She hoped that by heading toward the 7 July Memorial, the driver wouldn't be able to see her through the row of trees. That plan was also dependent on the men chasing her not catching her.

Sophie knew better, but she looked over her shoulder anyway and stumbled slightly. The men were closer than she thought. Two were clearly in shape and closing ground. The third one was behind them but not falling out of sight.

She needed her gun. Sophie could hear her mother yelling but couldn't make out the words as she shoved the phone into her coat pocket. She was reaching for her gun when the first man's hand fisted into the back of her coat. Sophie's scream was cut short as she was yanked onto the ground. She exhaled before hitting the ground so she wouldn't have the wind knocked out of her.

The ground came fast and hard as her back slammed into the walking path. The man who had taken her down stopped running and stood over her. Sophie could hear the second man slow behind her. She didn't make a move. Her coat still hid her gun and she could take the two men if the circumstances were right.

"Sophie! What's happening? The police are on their way. Remember everything your father and I taught you!" her mother screamed through the phone in her pocket.

The man who took her down smiled and held out his hand. "Hand it over," he said in an Irish accent.

Sophie held up one hand slowly and indicated she was going to reach into her pocket. She kept her eyes on the man in front of her. He was clearly the one in charge. She heard the man behind her relaying their location to someone else, likely a person in the van. The man in front of her was about five feet ten inches and lean. He was muscular, but not overly so. He would be hard to take down. He appeared to be quick and strong.

She heard the third man approach. He was breathing heavily. He'd be easy to take down. She didn't know about the man behind her. Sophie slowly moved her hand toward the phone in her pocket. She reached in, pulled it out, and held it out. Her mother was still screaming.

The man put the phone to his ear. "I'm sorry, Sophie will have to call you back," he said menacingly.

The threats that came from her mother had him arching an eyebrow before he turned off the phone, put it on the ground, and smashed it with his heel. "Interesting person you were talking to. Now, I need you to come with me."

Sophie took a deep breath. If she got into the van, she'd be dead. The man held out his hand for her and she knew she had her chance. She gently placed her hand in his before grabbing tightly and yanking him down with all her strength. He lost his balance, and as he fell toward her, she rammed the top of her head into his chin. It wasn't the perfect head-butt and it hurt like the devil, but it worked. The man was out cold.

Too bad for her, the other men were already reacting. Her arms were wrenched up from behind as each man took a side. She struggled to get to her gun, but the overly muscled bigger man had her arm on that side, and he wasn't letting go.

She fought and screamed like a madwoman as they dragged her through the tree line and out onto Park Lane. The sprint van was waiting for them. The driver was shouting out of the open window for them to hurry. Sophie dug her feet into the pavement, feeling the bumpy road cutting the soles of her feet as the men dragged her to the van. When the door opened, she was lifted with her feet suddenly finding nothing but air before she was thrown inside. She landed hard on the industrial-carpeted floor of the van. The tough carpet scraped the skin of her knees raw. Whatever happened next, she knew she wasn't going down without a fight.

Chapter Three

Nash saw her being taken. He had been keeping his distance and now he cursed himself for staying so far away. However, he knew Sophie would have spotted him if he were any closer, and she may have shot him. And she probably wouldn't have missed this time.

In that one moment, he was more scared than he'd been during all his years undercover with Red Shadow. Nash sprinted after them, eating up the ground he had to cover in order to get to her. He saw Sophie being dragged toward the street, and he fought the urge to reveal himself by screaming for them not to touch her. Surprise was in his favor, therefore he kept quiet so they wouldn't know he was coming. The man she had head-butted was stirring as Nash ran by. A quick kick to the head sent him sprawling back into unconsciousness while Nash broke through the trees and out onto the street.

A white sprint van sat half on the curb as the driver yelled at his cohorts to hurry. Nash didn't slow as Sophie was sent sprawling into the van. The two men leapt in behind her as the driver put the van into gear. The driver was on the opposite side of the car so Nash couldn't get a clear shot off with his gun.

It didn't matter anyway because when the van started to move, Nash shoved his gun into his waistband and jumped.

He landed hard against the passenger side door. The driver jerked the wheel hard in surprise, then started speeding up and swerving in an attempt to dislodge Nash as he hung onto the small lip above the door with his fingertips.

Nash heard a bellow from the back as Sophie fought her abductors. It was two against one and he needed to get to her fast. Dangling by one hand, Nash reached for his gun. His fingers burned and his shoulder stretched to the limit as he found it.

There was no sound. No warning. Nothing except the blood and brain smattered against the windshield to let Nash know Sophie had gotten to her gun as well. With the driver dead, the van jerked hard. Nash fired his gun into the window as a big man from the back leapt forward to take the wheel.

The passenger window shattered and the van sideswiped a truck on the driver's side, causing Nash to slam against the door and knocking his gun to the pavement. The big man stood grabbing the wheel as he tried to free the gas pedal from the dead driver's foot. Nash took the opportunity to pull himself up, planted his feet on the door as if he were rappelling, and pushed off. His fingers trembled with the force he used to hold onto the lip above the door as his body flew out into the street. He moved his legs into a pike position mid-air and when he swung back toward the van, his legs shot through the window. Nash let go of the van's exterior as his body slid sideways over the passenger seat.

"Nash!" Sophie screamed, although Nash couldn't tell if her voice rang with relief or annoyance.

He shot a look behind him at Sophie and couldn't help but smile. Sophie had her abductor lying on his stomach as she straddled his back. Her arm was wrapped around his throat in a firm chokehold. The man's eyes bugged and then closed, his body going limp.

The large man trying to drive looked back and saw he was outnumbered with his fallen compatriot now unconscious. He jammed his foot on the dead driver's foot, causing the van to speed up. Sophie rolled backward and slammed into the back of the van as Nash launched himself at the driver.

"Found it!" Sophie said cheerfully from the back. "Nash, get out of the way. I'll just shoot him."

The big man cranked the wheel hard to the right. The van crossed a lane and headed right for a row of trees.

"Get down, Soph!" Nash yelled a moment before the van hit a tree at full speed.

Nash felt every millisecond in that moment. For once, Sophie hadn't questioned him. She'd dropped to the van floor instantly. He never took his eyes off her. He reached for her, but he was already flying back through the windshield. He felt each piece of glass shattering as his back smashed through it. He saw her body being tossed like a rag doll. Nash's arms were still reaching for her when he soared over the hood and landed hard on the dirt.

"Sophie," he groaned, unable to move. He battled to fill his lungs with air. He was sure he was injured, but adrenaline hid everything except having the breath knocked out of him.

The big man had also gone through the windshield, except he went headfirst and straight into a tree. There was no movement coming from the van. The first pedestrian reached him. "Help me," Nash ordered a man frantically calling 9-9-9 for emergency services.

"Just stay down, mate," the man said before turning to talk into his cell phone.

Nash struggled to his feet. He swayed slightly as he gulped in air. The man didn't see Nash staggering toward the side of the van as he checked the pulse of the man who took a header into the tree. Nash could have told him the guy was dead. Other bystanders rushed forward. Sirens sounded in the distance as Nash pulled open the door.

"Are you injured?" someone asked.

Nash shook his head. "I wasn't involved. I just arrived," Nash told her, already trying to get out of the crowd. What he really wanted was to be alone with the guy Sophie had choked unconscious to question him, but that wasn't going to happen. All he could focus on now was getting Sophie out of here. They were one hundred yards or less from her hotel. He needed to get her out of the crowd and to her hotel before people started asking questions.

Nash climbed inside as bystanders gathered around. He put his fingers on Sophie's neck and was rewarded with a pulse. She'd hit her head and would have a concussion, but she was alive. Looking around, he saw that the other abductor was in a similar state. Nash turned to the group of people standing at the open side door.

"Can someone open the back doors and will the rest of you clear a space for emergency vehicles?" Nash asked. He knew he was bleeding from numerous scrapes. But he was going to play this concerned citizen routine if it killed him.

The people scrambled to do his bidding, happy to feel useful. Nash reached across Sophie and plucked a phone and wallet from the unconscious man. He shoved the items into the back pocket of his jeans before quickly searching for Sophie's gun. He found it under the front seat just as someone opened the back door. He put the gun in his waistband and pulled his shirt over it.

"Come on, sweetheart. We need to go," Nash whispered as he made a move to pick Sophie up. He hunched as he carried her out the back door.

"What are you doing? Shouldn't you wait for help?" a woman asked as she stepped back, giving Nash room to exit the van.

"I'm a doctor. This woman needs air," Nash said, the lie falling easily from his lips. "Go check the other man," Nash ordered. His authoritative tone sent her scrambling into the van. Nash didn't look back at the growing crowd as he strode away carrying Sophie.

"How is she?" Sophie heard Nash ask. She wanted to answer, but it took too much effort. She forced herself to open her eyes, though. It felt as if she were battling the weight of the world just to be able to blink them open.

A short, thin man with a bald patch on the back of his head stood blocking her view of Nash. He had a black bag with him and was setting a bottle of pills on the table next to the bed she was lying in.

"As you suspected, I believe she has a concussion. She's going to be very sore, as are you. Here's some medicine—" The doctor must have detected a change in her breathing as he suddenly turned to look at her. "Ah, Ms. Davies, welcome back."

Nash was by her side a second later. He knelt beside the bed and took her hand in his. "How are you feeling?"

Seeing the worry on his face made her want to cry. She had almost shot his balls off, and he'd still come for her. She could have saved herself eventually. But he'd come, even when she'd told him not to.

"Everything hurts. How did I get here?"

The doctor put on his stethoscope and shushed

them both. When he pulled the stethoscope from his ears and smiled down at her, Nash took that as his cue to begin talking again. "This is Dr. Famir. He's from the Rahmi consulate."

"Thanks for coming, Doctor. How am I?" Sophie asked.

"Nothing broken, just an ugly bump to the head. I want to do a neurological exam. If everything checks out, I can release you into Nash's care. You're going to be on bed rest for a couple days. I don't want you overdoing it."

As Dr. Famir turned to set his bag on the table and pull out his equipment, Nash kept her hand in his. His thumb slowly stroked her knuckles before bringing her hand to his lips and placing a soft kiss on the inside of her wrist. "When I saw you taken, Sophie . . ." Nash paused to place another kiss on her wrist. "We need to talk about us."

"Talk!" Sophie gasped as she tried to sit up too fast. Her head swam as Nash slowly lowered her back onto her pillows.

"Ms. Davies, please, you need to stay calm," Dr. Famir chastised.

"Nash, you have to do something for me," Sophie begged.

"Anything, sweetheart," Nash said instantly.

"I need you to call my mother."

Sophie saw Nash's eyebrow rise. "Okay, that wasn't what I was expecting. Kill someone? Yes. Call your mom? No."

"I was talking to her when I was attacked. She

heard the whole thing. She and my dad are probably going out of their minds," Sophie told him as she felt her own heart start to beat harder as she began to worry.

Nash leaned forward and kissed her on her forehead. "I'll do it right now. Is there anything else?"

"I don't suppose you want to break into the police station and steal my gun back out of evidence? I remember it flying out of my hand." Sophie closed her eyes and took a deep breath. That gun was worth her whole future. If someone found it before she turned it over to Ethan Storme, she might lose the contract.

"Don't you have any faith in me?" Nash asked with a trace of amusement to his voice.

Sophie opened her eyes to see him smiling down at her. "That's a loaded question." His smile slipped a little and Sophie wanted to kick herself.

"Your gun is in the room's safe. And before you ask, I've already moved all your things from your room, checked you out, and brought them here to my room. Gun included."

Crap. Now she felt like she needed to cry again. Sophie bit the inside of her lip. She was too stubborn to cry.

"Let's begin our exam, shall we?" Dr. Famir asked, defusing the situation.

Sophie nodded and watched Nash walk out of the bedroom of the suite and into the living room, shutting the door behind him.

Chapter Four

N ash had the curtains closed. He turned on the lights before pouring a drink. He tossed it back and pulled out his phone. Taking a deep breath, he dialed a number he'd committed to memory.

The phone was answered before the first ring was complete.

"Talk!" Annie Davies barked into the phone. It made Nash smile. So many men feared the father of the woman they were dating, but not Nash. He feared her mother. Not that he and Sophie were actually dating.

"Annie, it's Nash. Sophie is safe," he said quickly yet clearly. He heard a quick sob and then heard her tell her husband, Cade. There was a brief struggle over the phone before Annie and Cade agreed to put it on speaker.

"What's her status?" Cade asked in the typical, get-to-the-chase military way of his younger days.

"She's being examined by a doctor now. She hit her head during a kidnapping attempt but she's conscious now. As long as surgery isn't needed, she'll only need bed rest and protection," Nash told them.

"Where are you?" Annie asked, slightly calmer.

"In London at The Dorchester," Nash answered.

"How are you there? We haven't heard from you for two years and you're suddenly in the right place at the right time. Are you somehow involved in this?" Cade asked coldly. Okay, maybe if he'd ever dated Sophie, it would be *both* parents he needed to worry about.

"I was finishing a mission and learned Sophie was the target of a kidnapping by a very evil man. I came straight here to look out for her." Nash gulped at the silence on the other end of the line.

Cade cleared his throat a second later. "Well, I'm glad you were there. Now, bring my baby girl home."

"Yes, sir. I need to make a couple calls, though. No one can know we're heading back to Keeneston. I think the kidnappers who are now dead or caught are working for an organization. The leader of that organization already knows Sophie is from Keeneston. I'd like to buy us a couple of days for her to recover," Nash said.

"So, it's not over?" Annie asked.

"No, ma'am, it's not."

"What has our girl gotten involved in?" Cade wondered.

"I'm sorry, but she won't tell me," Nash said as his lips thinned in anger. If only she would trust him—but that had always been the problem.

"She'll damn well tell me," Annie said with

determination. "And whoever is after her has no idea what a pissed-off mother is capable of."

"Ares. His name is Ares. And I'm afraid he's all the things you try never to think about," Nash warned.

"I'll start gathering info. I'll call everyone and have a dossier ready by the time you get here," Cade told him.

Everyone wasn't your normal everyone. First there was Nabi, a computer expert and head of the Rahmi royal family's security. Cade was also a whiz with computers. Ahmed would be notified, and he'd scare the crap out of every informant he had across the globe to get information. Then there's political info from Mo, the Prince of Rahmi, Ryan Parker with the FBI, and Kale, who was finishing up his last year at MIT, would be brought in to hack whatever people wouldn't share. Kale put Nabi and Cade to shame with his computer skills.

It was what Nash had loved the most about Keeneston — the people. Even the ones who weren't in law enforcement were always there for you to shoot someone, to throw a pan at them, or to *thwack* them with a broom. They looked out for each other. While he wanted to drag Sophie to some isolated place in the Andes Mountains and hide her away, he knew that it was time to go back home.

"Have Mo send the plane. I need two people on it who match our description so we can trade places with them and have them walk around London for a little while so our return to Keeneston can't be confirmed. We can't draw any attention to ourselves," Nash instructed.

"Done," Annie and Cade said together.

Sophie lay in bed, trying to pay attention to the doctor, all the while trying to listen to Nash. Unfortunately he kept the conversations private and it was pissing her off. Why did he go into the other room? Sophie blinked for the doctor. Dammit. They did need to talk or they'd never be able to move on. She had felt as if the past two years had been nothing but her trying to forget when all it did was force her to remember.

"Well, you look as good as can be expected. Since you're talking and your eyes aren't dilated, there's only one more thing I need to see before I clear you," the doctor said, interrupting her thoughts.

"Yes?" Sophie asked.

"I just need you to get up and walk to the bathroom and back." Sophie got out of bed and walked across the room and back. "Good, good. The best thing is rest. Concussions are strange things we are still studying. Many doctors thought you shouldn't sleep. As long as you pass the neurological tests, sleep is fine. I find it helps in most cases. You may get a headache with stimulation such as television or working on your phone. For the next couple of days, I just want you to rest. No stimulation of any kind and then start reintroducing things to see what you can tolerate."

"Got it, thank you," Sophie said absently as she watched the bedroom door quietly open.

Nash stood with his arms across his chest watching the doctor pack his bag and say his goodbyes. As soon as he was gone, Sophie held out her hand. "Can I talk to my parents?"

Nash shook his head. "They're busy right now, getting everything set up for us to leave."

"Leave? What are you talking about?" Sophie asked.

"Mo's plane will be here in eight hours. We're going home, Sophie."

Sophie shook her head and winced. "Stop ordering me around. I have the biggest deal of my life to close tomorrow, and I'm not leaving until I do. And when I do leave, I need to go back to my lab, not to Keeneston."

Nash let out an annoyed breath and Sophie could see a muscle in his jaw start to twitch. "Ares is after you. As much as I would love to stick you in some remote location until I take him out, I know you won't stay there. Stop trying to control the situation and listen to me on this. I'm trying to keep you alive. Keeneston is the safest place for you. Now tell me about this deal and how I can close it for you so we can get you home."

Sophie closed her eyes. The past is the past. The future is now. She needed to get over what happened and trust again. "Ethan Storme is reviewing the contract to purchase the gun I developed—the one you saw. If he signs it, I can go back to Keeneston after I finish my final project for BLC Technologies. After that project, I can do whatever I want for the rest of my life: teach at the high school, farm, open a shop—anything."

"And this last project that you have to finish is why Ares wants to get you?" Nash asked as he took a seat next to her on the bed.

"Yes, but that's all I can say," Sophie told him sternly. She couldn't handle him pushing her right now. "Ethan has the contract and will be getting together with me in the morning to hash out the details. I can't leave until then."

Sophie watched as Nash thought about the situation. He didn't say anything at first. She could see him working through everything she had told him. Then he turned back to her. "Fine. But I'm not leaving your side. The negotiations are to take place at a secret location."

Sophie nodded. "It was after the meeting with him that I was attacked. They either followed me or they knew where I was going to be."

"What you're saying is that Ethan could either have a leak in his organization or he's working with Ares?"

"I don't think he is working with Ares, but I can't risk it. Let's just say what I'm working on is a game changer for the country or person with the technology."

Sophie felt Nash take her hand in his and she automatically leaned toward him before catching herself. "I'll take care of it," he said. "You just rest. I saw a phone near an unconscious man in the park. I take it that was yours?"

"Yes."

"I'll call Ethan and tell him you dropped your phone and he can contact me when he's ready. I'll stress the deadline as well."

Sophie stared at Nash and shook her head. "You can't just call up Ethan Storme and expect to get through."

"Sure I can. You're not the only one who knows people, Soph. Now, get some rest. We'll talk more in the morning."

Nash got up to leave and Sophie grabbed his hand. She couldn't explain it but the thought of him leaving her alone felt wrong. She swallowed hard. "You're not leaving, are you?"

Nash's face softened. He leaned over and placed a lingering kiss on her forehead. "No, love. I'm just going to make my calls in the other room so you can sleep. But I can stay if you want."

Sophie hated this. She hated feeling like a victim, and right now that's how she was feeling. In that one instance, when she realized he was going to walk out of the room and leave her alone, she knew she was scared. "Stay," she said softly, admitting defeat.

Nash only smiled gently and lifted the comforter to tuck her in. Sophie snuggled into the pillow and drifted off to sleep to the sound of Nash talking on the phone.

Chapter Five

Nash didn't like Ethan Storme. He had reached an agreement with the man during the early morning hours that consisted of him picking Ethan and his attorney up at eleven in the morning. Nash was driving and was the only one who knew where they were going. Ethan had wanted the deal bad enough to agree.

And now they sat at a pub table tucked away down an alley in Covent Gardens. The dark bar provided Sophie the relief from the light she needed to avoid a headache and the privacy to conclude the deal. Ethan had looked surprised when Nash had led them to the small pub. But it seemed like a good plan, considering the way the beer and negotiations flowed. The only thing irritating Nash was the way Ethan was blatantly hitting on Sophie. He touched her as much as he could. He leaned in close, pretending he couldn't hear her when she talked — perhaps not too much of a stretch since he was old enough to be her father. It didn't stop the old man from sending Nash a smirk that let him know Ethan didn't give a shit if Nash was aware of his intentions or not.

Nash sat across from them and next to the basically useless attorney. Ethan had a pen in hand and the contract in front of him, but he wasn't signing. Nash looked at his watch. The plane from Keeneston would arrive soon.

Nash stood up, the heavy wooden chair scraping against the old wood-paneled floor. "I'm sorry, Miss Blake. It's time for your next appointment."

"You're leaving me?" Ethan asked as he ran a finger over Sophie's hand.

"Yes. I told you it was a limited-time offer. I already have other buyers lined up and ready to sign," Sophie said sweetly.

Nash hid his smile as he saw Ethan's finger freeze on Sophie's hand. "Other buyers?"

"As we discussed, we needed a signed contract by noon. Well, it's 12:01."

Ethan yanked his hand from Sophie's and signed the contract. "There, now you can cancel the rest of your day."

Sophie signed the contract and handed it over to the attorney who also signed as a witness. "I'm sorry, but I have to get this over to Mr. McMillan. I look forward to working with you, Mr. Storme."

Sophie put the contract in her bag and stood up to shake Ethan's hand. He leaned in for a kiss and Nash jostled past him. "Oh, sorry, old man. I just needed to get the car for Miss Blake. Your driver will be notified of your location and should be here shortly." Nash tossed a couple pounds on the table. "Next drink is on me."

Nash smoothly cut between Ethan and Sophie, placed his hand on the small of Sophie's back, and led her out of the pub.

"That was rather rude," Sophie muttered.

"The man is a lecher," Nash defended as he moved to open the car door for Sophie.

"I know. I was talking about Ethan. I would have kicked him in the balls if that deal wasn't worth my whole future."

They sat in silence as they drove to Luton Airport. Nash had Sophie duck down as they drove past cameras and into a private hangar. The doors were shut and finally Sophie felt as if they were getting closer to home.

Five minutes later, the side door to the hangar opened and two people stepped through. Sophie recognized the man instantly as Gabe Ali Rahman, Prince of Rahmi. The second person wore big sunglasses concealing her face, but Sophie knew that lip quirk anywhere. "Piper!" Sophie called out happily as her cousin hurried toward her.

Piper was dressed in her normal outfit of T-shirt, jeans, and sneakers. Piper's parents were Tammy and Pierce Davies. Pierce's science background had rubbed off on Piper, who was now heading her own lab, researching viruses and nanotechnology, along with being one of the founding scientists of the Rahmi International Nanotechnology Lab.

"What is going on?" Piper asked as Gabe wrapped Nash in a tight hug before turning to give Sophie a hug.

"I can't tell you. I'm sorry," Sophie winced. Her friends and family had heard her say this too many times to count. "But it's big, and my life is in danger. So thank you for coming for me."

"I'd do anything for my cousin, you know that. Now come on. I have some temporary hair dye for us, and we need to swap clothes," Piper told her as she pulled her into the bathroom, leaving the hangar for the guys.

The second the door was closed Piper's friendly smile turned devious. "I know you won't tell me about work, but tell me about Nash. Have you two done it yet?"

Sophie's mouth fell open and she smacked Piper's arm. "Piper!"

"It's not as if it hasn't been coming. I mean, you two have issues and sometimes a good roll in the hay — or three — can work things out. And it isn't as if the entire town doesn't already think you two did it. At least, that's the leading bet on why you were so mad when Nash left. The loss of great sex can cause a woman a little anger," Piper said with way too much pleasure as she pulled out a box of dye from her bag.

"That's what everyone has been saying?" Sophie asked in horror.

"Well, when you try to hit on the town's priest, people will wonder what drove you to it. Now, bend over the sink." Piper shoved an outraged and embarrassed Sophie over the sink and stuffed paper towels around her neck.

"Do you know what you're doing?" Sophie asked as Piper slipped on a pair of latex gloves and got to work mixing the dye.

"I have a Ph.D. in nanotechnology. How hard can it be? It's just temporary. Now tell me about you and Nash. Aunt Annie said he rescued you?"

Sophie let out a long breath and told her cousin about Nash showing up in her hotel and rescuing her, and the deal she'd just signed. She never mentioned Ares or what he was after.

Piper sighed as she pulled off her gloves. "That's so romantic. I'm locked in a lab all day. Nothing like that happens to me."

"It's not romantic. Nash was just helping out."

Piper pulled Sophie over to the wall-mounted hand dryer and shoved her head under it before moving to dye her own hair. "Helping out is picking someone up at the airport, not flying across Europe to save them. And I think you're being too hard on Nash. He obviously loves you and you love him. Are you ready to tell me what you did to send him running?"

"Me?" Sophie yelled under the dryer. "Why do you think I did something?"

"Oh, it may have been accidental, but I've always thought you said or did something rash that sent him accepting whatever assignment it was. You're one of the smartest people I know. But bless your heart, you are clueless when it comes to men."

"I am not!" Sophie almost hit her head on the dryer but Piper shoved her down again as the hot air blew on her before Piper finished her own hair.

"I won't mention the whole priest incident again, so let's talk about Nate. Or Bryan. Oh, and let's not forget the disaster that was Ian."

Sophie cringed. "They weren't Mr. Right," she tried to defend.

"Admit it, Soph. You're not good at compromise. You have the finesse of a bulldozer."

Sophie nibbled her lip as her hair flapped around her. Piper joined her at the next dryer where she and Sophie stayed silent until their color was set. In the mirror, her golden hair was gone and replaced with a dirty blonde and one dark streak. Piper's hair had been turned golden except for . . . was that green?

Piper shrugged. "So, dyeing hair is not as easy as it looks," she admitted. "At least it comes out in three shampoos."

The cousins were close to the same height, had the same Davies hazel eyes, and the same tendency to bite their lip. Sophie was older by three years, but when Piper pulled Sophie's hair back into a sloppy ponytail, they looked as if they could be sisters.

"You really think I pushed him away?" Sophie asked instead of arguing with her cousin.

"Yup. And I should know. I'm the same way. I'm getting better about it, though. Aunt Annie is like that, too, so it shouldn't be too much of a surprise. I think it's because we're all in such male-dominated fields. I think we take any criticism, even constructive, as being an attack on our personal abilities. Ultimately, it's seated in our lack of confidence in ourselves," Piper explained as she started undressing and handing Sophie her clothes.

"That's pretty deep," Sophie said, looking at her cousin as if she were an alien.

"I've been talking to Sienna," Piper admitted shyly. Sienna Ashton Parker was a sports psychologist and married to their cousin, Ryan. Sienna and Sophie had been best friends nearly the entire lives.

"Ah, that makes sense. And maybe she has a point," Sophie conceded as she slipped the T-shirt on. "Why have you been talking about this with Sienna? Has something happened?"

Piper shook her head. "I'm just tired of all my relationships failing. And I can't even blame my father." Piper paused for a second. "Well, as much as y'all can. My dad is more relaxed about me dating. He bugged my phone and all, just like all of the uncles, but at least my dates weren't met at the door by someone who was armed."

Sophie snorted. All the cousins regularly commiserated over their dating lives with protective fathers. And in Sophie's case, it was overprotective parents.

"Ready to tell me what happened between you two?" Piper asked.

Sophie shook her head. She needed time to think

about all of this. "You really think he loves me?"

"Yeah, I do. And I think you love him, too," Piper said as she went to clean up the sink.

Sophie didn't say anything as she walked quietly into the hangar. It was large and cavernous. Nash was already changed and freshly shaven to match Gabe's appearance, who in turn was dressed in Nash's clothes. Gabe and Nash stood a good distance away with their backs to the bathroom, but Sophie could still hear them.

"The king is pissed," Gabe said.

Nash shook his head. "I couldn't leave her to be taken by Ares."

"I don't get it," Gabe said to Nash. "You leave two years ago on a mission for the king and we hardly hear from you. Sophie shuts down when you leave and barely comes home for more than a couple days at a time. Meanwhile, you succeed at your mission and are handed the job of your dreams, only to turn it down to play bodyguard to someone you haven't shown any interest in when you know a single phone call would have had Nabi or Ahmed by Sophie's side to keep her safe."

"Maybe I realized being the head of security for the king and his family wasn't the dream I thought it would be. Maybe something else is my dream," Nash said so softly Sophie could barely hear it.

"Or someone." Gabe stared at Nash before shaking his head as if coming out of a deep thought. "Keeneston folks will lose their minds when you get home. Oh, and watch out for Nikki. She's desperate now that Addison Rooney is making a play to become the president of the Belles. Nikki's trying to be *nice.*"

Addison was the daughter of the two town defense attorneys, Henry and Neely Grace. Her mother had been a Belle, and by rules Addison was a legacy to the supposed charitable organization. The Belles were intended to be a group of single women who provided charitable services to the citizens of Keeneston, but every once in a while they turned their mission into a husband-hunting popularity contest. Nikki had taken the charity and flushed it down the toilet along with all its tact. She ruled the Belles with bullying and the fear that, at any moment, some of her implants would explode and no one wanted to miss that. Unfortunately for Gabe, he was at the top of the most eligible list, which meant all the Belles were after him. But Nikki took it a whole different level.

Sophie listened as Gabe told Nash of Addison passing the bar exam and being sworn in recently as a new attorney. She was going to replace McKenna Ashton, Sienna's mom, as the town's prosecutor since Kenna just took over as judge. It would make for interesting family dinners.

But Sophie only half listened as Gabe talked. Instead, Gabe's and Piper's words flew around her head — *love, bulldozer, mission, dreams.* Sophie swallowed hard. Nash had turned down his dream job with the king to save her, and she'd just wanted to be bitter about their past, a past that apparently they both regretted.

The door to the bathroom opened and Piper came out. She let it slam shut and both men turned. "How does she look?" Piper asked.

Sophie twitched her lips to mimic Piper's smirk and Gabe laughed.

"Looks good. Now it's time for you to go," Gabe told her as he slung an arm over Piper's shoulder and stepped away from the plane. "We'll see you soon."

Nash held out his arm to indicate Sophie should start walking. "Are you ready to go home?"

Sophie nodded. She was ready for a lot more than just going home.

Chapter Six

N ash walked slightly ahead of Sophie as they
made their way to the plane. The family pilot
smiled at the bottom of the steps and welcomed
Gabe and Piper back on board just in case anyone was
listening. There were enough crew members
working on refueling and checking out the plane
who, if questioned, would say they saw the same
people get off the plane who got back on it.

"I'm sorry to hear that your father took ill,
Prince Gabriel. I know you two were wanting to
work on the lab in Rahmi." The pilot delivered his
lines perfectly. Nash nodded his head sadly before
walking up the steps of the plane. The pilot and the
flight attendant had been busy building Nash and
Sophie's cover for them. While in the hangar, the
pilot told the tower they'd just gotten word they'd
have to turn around and were requesting a short
refueling stop. The flight attendant would have told
the maintenance people the same story. A sick
father, a cancelled trip, and they all stressed that it
was Gabe and Piper on the plane.

Nash walked onto the private jet and took a seat

on the couch. He watched Sophie come in and take off Piper's sunglasses before sitting across from him on her own couch. She stretched her feet out and stared out the window of the plane as it taxied down the runway. As soon as the plane was in the air, Nash gave up watching Sophie. He had wanted to make a plan on dealing with Ares, but his mind was firmly in the past. Instead, he crossed his arms over his chest, closed his eyes, and let his mind take him back to two years ago.

Nash finally had his chance. Sophie was sitting alone at the Blossom Café. If he could run the gamut of Belles separating him from Sophie, he was finally going to do what he'd been wanting to for years. He darted around Emmeline, only to run into Nikki Canter, the queen Belle herself. She was all mahogany hair, over-injected lips, and enhanced breasts.

Nikki rubbed herself against him like a cat in heat. "All alone tonight, Nash? After what I saw, I'd be more than happy to keep you company," she purred.

"Because being a peeping Tom is such a turn-on, Nikki," Nash said tightly. He'd gone for a quick swim in the pond during the fall only to find Nikki had taken his clothes. She had stood ten feet from the water, forcing Nash to walk from the water nude to retrieve his things. Not that Nash cared all that much who saw him naked, but Nikki was something else, not someone else. He wasn't sure she was real. He still thought she was sent from aliens as a practical joke on humans.

"Hmm, I had to see if what the girls were saying was true," Nikki ran her hand down his chest and toward his

pants.

He grabbed her hand and flung it off. "Not happening, Nikki." He hadn't been a monk since moving to Keeneston, but the women he was with knew it was never serious. Nash had never found anyone he wanted to be serious with. He was too busy training to become an elite soldier to worry about anything beyond simple desire. That was until he started training with Sophie Davies.

It was an accident. He was alone in the training center at Desert Sun Farm working the punching bag when Sophie walked in. The training center started out for members of the security detail for Prince Mo and Princess Dani and then their children, Zain, Gabe, and Ariana, when they were older, but the Davies family used it, too. The oldest brothers, Miles, Marshall, and Cade, were in Special Forces and liked to train with Ahmed and Nabi. Eventually their kids began to use it as they grew up and their parents taught them how to defend themselves.

"Hey, Nash," Sophie said. Sophie Davies: his idea of perfection. Nash stopped hitting the bag and said hello. He had seen her on his first day in Keeneston. She smiled at him, and he thought he'd never seen anything so beautiful. But back then he was too afraid to ask a girl out and too busy training to have time to do so.

"I was supposed to meet my dad here, but he's gotten tied up with helping Uncle Cy on something," Sophie told him as she pulled off the oversized, baggy T-shirt, exposing a trim body in tight shorts and a sports bra. "Do you want to spar together?"

Nash cleared his throat. "Um, yeah. Sure."

Three summers, three Christmas breaks, and every chance they got they trained together. He learned about her hopes and dreams. He learned about boys breaking her heart and her breaking theirs. He learned she was scared of being herself, but she never seemed to have that problem when she was with him. And he learned that he loved her.

Nash pushed past Nikki and made his way to Sophie's table. "Hey, Soph. Can I join you?" Sophie looked up and smiled and Nash was man enough to admit he felt his heart trip.

"Of course. What are you doing out so late?"

"I've been helping Deacon and Sydney with some things. I was hoping to have a word with you before you head out on one of your travels and before I go to Indianapolis to help Syd out," Nash said.

"Sure. I need to stretch my legs a bit. I know it's a little cold, but do you want to take a walk through downtown?" Sophie asked.

"Sounds good. Here, let me." Nash laid down some money to cover the bill and helped Sophie on with her coat.

The night was brisk. The air was so clear that the stars seemed closer than usual. The moon lit the street as Nash walked quietly down Main Street and over to the park with Sophie. "Soph, there's been something I've been wanting to say, but sometimes I think actions are better than words," Nash said finally as they stopped close to the grove of willow trees.

Sophie turned to him and he went for it. He pulled his hands from his coat pockets and finally touched her the way he had always wanted to. Slowly, gently, reverently, *he ran his hand over her cheek. He saw her eyes widen in surprise at the intimate contact. "Sophie," he sighed and dipped his lips to hers.*

He kissed her then. Everything was in it. The hope that friends could turn into lovers. The honor, respect, and love he had for her. Everything. Sophie stood still for a second before kissing him back. She pressed her body against his, and Nash never wanted it to end. A moan sounded from Sophie as she opened her mouth to his. Nash deepened the kiss, turning love to passion. And then it was over.

Sophie pulled back quickly, her fingers going to her lips as she stared in surprise at Nash. "What was that?" she asked quietly.

"It's what I wanted to tell you. Do you have any idea how long I have wanted to do that? Sophie, I have feelings for you," Nash said with his heart pounding. "I was hoping you might return them."

Sophie shook her head. "I don't understand. We're friends, and I don't even live here."

"I know we're friends. I was hoping we could become more than that. Distance doesn't matter as long as we care for each other. We can find a way." Nash felt a weight settling on him as Sophie started to look panicked.

"Oh, Nash, it's not a good time. I've just been hired to develop something for the Defense Department. Something big. And if I start dating you, I will have to disclose it and I'm afraid I'll lose my position on the team because of you," Sophie said nervously.

"Because of me?"

Sophie cringed. "I don't think they'd like it if I was involved with someone like you."

"Like me?" Nash felt his anger rise as his pride took a second hit. "You mean someone who cares about you? Someone who supports you? Someone who has always encouraged you to go after your dreams? Yeah, I sound like a terrible guy."

Sophie shook her head. "No, Nash. It's not – "

"What was I thinking?" Nash asked out loud. "Ever since you took this job, you treat everyone else as if they're inferior to you because they don't have the security clearance to know about your work."

"That's not fair, Nash," Sophie said with tears in her eyes. "But if you think that, then you aren't someone I can be with."

"You already knew you couldn't be with someone like me before I even said it, Sophie. How stupid am I to think there was something between us?" Nash laughed to hide his pain.

"There is something between us," Sophie said quietly. Nash turned a cold heart to her. "We just missed our time. I want nothing more than to be with you. But I can't. I have to think of my future. You know how hard I've worked."

"Fine. You've answered my question on how you feel about me. Good luck with whatever this big project is. I hope it's worth it."

"Nash, let's talk about this tomorrow when we're not so upset so I can explain better. Wait! If you walk away from me, I'll never talk to you again!"

Nash turned and strode from the park not bothering to answer her. He slammed the door to his car when his phone rang.

"Yes," he snapped.

"Nash Dagher, this is King Ali Rahman's secretary. You have been ordered back to Rahmi to meet with the king for a new assignment. When can you leave?"

"I can leave within the hour," Nash replied.

Nash awoke with a jolt. Sophie was asleep on the couch. It was as if the two years hadn't passed at all. The same damn government contract was between them, but now it wasn't their love on the line. It was her life.

Nash let out a long breath and stood up. He walked to the refrigerator and pulled out a bottle of water. When he walked back, Sophie was sitting up and rubbing the sleep from her eyes. He felt it still — the pain of a broken heart.

Sophie watched Nash sit down and take a long drink of water. If Piper was right and Nash did love her, then he was lashing out like a wounded animal. And it was she who had wounded him. Sophie had hurt him. She had threatened never to talk to him again if he walked away. She had been immature when she issued that stupid ultimatum. That night in Keeneston was all she could think about since she boarded the plane.

"I need to take a shower, excuse me," Sophie said disjointedly as she got up, hiding the tears in her eyes. Was this all because of her? Two people going through two years of pain all because she had been too afraid to tell Nash the truth?

Sophie closed the bedroom door and turned on

the shower. With a start, she looked in the mirror to find someone else staring back with her eyes. It was time to do some soul-searching, and she was afraid she wouldn't like what she found. With the heat of the shower steaming the small glass enclosure, Sophie stripped off Piper's clothes and stepped into the shower.

I have feelings for you.

The first tear fell.

I was hoping we could become more than friends.

The second tear fell.

Nash had been right. She had feelings for him. Feelings that ran so deep that when he left, Sophie thought she'd die. She'd thrown herself into her work for so long she couldn't remember what it was like to just be herself. The woman who liked to laugh. The woman who liked to dream. Instead, she was the woman who, when she went to bed every night, dreamed of what her life would have been like if she'd said yes to Nash. If she had told him the truth — that she loved him.

But she had ruined it. Sophie had chosen her job over love. She was too afraid to stand up for herself to her boss, and that's what she would have had to do if she had started dating Nash. She would have had to publicly defend her relationship with a foreign operative. It could have cost Sophie her job, but now as she cried in the shower, hair dye raining down the drain with her tears, she realized she'd just been scared. With Mo's help, Nash would have passed the scrutiny, but Sophie had never given him that chance.

Instead of admitting she had pushed Nash away, Sophie blamed him. She blamed Nash for leaving her. She blamed Nash for running away from her. She blamed Nash for saying she cared more about her job, which she did by denying her feelings for him. She rested her head against the shower stall and let the water wash her tears away.

"Sophie? What is it?"

Sophie turned around to find Nash holding open the glass shower door, watching as she cried.

"I heard you crying," he said shyly as an explanation for why he was there. Sophie almost laughed at the way his eyes stayed glued to hers. But instead of laughter, more tears burst forth.

"I'm so sorry," Sophie cried.

"If we're finally going to talk, you really need to cover up," Nash said, handing her a towel as she turned off the water.

"I was hurt. I felt I had to choose between you or my job. I lashed out at you, and I shouldn't have. You were the one who always supported me. You would have jumped through all the hoops my company would have put you through and I should have trusted you enough to do that." It all rushed out of her. Sophie couldn't stop talking as Nash pulled her from the shower. It was cleansing to get out all the things she had wanted to say. All the feelings she had repressed and turned into anger against Nash.

"I loved you so much, and I didn't trust your

love. I took any question about my job as an insult and became defensive instead of talking to you. We could have worked it out. We could have been together. Instead, everything got so ugly so fast. We don't talk now; we constantly fight. All because I was too proud to simply tell you the truth. I loved you, and I was scared that by being with a foreign operative, I would lose my job on the biggest project of my life. A job where I'm the only woman. A job that now might cost me my life after already costing me you."

"Shhh," Nash said soothingly as he wrapped his arms around her shaking frame and pulled her to him. "You're not the only one with an overdose of pride. I walked away when I should have stayed and fought for you."

Sophie shook her head against his chest. "Not when I gave you that ultimatum. I never should have said that."

"Soph, look at me," Nash ordered. She lifted her head and looked into his dark brown eyes. They were warm and rich in color, and right now they were earnestly looking into hers. "I shouldn't have left. You're worth fighting for."

His lips captured hers, and Sophie almost cried with a mixture of relief and passion. For two years, she'd dreamt of Nash, and this time she wasn't going to let him walk out. He might think she was worth fighting for, but Nash was worth fighting for, too.

Nash deepened the kiss and his tongue stroked

hers as his fingers flexed into her hips. Through the towel, she felt his hardness, sensed the tight hold on his restraint, and all she wanted to do was watch that restraint snap. She pressed herself closer and felt a rumble in Nash's chest a second before he broke the kiss. They were both breathing heavily as they stood looking at each other with new eyes.

"As much as I want to continue this, we have something we need to deal with first. It's time to tell me everything. Why is Ares after you?" Nash took a step back and Sophie swallowed hard. She was faced with the same decision she had been two years ago. Could she trust Nash with all the secrets she held?

Chapter Seven

This wasn't two years ago. Sophie wasn't nervous about a job she no longer needed. What she needed was help. With the choice made, she nodded. Nash stepped out of the bathroom without saying a word, but Sophie knew he'd be waiting for her. She brushed her hair and dressed as quickly as she could. She found Nash sitting in one of the parchment-colored leather chairs with a small table between the matching chair opposite him. There were two glasses of white wine set on the table along with pasta in white sauce.

Sophie took the seat across from Nash and sipped the wine as she looked around. She might trust Nash, but that didn't mean she wasn't thinking twice about giving out classified information where someone could overhear them.

"The flight attendant is in the cockpit with the door closed. The flight crew is having dinner. We won't be overheard," Nash told her as if reading her mind.

Sophie took a deep swallow of wine. "Almost three years ago, the government contract I signed was to build a new kind of missile. They wanted a missile that utilized biometrics. It's coded with the target and won't detonate except when the target registers. Each missile is coded so that if someone, say North Korea, steals it and tries to shoot at South Korea, or if they try to use it for anything the missile is not coded for, the missile will explode either over an empty span of desert or the ocean, whichever is closest."

Nash's eyebrow raised but he didn't interrupt.

"And I did it. Not only that, but I did it years ahead of when others could. It's worth more money than you can imagine. If the technology got into the wrong hands, you'd see people like Ares developing smart weapons and . . . well, we can both guess what he'd do with technology like that."

Nash nodded. "Did you have any idea that Ares was after you?"

"No," Sophie said, taking another drink of wine. "I knew someone was. There had been two attempts to get into the lab. In both cases, the intruders never made it more than ten feet onto the property before they were chased off. My house and car were also broken into. I also think there's a mole in the lab. I'm very exact with how I leave my station, and one morning I came in and something wasn't right. I don't have proof, but I think someone went through my stuff."

"What were they looking for?"

"They were looking for my logs to learn how I built the missile, but I also knew they'd never find them."

"Logs?" Nash asked.

"Yes. Every developer is required to keep a daily log of their work, in case competing companies try to file the same patent. A judge will look at the logs to see who developed it first, and that company will hold the patent."

"So, where are these logs?"

"What passes enough for the courts aren't in Maryland, but the majority of my logs were here," Sophie tapped her head.

Nash's eyes widened slightly. "Why didn't you write it down?"

"Because I knew corporate spies would be after it as soon as I started to develop it. And I did write it down eventually. I have notes and enough information to prove it's my idea and to file for a patent in a lockbox in the Keeneston Bank. No one knows about it, and no one can trace it back to me. I put the evidence in an envelope and gave it to Kenna with instructions not to open it. She put it in the lockbox she has for her law firm. Ares will never be able to find it. And no one else will either."

"How would Russian, Iranian, or North Korean spies get into the lab? It seems like you went to extremes to protect the information, yet Ares found out about it anyway," Nash said out loud, but not necessarily to her. He was trying to figure out how Ares found out about her and the missile.

"The most connected spies aren't our rivals, they're our allies. Israel, France, the U.K., and I'm sure Rahmi all have very well-placed spies within our government and within U.S. government-contracted companies. It's why my team is small and handpicked by me. I also privately told each person on my team where I put the log, except I told each person a different place and have cameras set up to automatically turn on if the safes were ever opened. That way I'd know who is leaking the information by which location they go to," Sophie explained.

A slight smile tugged at Nash's lips. "And I thought I was paranoid. Though in this case, you were right to be. Did anyone trigger one of your cameras?"

"No. I don't know who is feeding information to Ares or how he found out about me. No one on my team has been acting differently as far as I can tell. But I know someone went through my things."

Nash took a drink and thought for a moment. "When are you finished with the missile? When it is ready to be handed over to the government?"

"It's just cleared the environmental tests, such as extreme heat, humidity, cold, and so forth. I just have one kink in some navigation software that we need to fix. Then I will bring in the heads of the defense departments and military branches to show them the missile and do another test. If all goes well, BLC Tech will start high-rate production on the government orders."

"And then it will become public?" Nash asked.

"No. I'll never be able to acknowledge the

missile unless I'm given permission. Even if one gets stolen, I have to pretend to know nothing about it, unless I'm told otherwise. If permission is given, I can only say that it's a new missile that utilizes biometrics. Everything else will go to the grave with me in order to protect our classified patent and intellectual property rights."

"Which is what makes you so valuable," Nash said, getting back to the fact someone was trying to kidnap her.

"Exactly." Sophie shuddered. She still remembered the feel of being dragged into that van. "The people on my team only know their part. I'm the only one who knows how to put all the parts together."

Nash thought about all Sophie had told him. Ares wouldn't stop until he had her and the knowledge she had locked away in her brain. "You know I need to stay with you, right?" Nash asked after a couple moments of silence. Sophie may have been overcome with emotion and said she was sorry, but Nash didn't know if it was real or because of the circumstances they found themselves in. He wished it were real. He wished they could start over. He knew their pride had been injured, but it wasn't something they could move from as if it never happened. Nash guarded his heart too closely now to open it again to love without making sure his feelings were reciprocated.

Sophie let out a sigh. "I was going to stay with

my parents, but I can't do that. I can't put them in danger. I know they're big bad-asses and whatnot, but that was decades ago. When was the last time my father or mother was in a shoot-out?"

Nash smiled. "I think you're underestimating your parents. They'd be thrilled to be in a shoot-out."

Sophie returned his smile. "I'm guessing after what Sienna and Ryan went through three years ago, you're right. The Rose sisters still complain that they were left in the car."

"So, either you stay at your parents' house, I stay with you at your house, or we stay at mine. Your choice," Nash told her.

"Um, you haven't talked to anyone from Keeneston for a while, have you?" Sophie asked. This didn't sound good.

"The last person I talked to was Matt, and that was over six months ago. Why?"

"Um, well, Matt and Riley got married," Sophie started.

"That's great. Matt's loved her for years," Nash said happily before clearing his throat, suddenly uncomfortable. Their situation was a little too close to Nash's own situation with Sophie. As far as Nash knew, Matt and Riley never had a fight like he and Soph did.

"Yeah, and Matt was appointed sheriff and so a new state trooper needed to be assigned to the area. You'll love DeAndre and his girlfriend, Aniyah. Well, Riley and her sister's house blew up, so Riley moved in with Matt, and Reagan is living at her parents' home while a new house is being built," Sophie rambled on.

"I guess Matt didn't fill me in all the way when I last talked to him. But he'll be a perfect sheriff. I'm surprised Marshall Davies actually retired," Nash said.

"It surprised us all. But," Sophie hedged, "DeAndre and Aniyah needed a place to rent, and since no one had heard from you . . . well, what I'm trying to say is you don't have a house anymore."

Nash blinked. He didn't have a home to come back to? He'd been dreaming of his little house on Desert Sun Farm for two years, and now it was someone else's home. "I guess I can stay at the bed and breakfast while I look for a new place. That is, as long as you're staying with your parents," Nash said tightly. He tried to keep the disappointment from his voice. It wasn't like it was his house. It belonged to the royal family. But for eight years, it had been home.

Sophie smiled a little too cheerfully. "Poppy and Zinnia will be thrilled to have you there. And the Rose sisters live next door with their husbands so they'll watch over the B&B for any bad guys."

"You know we need to tell them something. Showing up together after two years apart, plus your mom has surely told them about the attempted kidnapping, will set the town on its ear."

Sophie got a stubborn look on her face and Nash was worried she was going to fight him. "I can't. I know you're going to be mad, but I can't stress how important it is that this remains secret. I told you, and don't think I don't feel guilty for breaking my word and too many nondisclosure contracts to count. I'm trusting you, Nash. Only you."

"I'm not mad, Sophie. I understand. I just needed to know to be able to protect you."

"Why are you protecting me after how I treated you?" Sophie asked.

"I already told you. You're worth fighting for. Now, as for what we tell everyone. I think we tell them someone wants something from you that you're not willing to give. You don't know any more than that, but I do. I can tell them about Ares and have the town keep an eye out for any strange visitors. Let me take care of things for once," Nash said, holding his breath. Sophie wasn't good at letting go.

"I can't promise anything. How about I'll try? I don't want to be bugged with questions I can't answer, so I'll happily let you explain it to them."

"I'll take it. Besides, they'll be too busy placing bets at the café to ask you too many questions about work," Nash smiled devilishly, refilling their wine glasses.

"Placing bets on what?" Sophie asked.

Nash lifted his wine glass and toasted her. "On us, sweetheart."

Chapter Eight

Nash tried not to admit it, but he was eager to be back in Keeneston. He looked out the plane's window at the rolling hills and horse-dotted landscape as they approached the Lexington airport. He didn't doubt that Sophie's parents were waiting to pick them up and drive them back to Keeneston. Unfortunately, he wouldn't be able to return to his house, but he would be able to drown his disappointment in food from the Blossom Café. He was dying for some good Southern cooking. Poseidon may have lived lavishly, but for two years Nash had been living off sandwiches and ramen as if he were still in college.

They passed over Keeneland Race Track where horses were training and touched down soon after. Sophie had been quiet for the past hour. He had been, too. He was formulating a plan for dealing with Ares and hoping he could encourage Sophie to work on the software and hand off the project as soon as possible. However, even if she did, she'd still be in danger. It wasn't as if Ares would just give up because he'd been beaten to production. He wanted his own missiles. He wanted her technology, her coding, the software, and the guidance system. He would take all of that and bend it to his needs.

As the plane taxied to its hangar, Nash looked at Sophie. She seemed off. It was strange that she didn't appear to be relieved to be home. She had grown distant since she took her development job. He knew it was hard to keep confidential information, and working in missile development made working in the FBI look like child's play.

"It'll be okay, Sophie. I won't let anything happen to you," Nash said quietly as he reached across the table and took her hand in his.

"I've been in the shadows for so long that I just realized I don't know how to act. I don't know how to ask for help. I was in the shower earlier and came to the conclusion that I've lost myself. Since I can't tell people what I do for a living, I've pulled back from friends and family. I'm nervous. What if they won't help me? It's not like I've been part of the town for the past couple of years."

"I feel the same way. You're not in this alone, Sophie." Nash squeezed her hand as the flight attendant opened the door and lowered the steps. "Come on. Let's go home."

Sophie tried to pull back, but Nash didn't let her. He kept her hand in his as they came to a stop at the open door.

"Do you see what I'm seeing?" Sophie asked slowly as if trying to decide if the scene in front of her were real or not.

"If you're talking about the Rose sisters in skydiving suits arm in arm with three young men, then yes, I'm seeing it. Understanding it? No."

Lily Rae Rose-Wolf, Daisy Mae Rose-Lastinger, and Violet Fae Rose-Vasseur were in matching pink skydiving suits, their poufy white hair pushed back from their foreheads by clear plastic goggles. Their cheeks were red and the smiles on their faces could either be from adrenaline or the fact that they were eating up the attention the young men were giving them.

"John said you would land now and here you are. Good thing you didn't get here earlier or we wouldn't be here to greet you," Miss Lily said, coming to a stop at the bottom of the steps. "Welcome home."

Nash smiled then. A sincere smile, filled with the knowledge that some things never change and that it's always good to be home. "How did John know when we would be landing?" He didn't bother asking Miss Lily how her husband knew they were on their way home. By now, all of Keeneston would be expecting them. John Wolfe somehow had more information than the NSA.

"He has his ways. And that ol' billy goat won't tell me what they are," Miss Lily complained.

"I told you to go on strike until he answers you," Miss Daisy said with a shake of her head.

"I'm not going to withhold sex. I'd suffer just as much," Miss Lily said with a huff. Both Nash and Sophie cringed at the thought as though it were their grandparents talking about sex.

"Not sex," Miss Violet chided. "That's a young person's game. They're too young and dumb to know better. You withhold your cooking if you want to break them. No morning muffins. No fried catfish sandwich for lunch. No pot roast for dinner. And certainly no bread pudding for dessert. He'll break in less than a week."

"I put twenty dollars on him breaking in under a week," Nash said, fishing out his wallet as he walked down the plane steps. "It would break me."

"Don't say that too loud or our friends might torture you with bread pudding," Sophie said with a sarcastic tone to her voice but laughter in her eyes. Nash took a deep breath. It was so good to be home.

"Hmm," Miss Lily pondered. "I guess I can give it a try. We have to get Poppy and Zinnia to agree not to serve him at the café. Since we've retired and our dear young cousins took over, we're out and about enjoying our golden years and can't watch the place all day."

Golden years? More like ancient years. The Rose sisters were approaching one hundred years old and their husbands were just as old. Except for Violet who declared herself a cougar since Anton was *only* eight-nine years old.

"They'll do it," Miss Daisy resolutely said. It was done. John was cut off—poor guy. But Nash wasn't.

"Well, all this talk of food has me craving some. I have been dreaming of eating at the Blossom

Café," Nash told them as he reached the bottom of the steps.

Miss Violet grabbed him then and pulled him down—way down. She was barely five feet now. He sucked in a deep breath before his face was covered by her pillowy bosom. She hugged him tightly as he heard the muffled chiding of her sisters. Miss Violet had promised her husband when they married eight years back that she'd stop putting men's heads between her breasts. She had lied.

"It's so good to have you home. Anything you want, I'll make!"

"*Bwd pdng,*" Nash tried to say as she held tight to his head.

"What, dear?" Miss Violet asked.

"Let the poor boy breathe, Vi," Miss Daisy said, smacking her sister lightly on her upper arm.

With a roll of her eyes, Miss Violet let Nash go. "Fine," she grumbled. "Now, what can I make you?"

"I'd kill for bread pudding with the butter bourbon sauce," Nash told her, now free from the prison of her bosom.

"Done. And where should I send it?" she asked as she looked innocently between Sophie and Nash. Nash knew better. This was the most loaded question he'd ever been asked.

"To the bed and breakfast. Do you think Poppy and Zinnia have room for a boarder? I hear my house has new tenants." Nash saw the way their eyes shot to Sophie in surprise before looking slightly dejected. But when they turned back to

Nash they spotted a challenge. Uh-oh. He'd been tortured by people with less determination than these three old ladies had etched on their faces.

"I'm sure we can find room for you — for now," Miss Lily said with a sweet smile on her face that made the hair on the back of Nash's neck stand up.

"Annie's here. We better hightail it back to Keeneston so we can be the first to tell everyone the news of the homecoming," Miss Violet whispered as an SUV pulled into the private airfield.

"We'll see you two at the café," Miss Daisy called out as the three hurriedly shuffled to their large town car and took off at a surprising speed.

The door to the SUV opened before the car even stopped and Annie hopped out. Her red hair had turned a little lighter as the years had gone by and was in a messy ponytail with sprigs of curly hair escaping in all directions. She was in jeans and a Florida State University sweatshirt as she sprinted toward them.

"Sophie! Oh my God, Sophie! Are you okay?" Annie yelled frantically as Nash moved out of the way. Nothing was going to stop Annie from getting to her daughter.

Oomph. The sound escaped Sophie as her mother wrapped her in a tight hug at a full run.

"My baby! Are you hurt? Let me see," Annie ordered as she pulled away and started running her hands over Sophie's arms and took a look at her head as she made very specific and graphic threats against the people who hurt Sophie. Threats Nash would happily carry out if given half the chance.

"Dad!" Sophie cried as tears started to pool in her eyes. Cade wrapped his wife and daughter in a hug but didn't say anything. He didn't need to. The anguish on his face said more than words could.

Nash felt uncomfortable intruding on this private family matter. He was about to step back when Annie's hand snapped out and grabbed his arm. She pulled hard and Nash stumbled forward into the family hug.

"Thank you, Nash," Annie said with a voice tight with emotion.

The huddle broke up after Cade gave them one last squeeze. Silently he turned and held out his hand to Nash. Nash shook it as Cade gave him a simple nod of thanks. Cade's lips were white as he struggled to hold himself together.

"Now, your brothers are waiting at home. There's no way you're going to stay by yourself until these people are caught," Annie said in her mom voice that brooked no argument.

Nash saw Sophie open her mouth to complain, but one look from her father silenced her. Annie turned to Nash. "You'll come over for dinner tomorrow." It wasn't an invitation. It was an order. "I'll order from the café. They'll know all your favorites."

"Yes, ma'am. I appreciate it," Nash said with a tilt of his lips. Annie wasn't known for her cooking. It was passable, but it wasn't Blossom Café good.

"Where are you staying?" Cade asked suddenly.

"You do know about your house being rented out, right?"

"Yes, sir. I'll be at the B&B. The Rose sisters are already on their way into town to get a room ready and to tell everyone Sophie is back."

"Oh, I think you being back is the bigger news," Annie said, finally relaxing her hold on Sophie. "Come on, the town will be waiting to see you."

Nash let the sensations of the Blossom Café wash over him. It was the sound of gossip, the smell of fried chicken, and the warmth of a small town all in one place. But then they noticed him. The smells continued, but the talking stopped. Silence deafened the place as heads turned from Sophie to him and back to Sophie. Then chaos erupted.

The Blossom Café was gossip central and it was the only restaurant in Keeneston. The warm, cozy restaurant had large plate-glass windows on each side of a pale purple door. Inside, a row of booths lined the left side and a mix-match of booths and round, rectangular, and square tables filling the rest of the space. The kitchen looked out from the back of the old historic building. Tables were covered in bright tablecloths with mismatched chairs around them. A special table by the front was reserved for the Rose sisters and their husbands now that they had retired.

The Rose sisters had run a betting pool from the café since it started almost seventy years before. The money raised went to fund local charities and good deeds. But the Rose sisters had retired and their much younger distant cousins, Poppy and Zinnia Meadows, had come up from Alabama to help run the bed and breakfast and the Blossom Café. The elderly women had also handed over the betting books. And right now Poppy was running like a madwoman from table to table taking bets.

Damn, it was good to be home.

Poppy hugged Sophie and then held up her hands as Sophie went to greet her family. Everyone quieted down. "First, welcome back, Nash. We're all happy to have you home. Second, I'm ready to call the bet on whether Nash was alive or dead. The alive bets have it."

Cheers went up. It hadn't sounded as if there were many who had bet against him. It gave him the warm fuzzies—as much as a guy like him could feel warm fuzzies, that is. Poppy waved them to a seat as friends flooded in along with Sophie's very large extended family.

"Welcome back!" Matt Walz smiled as he thumped Nash on the back. Matt was the only person Nash had called while he was away. Matt cut straight to the chase and didn't ask questions. It was how Nash kept informed on what was going on in Keeneston. But now Matt looked different. Marriage to Riley agreed with him.

"What are you doing here? Aren't you supposed to be on your honeymoon?" Nash asked, receiving a hug from Riley Davies Walz.

"When I heard Sophie was in trouble and you were back, we decided to postpone it for a couple weeks. You're our friends, and we don't leave friends to fend for themselves. Plus I really wanted to see if my cousin kicked your ass or not. The fact that she's not shooting you with the taser farting gun she knocked Nikki out with before intrigues me," Riley said. With her red hair tied up in a sloppy bun and the toe of her cowboy boot tapping in contemplation, she looked at Sophie taking a seat at a table behind him and then back to Nash. "Poppy!"

Matt shook his head at his new wife as Riley pushed through the crowd to place whatever bets were raging. "I heard you're the new sheriff of Keeneston. Congrats," Nash said.

Matt filled him in on what was going on in town in under twenty seconds. "And finally the panty-dropper hit again at the wedding, but still no clue to the identity. I think the Rose sisters are planting cameras all over town. I had to remove two of them I found on trees in the park this morning."

"Or maybe they're John's and that's how he knows everything that's going on in town."

"I think ghosts tell him. Ghosts of past residents who can float between walls and never be seen," Matt said in a way that Nash couldn't tell if he was joking or not. Since aliens and the use of an Ouija board were the top guesses at this point, it wasn't too weird to add ghosts to the mix. "Hey, have you met DeAndre yet?"

Nash shook his head. "Is that the person staying at my old place?"

Matt look slightly guilty. "Yeah. And I'm sorry about that. I suggested it to Mo and Dani and they thought it was a great idea. I didn't think you were coming back. Well, are you back?"

That was the question, wasn't it?

Chapter Nine

Sophie was tired. She had told her kidnapping story so many times she never wanted to tell it again. First to her cousins, then to her aunts and uncles, then to the entire Blossom Café. Plus when Nikki Canter, the head nutjob of the Keeneston Belles came in and rubbed herself all over Nash, Sophie thought she was going to shoot her again. The first time she shot Nikki, it was with a taser she had in development. Now she had a gun in her purse. The trouble was, every place Sophie looked to shoot Nikki would involve a massive explosion—breast implants, butt implants, over-injected lips. There'd be saline and silicone all over the place, and that would just be rude to whoever had to clean it up.

"Honey, are you all right?" her mother asked.

Her mom hadn't left her side for the past two hours. Right now a bath and a long nap sounded perfect. "Just tired," Sophie smiled. "I'm ready to go home."

"Well, your old room is waiting for you. I haven't changed it since you went to college. You'll feel nice and safe."

Sophie cringed. She had meant her own home. She'd forgotten she was staying with her parents. Her brothers stood, forming a six–foot-two-inch wall around her. Colton, the older one by a year, was now twenty-two and had just graduated from college in May. His dark golden hair and trademark Davies hazel eyes took in everything around them as if someone from the town would suddenly become a threat. Landon was easily identifiable as Sophie and Colton's brother. He was in his final year of college and was home for fall break. He'd be leaving to go back to college in a couple days. However, unlike Colton, Landon's hair was lighter brown and his hazel eyes had more green than brown.

"We should bring Kale in on this. He could help us a lot," Landon said for the sixth time that night. Kale Mueez was Ahmed and Bridget's youngest child. He was Landon's age and the two were best friends. He was also at MIT working on an advanced degree in computers.

Sophie let out a sigh. "I know Kale is a good hacker in his own right, but he's just a kid. What can he do?"

"A lot. I texted him the info on that wallet Nash grabbed from the guy who kidnapped you, and he already found out it was fake and probably made in Munich. It had the signature style of a known associate to Ares who is famous for forged documents. What have you found out? And, I take offense at your remark. Do I look like a kid to you?"

Sophie looked at her younger brother. In her eyes, he was still a seven-year-old kid running around with shaggy hair and scraped knees. But when she really looked at him, she knew he was right. Her brothers were men now, much to her dismay. They had lost the lankiness of childhood and developed into tough men over the course of the past years. There weren't many things that scared them, except Winnie the Pooh. They were freaked out by the fact he had mitten hands.

"Fine. I promise to use Kale when needed," Sophie said before sighing. She was so tired.

"Stop giving your sister a hard time. Let's get her home," Cade said as he slipped his arm around her. "Nash," her father called out to where Nash sat with Matt, Zain, and the rest of the Desert Sun Farm group.

"Yes, sir?"

"We'll see you tomorrow for dinner. We're taking Sophie home. She's not to be alone until this Ares character is caught." The last part was directed to the entire town who nodded in unison. And Sophie had thought being a teenager in a small town was bad. It was hard to get away with anything then and your private life was never private. This was going to be a nightmare.

"Don't worry," her cousin Riley whispered.

"Yeah, we'll make sure you get some time away from the parents," her cousin Layne, Miles and Morgan's daughter, said with a wink.

"It'll be just like old times." Her best friend and cousin-in-law, Sienna Parker, smiled.

"Yeah, it's been a long time since you climbed out of your window and down that large oak tree," Reagan, Riley's twin sister, smirked.

"She may be too old," Riley taunted.

"Too old for what?" Cade asked, turning his attention away from Nash and back to Sophie.

"Too old to be staying out late. You know, you hit thirty and it's all downhill from there. Nothing but yoga pants and HGTV at night," her cousin Sydney, a former supermodel-turned-fashion-industry-CEO, said with a shake of her head. Okay, so it was a little too close to the truth—at least the yoga pants and HGTV part.

Cade looked at the cousins suspiciously but didn't say anything. As if he had room to talk. A couple years ago, Zain's wife, Mila, had gathered all the cousins and friends and shown them the truth of what their parents had done when they were Sophie's age. Sophie's parents had told her they had met when her mother had been hired at the Keeneston High School to teach drug awareness. Her father had been the biology teacher and football coach. The story had been it was love at first sight. They left out that her mother was there as an undercover DEA agent to take down a drug ring targeting kids. Not to mention they had been attacked and almost killed.

"Well, get some rest," Sienna said before hugging her. "Ryan and I will check on you later tonight."

"Yeah, *Property Brothers* is on," Reagan said without a hint of a smile although her eyes were laughing.

Sophie hugged her cousins and friend before her father, mother, and brothers escorted her out of the café. She looked over her shoulder and saw Nash watching her. Her body flushed at the intensity but then Nash disappeared from view as her brothers moved in to surround her. His look told her everything. He was going to fight for her. But was she ready to do the same?

Nash watched Colton and Landon close in around Sophie as they walked out of the Blossom Café. Zain was talking, but Nash wasn't paying attention. There was something bigger than Ares bothering him. He had loved the person Sophie had been. But over the course of two years, people could change. He wasn't the same and neither was she. They had been shaped by the events of that night and the consequences of walking away. The better question was, could they love the people they had turned into.

"Earth to Nash," Zain said, waving his hand in front of Nash's face. He blinked and looked at the group of his friends.

"Sorry, I was thinking," Nash said, not sounding sorry at all.

Zain looked back to Nash and grinned. "What you need is a guys' night. Let us welcome you home. Give you a break before this Ares thing takes over your life. How about dinner here at 7:00?" Zain suggested.

"Yeah," Matt agreed. "That will give you time to get your stuff from the farm and get settled into the B&B. By the way, I drove your SUV here. It's out front. As for tonight, I've heard the promise of Miss Violet's bread pudding. We can't miss that."

"Okay," Nash agreed. He needed time alone, but it would also be nice to have some time with his friends. And the bread pudding.

Nash left his friends as they told the Davies crew about the guys' night. Poppy was hurrying ahead of him to get a room ready so Nash decided to head out to his old house to pick up his things.

The drive to the farm filled him with mixed emotions. It was a life from the past, and it was the life he wanted for his future as well. He felt disconnected as he drove the narrow country road over rolling hills and around sharp curves. Horses ran in the cool fall air. Cows enjoyed the lush grass before winter set in. Pumpkins sat on carts with an old coffee can next to them on a couple of the farms he passed. He remembered getting his first Halloween pumpkin from one such place. You went to the cart, put some money in the can, and took the pumpkin of your choice. All honor system and never a problem.

Memories of the happiest times of his life filled him, but instead of happiness he felt sadness. It was the past. Nothing had been the same since the night he left. Was his desire to go back to the past hindering his ability to enjoy the present—to enjoy being back home, to enjoy being with his friends? Something was holding him back, and as he drove down the tree-lined drive of Desert Sun Farm he realized what it was. He needed to forgive not only Sophie, but himself.

He had spent the past two years blaming Sophie for turning him down, but now he knew why she did. It wasn't because she didn't love him. It was because she was scared of losing something she'd worked her whole life for. He knew how much that job meant to her, and instead of being supportive, he'd turned her job against her. There was enough blame to go around, and he needed to find a way to forgive and move on, or there would never be a future for him in Keeneston.

Nash parked his car and looked at the place that had been his home for eight years. Yellow, red, and purple mums lined the front of the house. A decorative flag with a pumpkin fluttered by the front door. It was no longer his house. His house had the touch of a woman now.

Nash walked to the front door and rang the bell. He waited and then knocked loudly before ringing the bell again. Nothing. Nash stepped behind a mum and looked into the window. Pink furry pillows on the couch were the only thing he saw. The house was empty.

Well, it was his house . . . Nash stepped back

onto the small entrance way and bent over. He ran his fingers under the concrete stoop he was kneeling on. There it was. The spare key he had attached underneath the overhang. He inserted it into the door and heard the lock tumble. He opened the door and called, "Hello! Is anyone home?"

Nash waited and heard nothing. He pocketed the key and went inside. The house was his, but it wasn't. Some of the furniture was the same, but the pink furry pillows, the bedazzled picture frames, and the lion skin rug was not.

He headed upstairs to where his closet had been. His bedroom was nothing like it had been before. A pink furry rug that matched the pillows downstairs was in front of the bed and a massive amount of brightly colored, sparkly clothes hung in his closet. Where had his clothes gone? Were his guns still there?

Nash struggled to push the clothes close enough together for him to reach into the back of the closet and feel for the hidden latch. He found it and shoved his way past a shocking amount of spandex to slide the door open. Inside a light automatically turned on and Nash sighed as he saw his weapons all in their rightful place.

"Freeze, asshole! What, you get some sick thrill sniffing women's clothing? And don't you be stealing my miniskirt you got your hand on. I don't care how good-lookin' you are from the back. You ain't pulling off that miniskirt with those hips of yours. They're too straight. You need curves to pull off a skirt like this."

Nash slowly pulled his hands from the zebra-striped miniskirt and raised them in the air.

"And what is that back there? I don't remember a light back there?"

Nash turned and heard the sound of a gun being cocked. An African-American woman stood wearing heels so high he didn't know how she stayed upright. She had on a V-neck sweater so low her considerable assets were on full display. She was the definition of curvy, and Nash figured quite a few men let out a low whistle when she walked by.

"I think we've started off on the wrong foot," Nash said calmly. He moved to hold out his hand to introduce himself and the woman fired the gun. Nash didn't move. He didn't need to. From the angle she was holding the gun, he knew she wasn't going to hit him. Instead she shot her miniskirt.

"Oh damn! Look what you made me do. That was my favorite skirt," she cried as she aimed at him again. This time it looked like she'd hit his pile of ammunition so he took a step back hoping she wouldn't fire again.

"Baby!" a man shouted as Nash heard the front door swing open and footsteps pound up the stairs. "Was that a gunshot?"

"I'm in our room, Sugar Bear! I caught an intruder getting off on sniffing my clothes! I think he was going to steal them for himself."

Nash felt his eyes go wide. Okay, being accused of theft is one thing, but this was completely different. "Hey, it's not like that."

"Don't say another word or I'll shoot!"

"Don't do that, Baby!" the man yelled as he rushed into the bedroom with his own gun drawn. "Get back, Baby. I got this. Step slowly out of the closet with your hands up."

Nash snarled. He was losing patience. "I've been trying to explain," Nash said between clenched teeth.

"Not another word!" the man in the state trooper uniform ordered as he pulled out his cell phone and called into the sheriff's department. He put it on speaker and handed the phone to the woman so he could keep both hands on his gun.

"Matt, it's DeAndre. Aniyah caught a man in our closet. I'm bringing him in."

"Tell him my name is—" Nash started to say.

"Not another word," DeAndre ordered.

"Wait a second," Matt said back. "Nash?"

"Yup," Nash called back as he heard Matt chuckle.

"DeAndre, is the man in front of you around six feet tall with lightly tanned skin, black hair, and dark brown eyes?" Matt asked.

"Yeah," DeAndre answered suspiciously.

"Then you can put down the gun and introduce yourself to Nash Dagher. He lived in the house for eight years."

"No shit," Aniyah said. "But ain't he the one who hurt Sophie? I should probably wing him for that." Aniyah aimed her gun again but DeAndre took it from her hands.

"Where did you get this, Baby? I thought I hid all the guns after you almost shot Matt the last time he came over."

Aniyah handed the gun over with a pout. "You know that was an accident. I was target shooting, and he got too close."

"Babe, he was twenty yards behind you. Just admit you're not the best shot."

"Maybe I'll get a taser," Aniyah said happily with her new plan.

"Sorry about that, Nash. I'm DeAndre Drews and this is my girlfriend, Aniyah." DeAndre introduced them as he held out his hand.

Nash shook it. "Nice to meet you both."

Nash kept an eye on Aniyah as she rose up on her toes and tried to peer over Nash's shoulder. "What were you doing in the closet? And where is that light coming from?"

"I have a gun safe back there. I knocked and when no one was home I used my key to get in. I just wanted to pick up my things. I guess I should have waited."

DeAndre shook his head. "Nah, it's your place, too. We just moved in, and they told us you'd lived here a long time. We felt bad moving your things, but Aniyah packed them up all nice and neat and labeled them. They're all in the guest room. Probably a good thing we didn't find this. Who knows what or who she would have shot next," DeAndre smiled lovingly at his girlfriend.

"Come on, Sugar, I'll show you to your stuff. Let me just kick off these shoes. I just got back from Frankfort. Do you know I work with Riley?"

Aniyah kicked off her heels and dropped five inches. She didn't even make it to DeAndre's chin. She looked to be only five feet tall without her heels. "Are you sure you weren't into my clothes? You can have that zebra skirt now. It even has a hole for you to stick your winky out of now that I shot it. Though from the condoms I packed up and the stories Nikki has been telling, you'd need another couple of inches on that skirt to keep from exposin' yourself," Aniyah happily rambled as she sashayed out the room.

"Wow," DeAndre said softly as he ignored his girlfriend's rambling. "This isn't just a little gun safe. I haven't even seen some of these guns before."

Nash finally turned from where Aniyah had disappeared into the hall. There had to be hidden cameras somewhere. This surely was a prank. "Um, yeah. It's my personal collection. Feel free to look while I load my boxes. I need to call Nabi and see if I can move my collection to the armory until I have a plan."

"Aw, I feel real bad. This is your home. We can find someplace else to live," DeAndre said sincerely.

Nash was tempted to take him up on it but he was starting to realize this dream he had of home wasn't really feeling right now that he was here. "Don't worry about it. I don't think I'll be around long anyway. The king isn't too happy with me.

After I catch this one last guy, I probably won't be working for the Ali Rahman family anymore."

"Well, you're welcome anytime. And you can feel free to keep your clothes here. Although, I might suggest moving your collection. My baby, bless her heart, loves guns but can't aim worth a damn."

"I heard that!" Aniyah yelled from the guest room.

"I appreciate it," Nash said as they headed for the guest room. He walked through the door and froze. Aniyah had packed and labeled all his things . . . in hot pink boxes with sparkling silver labels. There was even a small shoe-sized hot pink box with *condoms* spelled out in sparkling letters. Nash picked up a box of clothes and started to officially leave his old life behind with each box he carried to his car.

Chapter Ten

Sophie stared at her old room in horror. The ruffled comforter, the posters of her teenage crushes, and her mother unpacking her undies was the stuff of nightmares.

"Mom! I can unpack my own bag," Sophie cried as she snatched the undies from her mom's hand.

"It's just so nice to have you home. I'm going to be with you every second until this Ares guy is caught. We can have movie night tonight. Won't that be fun? I'll even let you pick: *Die Hard* or *Lethal Weapon*?" her mother asked as she grabbed some jeans from the bag and moved to put them away.

Sophie let out a long breath. She wanted to take a nap at her own home, in her own bed. "Sounds good. But I think I'm going to take a quick nap before dinner."

"I've made all your favorites. You just rest up. I'll be right downstairs if you need anything." Her mother pulled her in for a tight hug before leaving her room, making sure to keep the door cracked. She loved her parents. She really did. They could just be a little overprotective.

Sophie tossed her suitcase to the ground and crawled into bed. She wasn't really tired. She just needed some time alone to think — about Ares, about Nash, and about her future.

The door opened and Sophie cracked her eye to see Colton taking a seat at her desk with a book in one hand, his gun in the other.

"What are you doing?" Sophie asked, sitting up to glare at her brother.

"Dad said someone had to be with you at all times. I'm first. Landon got stuck on the night shift." Colton grinned.

"Get out!" Sophie threw a round pillow edged in lace at her brother.

"Sorry, Sis, but Dad—"

Sophie had had enough. She reached into her purse, pulled out the small taser and zapped her brother. He slumped in his chair and farted. At least she'd get a little time to herself. Sophie grinned as she snuggled into her pillows and closed her eyes.

Someone was in the room with her, and it wasn't her brother. Sophie didn't know how long she'd been asleep, but it was now dark out and the intruder smelled of expensive perfume.

"I know you're not asleep," the intruder said.

"Syd, what are you doing here?" Sophie asked as she flipped on the light to find her cousin sitting on the bed.

"The girls are here. Your mom invited us to dinner. She thought you'd like that. I was sent up to get you for dinner," Sydney explained. Her long, golden-blonde hair was pulled back into a sloppy bun and she wore jeans and a Kentucky sweatshirt. It was a far cry from the sexy lingerie or haute couture gowns from her modeling days, but this suited her more.

"Really?" Sophie perked up. "Sienna, Layne, Piper, Reagan, and Riley?"

"Yup. We're all here. Piper and Gabe just flew in. Ready for a girls' night in? Layne snuck in some Rose sisters tea, just like old times," Syd smirked, her hazel eyes sparking with mischief. It *was* just like old times and Sophie couldn't wait.

"This is exactly what I need!" Sophie hugged her cousin and scrambled off the bed. She stuffed her feet into slippers and looked to where her brother had been. "Where's Colton?"

"Your dad took him to see Dr. Emma. Uncle Cade found him slumped in the chair unconscious and farting," Sydney said, trying not to laugh. "I really want whatever that is. I mean, Nikki always looks at you suspiciously after you zapped her. It would totally be worth any price to zap her again. Colton must have really pissed you off."

"Dad ordered him to watch me sleep," Sophie whined as they headed downstairs.

"Um, so I don't know whether to tell you this or not," Syd said reluctantly as they stopped on the landing. "Promise you won't zap the messenger?"

"What now?" Sophie groaned.

"You know how one of the biggest bets in town

is on which of us will become pregnant first?"
Sophie gave her cousin a nod for her to continue.
"Well, your father just bought a baby monitor to put
in your room to look after you when one of them
can't be there."

Sophie blinked. "I'm sorry, what?"

Syd cringed. "Yeah, I'm afraid the betting pool
has gone mad. You're going to be mobbed with
pregnancy rumors the next time you go to the café."

"DA-A-A-AD!" Sophie yelled as she tore down
the stairs. Her father raced out of the kitchen with
his gun in hand.

"What?" He looked frantically around for bad
guys as her friends and cousins gathered to watch.

"You're putting a baby monitor in my room?
Are you serious?"

"Nothing is more serious than my baby's life,"
her father said, completely unapologetic. "Unless
you can guarantee you're *never* alone, that's the way
it's going to be."

Sophie caught Layne's eye from where she stood
behind the large group, pouring something into a
very large mug before putting the container back
into her duffel bag. "Here, have some hot tea to
relax you." She smirked. Bless her, Sophie thought
as she shook her head at her father and was
embraced by her cousins. They all understood
overprotective fathers.

An hour later, Sophie was back in her room with the
door shut, her girls surrounding her as they drank

out of the large canister of spiked iced tea, and the baby monitor dangled out the window so her father could enjoy the sound of crickets.

"I've missed y'all so much," Sophie said again as the girls laughed.

"Look who has found her Southern accent! It only took three glasses of iced tea and our cousin has come back to us," Piper teased.

"Now that Sophie has removed the stick up her ass, I want to know about Nash," Sienna smiled.

"Was it really a stick? Could it be a small twig?" Sophie asked, taking another gulp of her drink. She had said she felt lost, but this was exactly what she needed. She needed her friends to remind her of who she was and tell it like it is.

Riley shook her red hair. "Nope, it wasn't a stick. It was the entire tree."

Sophie tossed a pillow at her cousin and laughed. "I'm sorry, y'all."

"We know. And we love you anyway," Sydney told her, even thought she didn't need to. Sophie's family, even at their most annoying, were her everything, and she knew they'd go to the ends of the earth for one another.

"Now we got that out of the way, I believe we were going to be hearing about Nash and whether Nikki had been right about—" Sienna held up her hands as the group laughed again. The story of a naked Nash had been turned into something of a legend. The men wouldn't comment, and the women reveled in guessing.

Soph took another drink. "I can't say I've seen it, but things with Nash . . . well, it's complicated."

"Good thing I brought two containers of tea then," Layne said, pulling another full container out of the duffel bag. Sophie knew she wasn't going to get out of this. Her cousins were relentless when they sniffed a story, and she and Nash were the biggest story in Keeneston right now.

Sophie let out a long sigh. "I totally blew it with him two years ago."

Nash walked into the Blossom Café and took a deep breath. He'd live in his car for the rest of his life if it meant staying in Keeneston and eating at the café. It was easy to find his group for dinner. They had moved tables together in the back to fit them all and also to afford a little privacy. Zain, Gabe, Matt, Ryan, Deacon, and Wyatt were waiting. Deacon was Sydney's husband and Wyatt was Sydney's younger brother.

"Nash! Welcome home!" Wyatt said in his slow, smooth, deep Southern voice. "Sorry I didn't get to see you earlier. I was delivering a foal out at Ashton Farm for Carter." Wyatt's father, Marshall, had just retired as the sheriff and his mother, Katelyn, was the town's small-animal vet. Wyatt was the town's large-animal vet for some of the most respected horse farms in Keeneston, including Ashton Farm.

"And here's Carter now," Wyatt said, looking at the front door. Carter was Will and Kenna's son. His sister, Sienna, was best friends with Sophie.

"Hey, Nash. Did Wyatt tell you we have a new foal? It's a grandson of Naked Bootleg. We're really excited about him," Carter told Nash as he shook his hand. When Carter's father, Will, took on a managing role of the NFL team in Lexington, Carter had stepped up to co-manage the farm with his father. Every day Carter seemed to be taking over more and more of the responsibility, and the farm was thriving.

"I did. Congratulations. Do you think he'll be another racing champion like his grandfather?" Nash asked as they all sat down.

"We hope so. He's a great-looking foal already. But I think we're way more interested in hearing what you've been up to for two years than a new foal." Carter grinned as two dimples appeared in his cheeks. Nash could practically hear the women in the café sigh. When Nash had left Keeneston, Carter hadn't been on the Belles' radar as potential husband material. But Nash would be willing to bet he was now.

Nash waited for Poppy to take their order before he launched into the past two years. "I was undercover in an international gang who was stealing women and children from Rahmi and leaving behind drugs that caused crime to soar. The situation has now been resolved," Nash told them.

Ryan Parker, the son of Cole and Paige Davies Parker, leaned back in his chair. "Undercover!" he yelled out as some people groaned and Matt pumped his fist happily into the air.

"Did you all bet on me?" Nash asked though he didn't really need to. He should have expected it.

"And I just won," Matt said happily. "Mr. FBI big shot didn't even get it," Matt said, teasing Ryan. "Hey, Poppy, did anyone else get it?"

Poppy came over with her notebook. "Yup. Four others. Abby Mueez."

Okay, Ahmed's daughter wasn't a big shock. She's in DC now, supposedly.

"Dylan Davies."

Well, as for Dylan, like recognizes like. He may or may not be undercover himself, but he sure knew secrets.

"John Wolfe."

Of course. John knew everything. The CIA would kill for his abilities.

"And last is DeAndre Drews."

That rose Nash's eyebrows.

"DeAndre?" Matt asked surprised as well.

Poppy nodded her reddish-blonde hair. "Yup, he was quite adamant that he was right."

The guys looked at each other and shrugged. So it was a lucky guess by the town newbie.

"I, for one," Gabe started out, "am enthralled by your undercover work. However, let's cut to the chase. We want to know what's going on with you and Sophie."

Nash looked around the table as the guys leaned forward. Well, he could use some advice. "Two years ago . . ." he started as the guys leaned even closer to hear the best-kept secret in Keeneston.

"Oh my gosh!" Sienna cried. "And he just left?"

Sophie nodded her head as her cousins shook theirs.

"I can't believe Nash didn't let you explain," Riley said, full of indignation for her cousin.

"Well, to be fair, I wouldn't have really explained. I thought I was such a big shot working on a secret project. I guess that's when the stick got lodged," Sophie said with an apologetic tilt of her lips.

Sydney looked up at the ceiling, her lips moving quietly as she thought about something. "Yeah, that's exactly when you changed. I always blamed Nash."

"When all along it was my fault," Sophie said sadly. "I'm so sorry. I have to apologize to all of you. You took the brunt of my anger and bitchiness, but I do love y'all."

"We know that," Layne said as she moved forward to hug Sophie.

"And we love you, too. After making Nikki pass out and fart, that video Miss Lily took went viral. I'll forgive just about anything," Reagan teased.

"And don't forget about hitting on Father Ben. That was the best." Sienna laughed and Layne blushed. Sophie wasn't the only one who had hit on the town's new priest.

"But what about Nash now?" Piper asked. "You

loved him then, but what about now?"

Sophie took a deep breath and blew it out. "Of course I do. I never stopped. Even when I was mad at him for walking away. Today he told me I was worth fighting for," Sophie said a little shyly.

"Holy-moly," Piper whispered, fanning herself. "Then what are you doing here?"

"Yeah, the man you loved and then messed up with just gave you an opening for another chance. You gotta take that," Sienna told her.

"It's clear as day you two belong together," Layne declared.

"Now you just got to show him you're interested," Riley said as if it was easy.

"And how do I do that?" Sophie asked.

"Just give him all those hints women give. You know, find an excuse to touch him. Tell him how strong he is. The usual." Reagan shrugged.

"And if that doesn't work?" Sophie looked to her friends sitting around the room for help.

"Men are so simple," Layne said with a smile. "Get naked."

"Women are so confusing," Gabe said as he put down his drink.

"Hell, I'm married and I still don't understand half of what Sydney does," Deacon said with a shake of his head.

"Don't ask me," Carter said with a sigh. "They're as clear as mud."

"You can borrow my polygraph machine," Ryan offered with hope before his face fell. "Never mind, Cade and Annie are her parents and they would have taught her how to beat one."

"Wait," Zain said, holding up his hands. "Do you even want to be with her? I mean, you've only told us that she chose her job over you. Why do you think she's changed?"

"Or the better question is, do you want a second chance now?" Wyatt asked.

The table went quiet and the only thing Nash heard was the sharp, high-pitched sound of a hearing aid being adjusted behind him. "It wasn't just Sophie who chose wrong. I could have stayed. I could have fought for her. I'm going to now, though. We talked about it, and I think there's an opportunity to right the wrong. I just don't know how. It's easier to assassinate an international crime boss than to figure Sophie out."

"We've all been there," Ryan said sympathetically.

"But now you've got to win her over." Gabe smiled at the group of married men at the table. "It can't be that hard, right?"

Chapter Eleven

Sophie followed the girls outside. It was late and they were heading home after spending hours locked in her room talking about everything under the sun. Sophie was tired but energized at the same time. She had a network of friends who would look out for her, help her win over Nash, and take down any bad guy who dared step into Keeneston.

Sienna hugged her and when she pulled back, Sophie could see the concern in Sienna's green eyes. "Promise me you'll be careful. And if you have anything you need to discuss professionally, you know I'm here for you."

"I know. And I appreciate it," Sophie said, squeezing her best friend's hand.

"I'll call you tomorrow!" Sienna called and got into her car.

Sophie held up her hand and waved as Sienna, the last to leave, backed her car up and turned around in the driveway. The two beams of light swung over the patio, across the yard, and into the woods before aiming down the long driveway. In that split second, the lights moved past the tree trunks, and Sophie's hair stood on edge. Her brain recognized the threat before she even saw it. The dark figure of a man had been among the trees.

Sophie narrowed her eyes into the darkness, but it was too far away to see now. She turned to run inside at the same time she heard something hit the house where she had just been standing. Going on instinct, Sophie dove through the door, landing hard on the floor at her father's feet.

"Soph?"

Sophie didn't have time to explain. She rolled over, kicked the door shut, and grabbed the rifle her father had leaning against the wall. In seconds, her family was around her with guns drawn.

"What happened?" her mother whispered as she checked the security camera feeds.

"When Sienna was leaving, her lights caught a figure in the woods. A second later, something lodged in the house right where I was standing."

Her father looked to her brothers who simply nodded in return. Quietly and with a natural ability to work as a group, the three of them went about turning off the lights in the house and checking all the locks. Years of working together to win the Annual Davies Family Paintball Tournament came in handy when someone was trying to kill you. Her brothers and father silently slipped from the house from three different routes. However, this wasn't a game. And it wasn't paintballs being shot either.

Sophie made a move to open the front door and Annie stopped her. "Not this time."

"Mom, you know I'm perfectly capable—"

Her mother just shook her head as her eyes narrowed. The look screamed *don't mess with me*. Her mother had always been laid back, but right now Sophie could see why she'd earned the reputation as a badass.

"Tonight you do what I say and I'm telling you to go the armory, lock yourself in, and arm yourself. Shoot anyone who opens that door unless you hear two raps with five seconds between each rap on the wall. Got it?"

"But what if they get in?" Sophie asked as the seriousness of the situation just went to a whole new level.

"Then they'll have to get through me. Now go."

Sophie quickly hugged her mom tight before running to her dad's office. She found the hidden latch and opened the door to the armory. Her parents had bonded over the weapon collection. They had taught their children to respect and use all the guns in the hidden room. As Sophie locked herself in, she prepared for the longest night of her life.

Two hours of silence is what Sophie endured. She heard herself breathing. She heard the house settling and aimed her gun at the creaking noises. Sophie was so rattled that when the first knock on the wall came, she almost fired her gun. She didn't breathe or move until the second knock came five seconds later. The door then opened and she flung herself into her father's arms.

"What happened? Did you find him?"

Cade shook his head. "No, but we found evidence of someone watching the house. There were some candy wrappers and the grass had been trampled in several places. I'm afraid you'll need 24/7 guarding. Landon will take first shift tonight."

Sophie followed her dad into the living room where her family was waiting. They looked tired and edgy. Tight lines of stress were etched on her brothers' faces. Her mother suddenly looked as if she'd aged ten years, and it was all Sophie's fault. She'd put her family in danger all the while she'd been hiding. This was her mess. She was going to fix it. She needed to get out of her house for her family's own safety and there was only one place she could go for help.

"What did he shoot at me?" Sophie asked instead of telling them what she was planning on doing at first light.

"It was a tranquilizer dart fired from a rifle," her mother explained as she held up a nasty-looking dart with a puffy red marker on one end and a long needle on the other.

"They wanted you alive," her father said grimly.

"Come on, Sis. Let's get you to bed. We can talk about this in the morning and come up with a better game plan," Landon said, taking her arm and turning her toward the stairs.

Sophie let him lead her upstairs to the guest room. All the blinds and curtains had been shut and the lights were off, making it hard to detect movement. Landon settled himself in a chair with a tablet in his lap. Its screen was filled with green night-vision live camera feeds from outside. No one could approach the house without being seen.

"Where's everyone else?" Sophie asked.

"They're sleeping downstairs in shifts. Are you ready to tell me yet what you've done to have someone like Ares coming after you? Kale sent me some information on this guy. He's not your average bad guy. He's wanted worldwide for murder, political assassinations, arms dealing, sex trafficking, cyber warfare—the list continues another mile after that. And let's not forget what Ares does to those he captures. Torture the likes no one has seen before. It's obvious he is the embodiment of his name."

Sophie swallowed hard. She'd researched the Greek mythology of Ares. He was bloodthirsty. He killed for the sake of killing and showed no mercy. And knowing that Ares had found her only made her decision easier. Tomorrow she was getting away from her family so that they would be safe.

Nash woke to the sound of someone tapping the glass of his second-story window. His gun was off the nightstand and in his hand before his eyes opened. A figure, dressed in black, was balancing on the tree limb of the old maple tree out front of the bed and breakfast, waving at him. Nash put down his gun and shook his head as Sophie pressed her face to the glass and mouthed, "Let me in."

Nash flung back the cover to open the window and saw Sophie's eyes go wide. He had forgotten he slept nude. Nash grabbed a pair of sweats from the nearby chair and stepped into them before opening the window.

Sophie, her face covered in a becoming pink blush, climbed into the room. The sky was slowly changing from the darkness of the night to the deep reds and oranges of dawn as the sun grew closer to the horizon. Nash looked down at the road and didn't see a car or anyone from her family.

"How did you get here?" Nash asked as he closed the window.

"I ran."

Nash felt his eyebrow rise. "That's six miles."

"Well, it was the only way I could get here," Sophie said defensively as Nash turned on a lamp and looked at her. She was in shorts a size too small and a sports bra that looked so tight it had to be uncomfortable, but he wasn't the only one looking somewhere south of the face. Sophie's eyes hadn't traveled up to meet his yet, and Nash had to admit he enjoyed the way her blush deepened.

"Why don't you fill me in on why you're wearing clothes from what . . . college? And why you had to run through the dark to see me. Not that I mind." He smirked, finally drawing her eyes to his.

Nash watched as Sophie adjusted her breasts in the too-tight sports bra hidden under a skin-tight, long-sleeved T-shirt. "High school. These clothes are from high school and are way too small, but I couldn't run out here in what I had on."

Now it was his turn to have trouble meeting her eyes as he watched her hands adjust her breasts.

"I saw someone tonight."

That did it. Nash tore his eyes from her breasts and onto her face. How come he hadn't seen the tight lines of worry before? Nash felt slightly guilty when he realized it was because he hadn't been looking at her face.

"Who was it?"

Sophie shook her head. "My dad and brothers couldn't find him but found evidence of someone watching the house. I only saw him for a split second when Sienna left and her headlights illuminated him as she turned to leave. That's why I'm here. I need your help."

"You've already got my help. I'll do anything for you," Nash told her and he knew he would. He'd give his life for her in a split second, and that was a very real possibility since they were dealing with Ares.

"To protect my family I need to get out of my house. They were driving me crazy before by smothering me. But this is different. I can't put them in danger. Tonight my brothers and father went after one of Ares's men while my mom stood guard, ready to die for me. I have to protect them. I can't hide away doing nothing. It's me Ares is after, and it's only me that needs to be in danger."

"I'll protect them and you," Nash promised.

Sophie shook her head. "I can't put you in danger either. But I need your help to disappear. It's the only way to protect y'all."

Nash didn't answer right away. As a trained operative, he was able to run scenarios through his mind one after another, dissecting them for rate of success versus failure as quickly as possible. In the span of a few seconds, he'd come to the conclusion that disappearing all together wasn't an option, but that becoming harder to find would be a good thing.

"I have a better idea. No matter where you go, Ares will find you. If you are here in Keeneston, then we will know where Ares will eventually be. However, having you hard to find will in turn make it easier for us to spot Ares and his men," Nash told her.

He saw Sophie think about what he said. "So, if I'm here in town and I make appearances here and there but he can't find where I'm staying, it'll make his men have to be out in the open more as they search for me. Is that it?"

"That's it exactly."

"We'll need the town's help," Sophie said, already adding her input to the plan. Nash grimaced at the same time Sophie did. They were both thinking the same thing.

"And we'll have to tell my parents," Sophie groaned.

Chapter Twelve

Sophie and Nash walked slowly up the patio stairs as Cade and Annie stood waiting with their arms crossed over their chests, staring daggers of disapproval. Nash had never felt such fear as he had now. He was about to ask Sophie's parents to put their complete trust and Sophie's life into his hands. This had to be worse than when Matt had to ask Cy's permission to marry Riley.

"Where have you been?" Cade asked, his voice a deadly calm.

"And what did you do to your brother? You need to hand whatever you've used on them over to me right now young lady," Annie said, holding out her hand.

"I don't know what you're talking about," Sophie said so innocently Nash almost believed her as they walked into the house.

Annie just narrowed her eyes at her while Cade shifted his attention to Nash. "What are you doing here? Why are you two together?"

"Not that we aren't glad to see you," Annie said into the deafening silence that had followed Cade's question.

"Mom, Dad, we need to talk about something personal. I asked Nash here because it involves him, and now it's not just he and I—" Sophie started to say seriously.

"You bastard," Cade growled and launched himself at Nash. "First you break her heart and now you got her pregnant!"

Nash ducked the punch, but Cade still managed to take him down.

"Dad!"

"Cade!"

Nash heard Sophie and Annie yell and moved to avoid another punch as he refused to fight back, which only infuriated Cade further. Nash rolled to the side, avoiding an elbow to the face as Sophie waded into the fight.

"Dad! Stop it!"

"I'll not have you defending his actions. He took advantage of you and your feelings for him. I should have known when you showed up in town together things had changed," Cade growled, fighting to put Nash into a headlock as they rolled on the ground.

Nash couldn't argue for himself, he was too busy trying to avoid being killed. He heard Sophie's grunt of annoyance as suddenly she joined the fight. Together they formed a train of headlocks: Nash on his stomach with Cade on his back, the two of them struggling for control as Sophie wrapped her arm around her father's neck and pulled.

"I said stop it!" Sophie yelled.

"You shouldn't be involved in your delicate condition!" Cade grunted, still struggling to get a hold on Nash as he tried to avoid being choked out by Sophie.

"What's going on?" Colton asked sleepily, coming down the stairs.

"Sophie left in the middle of the night and showed back up with Nash to discuss something personal involving them and a third party," Annie said, amusement laced in her voice as she took a seat on the sofa to watch the show.

Nash looked up and saw Colton's face go molten in color. "You asshole! I'll kill you for touching my sister!"

"Who touched Sophie?" Landon asked as he stumbled into the room, his hair sticking out at all angles.

"Nash did. He was out with her last night," Colton growled as he raced forward to remove Sophie as Landon leapt onto Nash and Cade.

"Be careful, your sister's pregnant," Cade yelled.

Nash saw Annie grin and shake her head as she crossed her arms over her chest and sat back.

"Not pregnant," Nash tried to say, but with Cade choking him no one else heard him.

He felt the added weight as Sophie leapt onto her brothers' backs. "Get off of him!"

"We'll take care of this, Soph, go upstairs," Landon ordered as he shook her off.

"Don't make me tase you again!" Sophie threatened as she got a lock on Colton and squeezed.

Annie put her fingers to her lips and blew. The
sharp whistle pierced the air and everyone froze.
"As fun as this has been, I think we need to hear
what Sophie and Nash have to say since there's no
way she's pregnant."

"What do you mean not pregnant?" Cade asked.

"They just got together the other day.
Remember she still *hated* him at the wedding,"
Annie said, using air quotes. "And I would think
you would know after having three children that
you can't tell you're pregnant after just a couple of
days. I think they're here to tell us we are being
replaced."

Nash tried to nod his head as Cade loosened his
grip around his neck. "Is this true, sweetie?"

"Yes, Dad," Sophie said as she let go of her
brother.

"Oh, well, sorry about that," Cade said as he
released Nash, and Landon stumbled off the pile.
But then he leaned down to whisper into Nash's ear,
"You hurt her and no one will ever find your body."

Nash got to his knees as Colton and Landon
took a seat on the opposite couch from their mother.
"I thought you'd be a better fighter and all," Colton
said with disdain in his voice. He still refused to
believe Nash hadn't been with Sophie. And he was
right not to. Given the chance, Nash wouldn't think
twice about stripping her naked and spending hours
lost in her embrace, but Nash figured they probably
didn't want to hear that.

"Sophie came to me tonight to help her. She told

me about the man outside your house," Nash said instead. "I have an idea, and I want your help with it."

Sophie came to stand by his side as her father took a seat on the couch next to Annie. He slung his arm around her shoulder as he waited for Nash to continue. Nash didn't miss the reassuring squeeze Cade gave Annie's shoulder or the way her hand went to rest on Cade's thigh. They still loved each other after all these years, and more than that, they were partners. They would have each other's backs through thick and thin. Nash looked quickly to Sophie standing next to him and felt a pang of longing. He wanted that, and there had been only one woman he had ever wanted that with.

"Sophie wanted to disappear in order to protect you. I could make that happen, but no matter what, Ares would find her. He's ruthless, fearless, and will hurt anyone just for fun—innocent or not. If Sophie disappears, then so does Ares. But if Sophie is known to be in Keeneston but can't be found easily . . ." Nash explained as Annie and Cade's heads started to nod. They were already following his train of thought.

"Then you know where he'll be," Annie said grimly.

"And you'll force him out into the open," Cade sighed unhappily. "Damn, it's a good plan."

"Why is that a bad thing?" Colton asked.

"Because Sophie can't stay here. We have to find a place to hide her," Annie answered.

"A place I already have," Nash told them. "A place hardly anyone knows about where I will watch her."

"Like hell you will," Cade snapped. "That's my daughter and I'll watch over her."

Nash was about to answer when Sophie gently placed her hand on his arm to quiet him. "No, Dad. I want Nash with me so you can protect Mom. I won't have it any other way. This is my mess, and I'm already placing everyone in town in enough danger."

"I think it's about time you told us the truth, Sophie. All of it," her mother added pointedly.

"I can't. I signed nondisclosures and the clearance levels . . . if I told you, I would be in serious trouble," Sophie said.

"I think you're already in serious trouble. And don't get me started on clearance levels. Your father has more than enough clout to get them if he doesn't already have it. Or do we need to call Bridget's father and just ask him?" Annie challenged. Bridget Mueez's father had been the head of the military for years. He had since retired, but he could still get whatever information he needed in a single phone call.

Nash felt Sophie stiffen beside him and then relax. She'd decided to tell them. "I designed a smart missile. It's worth billions. I have one more fix to do, and then it'll be sent for testing. If the testing goes as planned, the U.S. government will have the most advanced and accurate weapon in the world."

Cade blinked and her brothers let out a low whistle. However, her mother didn't look surprised. "About time you came clean. Do you have any idea how hard it is to pretend not to know what you've been up to."

"How did you —?" Sophie started to ask.

"John Wolfe," her father and mother said together.

With that, the tension left the room. Sophie felt the weight being lifted off her shoulders. Sure, she was going to lose her job over this and possibly end up in jail. But when it came down to her life, she trusted her family with all of her secrets. Plus, it wasn't like she even needed her job anymore. She just hoped she didn't end up in jail or dead at the end of this.

"Where are you taking her?" her father asked Nash.

Sophie looked over at him standing next to her and realized she was still holding onto his arm. He moved then, just enough to dislodge her hand but before her arm could drop to her side, his fingers laced through hers. He squeezed it, supportively holding her hand as if they did this all the time. The way her heart sped up was the only indication to her that this was new. She leaned toward him and saw her mother's eyes drop to their linked hands and flutter back to Nash's face as he began to explain.

"I think it's better that no one knows exactly where. I don't want any of you visiting and being followed," Nash said with a slight cringe.

"You think I can't tell if I have a tail?" her father asked, insulted.

Her mother remained silent.

"I can tell you it's on Mo's property, but that's all. She'll be safe. I'll guard her with my life. You have my word," Nash pledged.

Her father made a move to argue, but her mother simply squeezed his leg to silence him. "You promise not to leave her side?"

"I swear to it," Nash said solemnly.

"Then what do you want us to do?" her mother asked, shushing her husband who began to argue.

"I want Sophie to pop up over town as if it's not a big deal. We'll have dinner tonight at the café instead of here. I want lots of people around. Make it easy to see her. Then we'll need help getting out of downtown Keeneston to where we stash our car without being seen. I want to confuse Ares's men. They will likely grow bolder so don't be surprised if they are still watching the house. If you see anyone, let me know. I'll take him down. I'll need you and the town to be our eyes and ears."

"Easy enough." Annie smiled as she patted Cade's leg and stood up. "Come on, Soph, let's get you packed. Cade, don't kill Nash while we're upstairs. He's going to save our daughter. Or our daughter is going to save him. Either way, don't kill him."

Sophie looked between her parents and Nash in surprise. She thought they'd have to fight for their plan. Although, by the look her dad and brothers were giving Nash, she figured she might not want to leave him alone with them. And Nash and Sophie weren't even a couple. It was the nightmare of high school all over again.

"Behave," she said, pointing her finger to the men in her life before following her mother upstairs.

"Start packing. I have to get you something special. And Sophie, I like Nash. I always have. I don't know what happened two years ago, but there's nothing that brings out people's true feelings like a life-or-death situation," her mother said as if giving her a lecture on the birds and bees. "I'll be right back with something for you. Safety first!"

Sophie watched her mom leave the room and shook her head. Please don't be the birds and bees talk. If her mom came back in with a book about sex, she'd die. She was a couple decades past that talk.

Sophie pulled out her old cross-country duffel bag from high school and looked for the few clothes she'd had brought over from her house. She tossed them into the bag along with some of her old clothes that still fit, well, at least fit better than her running clothes from high school.

"Here we go!" her mother called out from the hall. "The most important thing for a woman to have in a situation like this."

Oh no. Please, not a box of condoms. Her mother held out a black lace corset instead, and Sophie was ready to expire on the spot.

"Every woman needs—"

"Mom!" Sophie cut in. "I know about sex. We

don't need to talk about it."

Annie rolled her eyes and held out her other hand with a compact, yet powerful Smith and Wesson in it. "A great way to conceal her gun."

"Oh," Sophie replied sheepishly as she took the corset in hand. It wasn't a traditional corset. It had three places to hide a gun: one under each arm and at the small of her back. "This is really nice. Thanks, Mom."

"I know you have that gun you invented, and I'm sure you have more at home. This was going to be your Christmas present. I thought it would come in handy now, though. As for sex, are you and Na—?" Annie started to ask.

"Mom! Nope. Not going there." Sophie felt herself turning bright red. She'd rather face Ares than talk about her desire to have sex with Nash, especially after seeing him naked that morning. And Nikki must have caught him coming out of cold water because she'd understated things.

Her mother shrugged. "Do you want me to pack some things from your house and bring them to dinner at the café tonight?"

"That would be great, thank you."

Her mother waited for Sophie to put the corset and gun into her bag before pulling her into another mom hug. "When your life is on the line, feelings can't be hidden. Remember that when trying to make your decision about Nash. And know we will be right here to help with Ares. We won't let anything happen to you."

"Thanks, Mom."

Nash moved toward the door as soon as Sophie headed upstairs. By the way Cade, Colton, and Landon were looking at him, he worried a broken bone or two was in someone's future.

"We used to like you, Nash," Colton said quietly as he cast a sidelong look up the stairs to make sure Sophie was out of earshot.

"But then you left town and suddenly Sophie hated you. You see, it leads us to believe you did something to hurt her," Landon said as he moved closer.

"And you left my baby broken-hearted," Cade hissed.

How long could it take Sophie to throw some things into a bag? "It didn't happen like that. What it comes down to is that it's none of your business. What happens between Sophie and me in the past, present, or future is private."

"I owe you for saving her in England. But if you think I'll just sit back and watch you break her heart again, you're wrong. You're to protect her only. That's it," Cade warned.

"You step one foot out of Friendsville," Colton cautioned.

"Sophie! Are you all ready?" Landon said loudly, ending the threats.

"Leave him alone," Annie chided with a smile on her face as she followed Sophie down the stairs. She rolled her eyes as she saw how Nash was partially surrounded by her father and brothers.

"Boys, take your sister outside. Here, Nash, carry this," Annie said, taking the bag from Sophie and tossing it to Nash as the men grumbled but went outside to lead Sophie to his SUV.

"You're a good man, Nash. Remember that love is worth fighting for."

"I plan to," Nash admitted softly.

"Good," Annie beamed. "But if you screw it up, it's not my husband you need to worry about."

Yeah, Nash was worried about that almost as most as facing Ares.

Chapter Thirteen

Nash drove all around Keeneston, making sure he didn't have a tail. When at last he was positive no one was following him, he headed toward Sienna and Ryan's house. Sophie had stayed quiet the entire drive up until then.

"We're going to Sienna's? That's where we are staying?"

"No, but that's where we are going to hide my car," Nash answered. "Nabi and Ahmed showed me a small historic cabin deep in the woods of the farm. There's a deer path that leads to it, but the fastest way to it is to climb the fence at Ryan and Sienna's and hike the two miles. Ryan also has a garage with no windows for me to put the truck in."

"Won't being isolated be bad if Ares finds us?"

Nash shook his head as he turned into the driveway at the Parker house. "Ahmed and Nabi made me live there for a month for survival training. I wasn't allowed to leave the woods. I thrived. I know every inch of those woods and can set traps to alert us of anyone approaching. Plus now I have weapons and technology to help. I've told Ahmed and Nabi. They're the only ones who know where we are and they should have the cabin stocked by now."

Ryan walked out of the house in jeans and a T-shirt, looking surprised to see them. The earth shook as Sophie and Nash got out of the car. The house jiggled as thunder roared. Then, on an excited *woof* that echoed across the entire state of Kentucky, the ugliest dog Nash had ever seen stampeded his way past Ryan. Pumpkins and flowerpots filled with mums went crashing off the porch as Ryan stood, shaking his head.

"I don't know why Sienna even bothers," he sighed. "What are you two doing here this early?"

Nash would have answered, but Hooch, their massive beast of a dog, was currently shoving his drooling, basketball-sized head between his legs, trying to sniff his crotch. Sophie's uncontrollable laughter wasn't helping things.

"Knock it off, Hooch. I've got a bone for you," Ryan called out as he lifted up a bone the size of a baseball bat.

Hooch pulled his head from Nash's crotch and wagged his tail, denting Nash's SUV in his exuberance at seeing the bone. Ryan tossed it off the porch and Hooch lumbered over to the bone, taking out a birdbath on his way.

"That will keep him occupied for the next hour. What's going on?" Ryan asked as he walked down the steps toward them. "Is this about Ares? I've been looking into him. That's one bad man."

"Yes, he is. I'm making Sophie a little scarcer. There was someone watching her parents' house last night. I only want her seen in town surrounded by people. And to do that I need to take her someplace out of the way to stay," Nash explained.

"So you can draw Ares and his men out when they look for her. Got it. You need to stay here? I can send Sienna to her parents' house," Ryan offered.

"No. I have someplace in mind, but I need to hide my truck in your garage," Nash said, trying to ignore the horrendous slurping sounds of Hooch gnawing on the bone.

"Of course. I'll keep an eye out for anyone suspicious and alert my office about the situation," Ryan told him. Having the local FBI office ready to assist would be good if Nash intended to turn Ares over. However, he wasn't intending anything of the sort. Not when Ares was a threat to Sophie.

"Thanks," Nash said instead as he moved to pull the car into the garage. By the time he closed the garage door, locked it from the inside, and walked back outside through the house, Sienna was in deep conversation with Sophie. The second Nash appeared the conversation stopped and they both looked guiltily up at him while Ryan was picking up the destruction Hooch left behind.

"Ready?" Nash asked Sophie, who simply nodded.

Everyone agreed to meet for dinner at the café that night and then said their goodbyes. Nash crossed his bags containing weapons and clothes over his shoulders and tried to reach for Sophie's but she shook him off.

"It's okay, I can carry it," she said as she climbed the black, four-plank fence and dropped onto the farthest part of Mo and Dani's farm.

Nash followed and then took the lead as they headed toward the dense woods. As they neared the woods, they walked silently next to each other. Nash glanced at Sophie, her face set in deep thought, and looked quickly away. Why were women so complicated? Did she just want his help or did she also want him? He knew he wanted her in more than one way. He didn't want to protect her because it was a job. He would lay down his life for her because he loved her. The question at hand: Was he brave enough to put his heart on the line again?

Sophie kept her eyes on the trail ahead of them as they entered the woods. The morning sun shone through the fall leaves, lighting up the brilliant reds, oranges, and yellows. Sophie felt at peace as they walked through the woods. They saw deer and rabbits nibbling on their breakfast. Squirrels were searching for nuts to ready themselves for winter, and Sophie was preparing herself for sharing a cabin with Nash.

The girls had said guys were easy to read. Well, Nash wasn't. His face was impassive and she couldn't tell what he was thinking about. He had said she was worth fighting for, but did he mean for her heart or only for her life?

Bird chirps drew her eyes up from the fresh-fallen leaves to the trees around them. The path they were on was obviously an animal track. It had started off wide, but the further they walked in the woods, the narrower the path became. It followed a small stream to the left that brushed up against the path before winding its way off into the woods only to come back to the path again. Was that what she and Nash were doing? Did they run off course only to be returning together now?

Thirty minutes later, the path widened again to a small clearing surrounded on two sides by the creek. Sitting in the middle of the clearing was a small, one-story cabin with an A-frame wood-shingled roof that sloped over a porch running the length of it. Two rocking chairs and a small table sat under the roof to the left of the front door and between two small glass windows.

"How old is this place?" Sophie asked in wonder. There was no sidewalk, no driveway, and based on the size of the river rock fireplace and lack of electrical lines, no electricity either. There was a small lean-to filled with firewood not far from the house and a small second structure that looked to be an outhouse.

"Early 1800s is our best guess. Nabi did some research on the farm and found it had been settled as people started to make their way West, but he couldn't find out what happened to those who lived in the cabin. It had been falling down, but I renovated it while I was out here for that month. It's nothing fancy, but it'll keep us safe and warm," Nash said as they walked across the tall grass that had been bent by the weight of the fallen leaves and animals crossing to the creek.

"It's beautiful out here," Sophie said with wonder as she listened to the creek babbling over stones, the slight breeze rustling the leaves, and the sound of animals preparing for winter.

"I thought so, too. I ended up coming out here quite often to finish my renovations even after I had returned to the farm. We're about five miles from the main part of the farm. It seems as if we stepped back in time here," Nash said as he climbed the front steps and pulled out a set of keys.

Sophie took one last look around while Nash unlocked the door. She may feel at peace out here, but it was an illusion. Not only was her personal life in upheaval, but also her actual life was on the line. There was one thing she could do to fix that, though. She could figure out how to fix the final kink to the guidance software her team was battling so the weapon could be tested. The sooner the missile was turned over to the government, the better. If only she could get over the mental block she was having on the system. When she got these blocks, she found that relaxing completely and letting her mind wander usually helped. Eventually her mind would wander to the solution and, like a lightning bolt, she'd sit up with the answer. Maybe the peace and quiet of the cabin and the beauty of nature would help.

Nash unlocked the door and held it open for her. Inside, new wooden floors gleamed. The entire log cabin was open and clean. A wood-burning stove surrounded by cabinets sat against one of the sidewalls with a small kitchen table and two chairs under one of the windows. The back wall was nothing but a log wall. A bed with a thick, colorful Shaker quilt was against the back wall. On the opposite wall was the large river-rock fireplace. The brown, tan, red, and gray rocks were stacked to make the chimney along with a hearth big enough to sit on. In front of the fireplace were two overstuffed chairs and ottomans with a rug on the floor.

"This is beautiful," Sophie said as she looked at the exposed beams running across the angled ceiling. "I can't believe you did all this."

Nash lifted the bags from his shoulders and set them on the bed. "I like to come out here every now and then. It's rejuvenating. I'm glad you like it."

Sophie placed her bag on the bed next to Nash's and glanced at the chest of drawers with an oval mirror attached to it next to the bed. "Want to share the drawers?"

"There's plenty of room. I have some stuff out here already, or at least I should. The bottom two drawers are open and all yours. I'll let you get settled while I put up some motion-activated wireless cameras. It won't take me long."

Nash reached into one of the bags and pulled out a box filled with tiny cameras, went to one of the cabinets in the kitchen area, and pulled out some tools. "There's food in the cabinets if you want anything. And there's water over there," Nash said, pointing to a huge five-gallon water dispenser sitting on the counter. "I'll be right back."

Sophie moved to the window and watched as Nash pulled out a ladder from the lean-to. She didn't know how long she stood watching him before deciding that maybe Layne was right—she should just get naked and see what he'd do because right now she couldn't get a read on him. With a sigh of both frustration and longing, Sophie began to unpack. If only the world outside this cabin would vanish, leaving her safe and in Nash's arms.

Opening the drawers, she put away her clothes and then went to explore the cabin. There was plenty of food, pots, pans, and toiletries. They could live here for a month if need be. Unfortunately, her presence was required in Keeneston for dinner that night. Well, she might as well make lunch. She pulled out bread, peanut butter, and jelly. It wasn't gourmet, but at least she was doing something.

Chapter Fourteen

Two hours after arriving at the cabin, Nash came inside. Sophie had set the sandwiches and chips on plates at the table and had two glasses of water waiting. She took a deep breath as Nash looked around and set his things down. She had made a decision. No more waiting to see what Nash felt. No more wondering what was going to happen between them. She was going to find out once and for all where they stood and where they were going.

"I thought we could have a date," Sophie said with courage she didn't feel. Nash had put his heart on the line before and now it was her time to do so.

A smile tugged at his lips, accented by a day's growth of his whiskers. Sophie's stomach flipped and then swirled as he moved close enough for her to smell. He smelled of fresh leaves and something she recognized as a scent belonging solely to him.

"A date sounds great," Nash said, taking a seat at the table. "Thank you for making brunch."

Sophie sat down opposite Nash at the small table. He said he'd changed. She had said she'd changed. Now it was time to see if that was really true. "Tell me about your time with Poseidon."

"I guess it's only fair since you told me about your missile, but it's not a pleasant conversation," Nash said, popping a chip into his mouth. A mouth that was suddenly tight with tension.

"I figured as much, but I want to know anyway," Sophie decided.

"It started with a couple missing people from the illegal brothels of Rahmi, then some teenagers who were deemed runaways. Suddenly a lot more drugs were appearing in our schools, on the docks, and in the clubs. Not saying Rahmi is utopia, but there was an epidemic almost overnight. Then the king's secretary's daughter went missing. The king sent a small task force to try to find her. She was eighteen and was starting university in the fall.

"The task force found she'd gone to a club. Video showed her taking drugs and passing out. A man carried her out with her friends stumbling behind her. They got in a van and just like that, five girls were gone. The task force followed the drugs and found it was a highly addictive, synthetic heroin. Stores were being robbed to pay for the addiction. Women were selling themselves or just disappearing. The king called me in when his team discovered the customs minister was being blackmailed," Nash told her as he looked out the window.

"I was brought in and discovered drugs, prostitution, and blackmail were a signature of Red Shadow, an international gang led by a mysterious man who went by the name Poseidon. It took a couple of weeks of crime, but I was finally asked to join. I found the secretary's daughter. She was so hooked on drugs she couldn't speak. She was at brothel in India. I burnt it to the ground and shipped the women back to Rahmi. But selling sex wasn't the main moneymaker. It made a lot, don't get me wrong, but it was the drugs and blackmail that brought in the most. Red Shadow was nothing more than the mafia on steroids. To get in, I had to kill a politician who had helped keep the police off Red Shadow's tail as they set up a drug trade in France. The politician wanted a larger cut of the drug profits."

"What did you do after you got in?" Sophie asked quietly. Nash was trained to combat evil and to do that you had to have a pure heart. Anyone pure of heart would have trouble seeing the things he saw, and it must have been hard for him to do what he did.

"I beat up dealers who weren't paying on time. I was paid to take out competition for Red Shadow or for people who paid Red Shadow to do their dirty work for them. When I could, I would save those I could get to safety. The children especially. I might have shot a couple of dealers who peddled to the weak instead of helping them. It all depended on whether I was alone or not. I advanced until I was assigned to Poseidon himself. Through this period, I learned of Ares. He'd been Poseidon's mentee. He taught Ares all he knew. Even gave him the name and was the only person to know Ares's real name. Then one day, Ares killed a whole shipment of prostitutes because he deemed them unfit to service him. While Poseidon believed in killing, he never did unless it served his purpose or he was paid for it. When he confronted Ares, Ares challenged Poseidon for leadership. When he lost, he left with the most evil of Poseidon's men and started his own gang where nothing was off limits."

Sophie took a deep breath. "And you killed Poseidon and his men?"

Nash looked at her then and with a completely emotionless face said, "I told you before, I slit his throat and blew up everyone on his yacht."

Sophie watched him. He was trying to shock her. "I have a feeling that's not all you did. Knowing you, you also dismantled his entire organization."

"Don't let that sway you, Sophie. I did what I was ordered to do. I lied, I cheated, and I killed. I was not a saint."

Sophie could tell he was watching her reaction closely. He was expecting her to be revolted. He was expecting her to tell him he was wrong for what he did. But she couldn't. "You did horrible things in order to make the world better. I can't say I understand. I'm not a soldier. I might have trained in combat with you, but I don't know how it is to take a life, and I hope I never do. You did what you had to do to take down a massive organization hurting thousands of people, and I have nothing but respect for you, Nash. Like I always have. You're a good man with a good heart. It's one of the things I love about you."

Sophie snapped her mouth shut. She hadn't meant to say that right now. She was going to feel out the situation a little more before dropping the L-word. Nash's face didn't change except for the tic of the muscle along his jaw. He took a sip of water and then let out a breath.

"And you. What changed with you?" Nash asked, ignoring her mention of love.

"I spent the last two years proving I was good enough to hang with the boys. I forgot who I was. I didn't come home much because I would be accused of not caring enough about the project. So I worked night and day. Eventually I won them over, but I realized it wasn't me who won them over. It was the nondescript lab worker I had become. I didn't laugh. I didn't crack jokes. I couldn't show emotion. If I did, it was because I was a woman and the guys would snicker and roll their eyes. And so here I am, ready to go home as soon as I can figure out one last thing before someone tries to kill me," Sophie said with a sigh. It had been a tough realization to come to that she wasn't the same confident Sophie she'd been in college, and she was determined to find that person again.

"Since this is a date," Nash said with the slightest tilt of his lips, "let's go for a romantic walk in the woods."

Nash stood and held out his hand. Sophie didn't know really what he was thinking but her heart beat a little faster at the idea of him liking their fake date enough to continue the charade. She placed her hand in his, and he laced his fingers with hers as he led her outside.

"Remember the tricks we used to play on each other?" Nash asked with a chuckle.

Sophie smiled as she remembered their past. "You used to hide and try to take me down by surprise."

"But you got me that one time at the pool with Zain and Gabe," Nash playfully chided as they walked closer to the stream. He stopped walking and she looked down at the water rolling off the stones and into a little pool about two feet deep.

"I planned that for over a week. I had Gabe call you to the pool, and *BAM*, I was able to shove you into the pool as you passed by my hiding place. It was the only time I ever got you." Sophie laughed as she remembered Nash flying into the pool. She also remembered him coming out of it with his clothes clinging to him.

"I remember."

The grin that suddenly broke out on Nash's face was the only warning Sophie got. The next thing she knew she was on her bottom in the creek. She gasped at the coldness of the water in the shallow pool. A frog croaked and jumped off the pile of stones that caused the formation of the pool and disappeared downstream.

Sophie's mouth opened and closed and then she felt it. The laughter started all the way down at her toes and finally burst from her mouth. Not the fake laughter she had perfected for her coworkers' stupid jokes in the lab, but a real laugh from her soul.

"There you are. Welcome back," Nash smiled down at her from the bank of the stream.

Sophie tried to stand but teetered and fell back again, laughing so hard tears were rolling down her face. She felt alive, cold, and mischievous. "I can't get up," she said as she tried to catch her breath.

Nash crouched down and held out his hand. Sucker. Sophie grabbed his hand and let him help her up. As soon as she felt his muscles relax, she tightened her grip and fell back into the stream, taking him with her.

She laughed when she heard him draw in a surprised breath as he hit the cold water. "Gotcha," Sophie smiled proudly from under him, but it was his smile that made her worry she'd fallen into his plan.

"I'm pretty sure *I* got you," Nash said, looking into her face. They were chest-to-chest, hip-to-hip, and nose-to-nose. Instead of getting up, Nash tilted his head slightly and kissed her. It was soft at first and over too quickly.

"Finally," Sophie whispered, her voice husky with emotion. She wiggled under him, trying to get closer, and Nash obliged. He wrapped his arms around her and pulled her to his chest as his kiss went from soft to not. It was two years of anger, love, desire, and longing rolled into a single moment. His tongue was masterful, his fingers magnificent, and when he rocked his hips into hers and hit just the right spot, Sophie saw stars.

Without breaking the kiss, Nash moved his hands from her shoulder blades to her waist. He sat back on his heels, bringing her with him. Using his hands to give her directions since their mouths were otherwise occupied, Nash moved her legs around his waist. His hands moved to cup her ass and then they were out of the creek. Sophie hung onto his neck as Nash carried her back toward the cabin. He stroked her tongue with his, squeezed his fingers so he was massaging her bottom as he pressed her against his erection. By the time they made it to the cabin, Sophie had forgotten all about being cold. Her body thrummed with passion and heat. The only thing that could satisfy the building tension was Nash.

Nash pushed open the door and left it open. The sun streamed in through the door and windows of the cabin. He sat on the hearth of the fireplace and finally pulled back from her. She felt the loss instantly.

"I just need to light the fire," his graveled voice said as he moved to strike a long match he had nearby. Paper flared, kindling caught fire, and warmth spread.

"Nash," Sophie said, reaching for him again.

"Wait," Nash said softly. "Sophie, as much as I want to get carried away in the moment and blame whatever happens next on that, I can't. I respect you too much and care about you too much to do that.

It's all or nothing and only you can decide which you want. If we go forward, then we go forward together." Nash ran his hand over the wet hair surrounding her face and cupped her cheek. He bent forward and placed a loving kiss on her lips. "The question is, what do you want, Sophie?"

Sophie pulled back from his gentle hold and stood up. She faced Nash and saw the emotion in his eyes. It was two years ago all over again. Only this time Sophie knew what it was like to walk away from love, and she was determined never to do it again.

She reached down to grab the hem of her shirt and peeled the wet fabric from her skin. Nash's eyes flared with appreciation, but he didn't move from where he sat on the hearth. "You. I want you, Nash."

Nash looked up at the woman he'd loved since the first time he saw her in a crowded ballroom. Some people got second chances, but in Nash's career they were as rare as unicorns. A second chance came when the bullet ripped your shoulder apart instead of your brain. But now Sophie was standing half-dressed in front of him offering him just that, a second chance.

He told her she was worth fighting for, and he intended to do just that, not only with his heart, but also with his life. Ares wouldn't rest until Sophie was his. If Nash got between Ares and his goal, Ares wouldn't hesitate to kill him. Before this was over, one of them would be dead. Nash didn't think he could walk away from Sophie, knowing there may not be another chance.

The anger, the regret, and the desperation of the past two years had melted as soon as Sophie laughed. She was drenched sitting in the creek and it had been the sexiest he'd ever seen her. Sophie had been hiding for two years, just as he had. And now it was their time, their time to love, and their time to make their own future.

"I've always been yours," Nash told her, keeping his eyes locked with Sophie's.

Sophie reached behind her and a second later, her bra fell to the floor. Nash swallowed hard. She was even more beautiful than he imagined. Rounded breasts that begged to be worshiped gave way to an athletic waist. As she pushed down her jeans, he admired her long, shapely legs.

Sophie stood nude before the fireplace, looking down at him. Nash fought every instinct he had to grab her and make her his right then and there. Two years before, she turned away from him, and now he'd give her one last chance to do so. If she didn't, then he'd be hers forever . . . or as long as he had left on this earth.

"You said you want me so come take what you want," Nash challenged. This time Sophie didn't look confused. She didn't hesitate as she walked forward only to stop and kneel down in front of him. She pushed her way in between his legs and reached for his shirt.

In minutes she had undressed him. She'd

moved slowly and confidently taking off his shoes, his pants, and running her hands over his chest, down his stomach, and grabbing onto what she wanted. Nash's head fell back as his breathing quickened. He'd given Sophie the power not only to choose her own future, but their future as well.

Sophie moved slowly as Nash held her tight. The warmth of the fire behind them was nothing compared to the heat between them. She knew Nash had given her an out, but that was the last thing she wanted. She wanted him. She had for years. The only thing stopping her had been fear. Fear to put herself out there, fear of ruining a friendship, fear of losing her job . . . but now the irony was that fear for her life was what gave her the courage to stand up to her past fears.

Nash's fingers dug into her hips as he held her tight, the friction causing her to gasp for breath. And she thought undressing him had been arousing. He was all muscle from his years of training. When she pulled the shirt from his body, she saw that even in the two years he'd been gone he'd changed. The breadth of his shoulder, the rippled muscles of his abdomen, the definition of his arms — it was different. He'd matured not only in what he'd had to do and see, but his body had, too. Gone was any trace of the boy he'd been when she'd first seen him. In his place was a mature man. A little more serious than when she left him, but then again so was she.

Their bodies moved in unison and Sophie knew

this was more than sex. She didn't need Nash to tell her he loved her. She knew this was an expression of love, of trust, and of partnership years in the making. Nash moved his hands from her hips to her breasts. He pushed them together and dipped his head. His tongue flicked the taut peaks and Sophie stopped thinking.

Chapter Fifteen

Sophie groaned when Nash got out of bed. She knew it was coming as the shadows grew long across the hardwood floor. It was time for dinner. Time to leave the cocoon of the past hours and go to the Blossom Café.

"We have to go or your parents will tear the town apart looking for you," Nash said as he pulled on a new pair of jeans. That wasn't the only reason Sophie was grumbling. Nash was no longer naked.

"They're going to take one look at me and know I've been having sex and then all bets are off — or should I say on," Sophie told him as she finally got out of bed.

Nash smiled proudly. "I know."

"Really? You're proud of that?" Sophie asked as she hunted for her bra.

"Of course I am. What man wouldn't be? And before you ask, yes, I want every man in the entire world to know so they don't get any ideas about you and them."

Sophie rolled her eyes. "Should I just wear a sign?"

Nash thought for a minute. "Sure. It could say *I am well loved by Nash Dagher* and it will match the satisfied smile on your face perfectly."

"Hello, Ego, I've found someone bigger than you," Sophie teased.

Nash stopped getting dressed as he reached under a chair and pulled out her bra. She turned so he could help her put it on. "I'll happily tell anyone who wants to know I have no interest in anyone else and that Sophie Davies has loved me well."

Sophie smacked his arm. "You'll be a dead man. My father—"

"—has a pretty good idea what's going to happen between two people in our situation. After all, I believe he met your mother during a drug operation, right?"

"I don't think he'd care to be reminded of that," Sophie said under her breath as she finished getting dressed.

"Don't worry. Our friends and your family are the least of our concerns."

"You've been gone too long if you think that," Sophie said, slipping on her coat. The sun was down and a chill was settling in the air.

"Grab your cell phone and charger. We'll recharge during dinner. And stop worrying. Everything will be fine." Nash grinned before kissing her senseless.

Sophie froze in place. It was like a bolt of lightning hit her. "I've got it!"

"Got what?" Nash asked as he put on his boots.

"The solution to the software glitch for the missile. It just came to me. Quick, get me something to write with," Sophie ordered as she closed her eyes and started repeating the solution over and over again. There was no way she would take a chance of letting the thought disappear.

"Here." Nash shoved a pad of old yellow ruled paper and a pencil into her hands.

Sophie didn't move as she wrote and wrote. She filled the page barely breathing and turned to the second page. The ideas flowed from her head as her fingers had trouble keeping up. After the fourth page, two diagrams, and an untold amount of talking to herself, she set the pad down and took a breath. If she got this fix to the lab tomorrow, they could test it in a couple days. The sooner she handed this missile off to the government, the better.

Nash pulled up to the café to find it filled to the brim. Cars lined both sides of the street and every citizen of Keeneston seemed to be inside. For all the teasing Nash had given Sophie, he was worried, but not because of her family. They'd wait to kill him until after Sophie was out of danger. It was Ares he was worried about. The person who had been spotted hadn't been caught and had definitely seen Sophie. He would be reporting her location back to Ares, and Nash expected to come face to face with him soon enough.

"I'm going to park at the courthouse," Nash told

her as he pulled into the parking lot and took a reserved space.

"You'll get a ticket," Sophie warned.

"It's okay, I know the sheriff," Nash teased, reaching for his gun when the door to the sheriff's department opened.

"You can't park there," a young man said. He was in jeans and a brown fleece with a gold star embroidered on the chest.

"Who's that?" Nash asked, pulling his gun from his hip.

"Cody Gray. He's a new deputy. Well, new to you," Sophie said, opening her door. "Hey, Cody, it's me."

"Oh, hi, Sophie. Are you here to see me?" he asked hopefully.

Sophie heard Nash's choice response to that before his door opened, too. "No, we're not. We're going to the café, but there's no place to park, and I need the car close to the café in case I need to get Sophie out fast," Nash explained, flipping open his wallet to identify himself as a royal guard of Rahmi.

"You must be Nash. Cody Gray. Matt filled me in. You can put that away. From what Matt said, you may be out of a job. But I'll do anything to help Sophie out. Why don't I escort you across the street," Cody said to Sophie. Cody was a wonderful guy, polite, brave, and gentlemanly. But he was young and eager. And right now he seemed like a little boy compared to Nash. She blushed as she looked at Nash who in return lifted his frown into a smile as if reading her mind.

Sophie positioned herself next to Nash and let Cody lead the way across the street. Through the large plate glass windows of the café, they could tell the second they were spotted. Heads swiveled to the door as they came in. Nash gave a quick glance around and confirmed what he thought. The entire town was there. Everyone from professional PTA president Pam Gilbert, who had turned into a fraternity mom now that her sons were in college, all the way to elderly Father James who looked relaxed in street clothes tonight. Nash hadn't seen most of these people in years. Though he greeted his friends when he arrived, he didn't see Mo and Dani, Kenna and Will, Paige and Cole, and the others whom he considered practically family.

As Cade and Annie rose to greet Sophie, Gabe, Zain, and Mila waved Nash over to their table. Nash smiled and shook Mila's hand. The wavy brunette beauty smiled at him warmly. "It's nice to finally get to see you in person," Mila said with just a hint of German accent left.

"I'm sorry I couldn't make it to your wedding," Nash said, letting go of her hand.

"I'm just happy you were there to help us out when you did. Besides, I feel as if I already know you from all Zain and Gabe have told me." Mila smiled as her gray eyes sparkled. He could see she was perfect for Zain, who seemed more settled and sure of himself and of his role in the royal family. Even though Zain was still heir apparent, he didn't seem bothered by it as he had in the past.

Zain gave him a pat on the back as his father and mother walked up. Dani, so unlike the rest of the royal family with her informal ways, pushed past her sons and wrapped Nash up in a tight hug. "I have missed you so much. Please tell me you are here to stay." Also unlike most royals, Dani, clad in jeans and a sweatshirt, had her dark hair, sprinkled with gray, pulled back into a braid with springs of hair tucked loosely behind her ears.

On the other hand, Mo, the Prince of Rahmi, was in a suit and looked as if he had just stepped out of a meeting with the president, which could be a possibility since Mo gave up his right to be king. Instead, he had taken on a diplomatic post for his brother, King Dirar, in the United States.

"Let go of the poor man, my dear," Mo said with his smooth voice.

Dani rolled her eyes and kissed Nash's cheek. "I'm so glad you're home."

"I don't know if I'm really back or not yet," Nash said as Dani let him go. "I disobeyed King Dirar."

Mo held out his hand and Nash was surprised by the tight grip a second before Mo pulled Nash in for a slap on the back. "You're home if you want to be. All you have to do is say the word and I'll talk to my brother."

"You mean that?" Nash asked.

"Of course I do. You're the one man my sons trust. Sure, we have Ahmed and Nabi, but Ahmed is retired and Nabi could use the help. If you choose to stay, you'll be in charge of Zain and Gabe. You'll be second in command to Nabi with the express agreement of King Dirar that you will replace Nabi when he chooses to retire."

Nash blinked. He was overwhelmed. "Of course I want to be home. I'd be honored to serve your family, Prince Mohtadi."

Mo waved his hand. "It may take a while, but I'll get to work on my brother tonight. If all else fails, I can hire you privately. One way or another, it means you're finally where you're supposed to be— home in Keeneston."

"We've all heard you did great work these past two years," Zain told him as the group nodded their agreement. "You served Rahmi with honor and brought home so many lost souls. We can't thank you enough. However, I agree with my father. This is where you belong."

"Welcome back," a deep voice said from behind Nash. When he turned, he nodded respectfully to Ahmed and then Nabi, who was standing next to him.

Nabi held out his hand. "I hope you take Mo's offer. You wouldn't believe the idiots I've been working with for the past two years. Plus, Faith misses Uncle Nash and I think Grace misses Monday dinners with you. She'd saves your spot at the table every week just in case."

"I'll be there Monday. I'm looking forward to seeing Faith. I can't believe she's eleven already. By the way, thank you for stocking the cabin," Nash said softly so no one could hear him as he thought of the little girl in pigtails he'd left two years ago. Nabi and his wife, Grace, had been like parents to him since his arrival. Grace baked him cookies and invited him over for a weekly dinner. Nabi taught him everything he knew and helped him become the man he was today.

"Good. We'll see you Monday. As for the cabin, I also left a generator and some other supplies in the lean-to if you need them. In the meantime, what do you want us to do to help you?" Nabi asked.

"Feels strange to be on this end of it," Nash said as he watched Ahmed and Nabi waiting for orders.

"Don't get used to it," Ahmed said seriously. However, his wife blew his tough man routine by smacking his arm when she walked in with a red short-haired dog on a pink leash. "He knows I was joking," Ahmed said to Bridget while pinning Nash with a stare that told him otherwise.

"And what is Satan's spawn doing here?" Ahmed asked, looking at the Vizsla wiggling around his legs.

"Robyn trained today in tracking and I told Sydney I'd bring her here so she didn't have to drive out to the kennel," Bridget said. She had built a state-of-the-art K-9 training facility to train military and police dogs . . . and then there was Robyn. The Vizsla currently had hold of Ahmed's sleeve and was tugging it playfully as Ahmed cursed.

"Robyn!" Sydney called from the back of the

room. The dog immediately dropped Ahmed's sleeve, tore from Bridget to race across the café, and leapt into Sydney's arms. Syd caught all forty-eight pounds of dog on a laugh as Robyn attacked her face with kisses. "How's my big bad police dog?"

"She has a knack for finding more than just designer shoes. She was able to follow a scent trail for five miles today," Bridget started to explain, walking over to see Sydney and Deacon.

"I don't care how good she says that dog is, she has a pink rhinestone collar, for crying out loud, and is Satan's spawn. She stares at me. I'm pretty sure when she does, she's thinking she's smarter than me," Ahmed grumbled.

Nabi tried to hide his smile. "Tell us about Ares and what we can do."

Nash turned back to his team and started outlining a plan of action.

Chapter Sixteen

Sophie said hello to her parents and brothers but was quickly surrounded by her cousins. They were talking a mile a minute as their husbands sat at a nearby table talking football and generally ignoring the commotion the women were making.

"You totally did it," Sydney whispered.

"Definitely. She's glowing," Piper smiled.

"Told you getting naked would work," Layne said smugly.

"Sophie," Cade called out and all the women slammed their mouths shut and turned to innocently look at her father.

"Yes?" Sophie asked.

"Poppy's ready to take our order," Cade said, getting Nash's attention.

"Coming," Sophie said, watching Nash finish his conversation with Ahmed and Nabi.

"In more ways than one," Layne said under her breath as the women all turned to stare at Nash at once.

"I hate y'all," Sophie hissed.

"Nope. We're family. You're not allowed to hate

us." Riley grinned as Sophie rolled her eyes and headed to the table.

Her cousins took a seat nearby and Nash sat down next to Sophie as they faced her parents. She swallowed hard as her parents looked at her. Oh my gosh, they knew. Sophie tried to act casual, but when Nash slid his hand onto her leg under the table, she jumped.

"What is it, dear?" Annie asked with concern.

"Can you order me a hot brown? I need to go to the bathroom," Sophie said as casually as she could. She hurried from the table when Nash started silently laughing behind the menu he held up.

Sophie opened the door at the back of the café and locked it. She took a deep breath and looked into the mirror. "You have got to keep your cool. Mom taught you better than this," she said to herself in the mirror.

Like everything in the café, the bathroom was comfortable. It was a small room with a farmhouse-style vanity and a cracked window that let in cooling air to compensate for the hot kitchen in the next room. Fresh flowers were on the vanity along with an assortment of homemade soaps and lotions.

Taking a moment to collect herself, Sophie began sniffing the lotions when she heard the crunch of gravel by the window. There was a small parking lot behind the café so Sophie didn't think anything of it until she heard a curse and someone fall.

"Oh, no! Someone, I need help!"

She heard a voice she couldn't place from outside. Sophie set down the lotion and shoved up the window to look outside. The second her head was out the window, a hand fisted her hair and another hand reached for her neck and pulled.

Years of training kicked in, but the most effective action was one anyone could do. She screamed. The hand on her hair yanked, and Sophie almost sailed through the window. The man cursed as a van spun around and slid to a stop in the graveled lot. There was no way she'd be taken.

"NASH!" she screamed as loud as she could as she let her body go limp toward the floor. The man would have a hard time lifting her from the window as dead weight.

She heard the door jiggle and knew help was there. She just had to fight them off until the café emptied. By the sound of nearing voices, it wouldn't be long.

"Two men, armed with Glocks," Sophie shouted out. "One is driving a black van."

"Shut up," the man cursed as he let go of her neck and landed a solid punch to her head. Sophie blinked the pain away but then her vision filled with rage. How dare someone try to attack her while out to dinner with her family? "Help me. Hurry!" the man yelled to the driver.

Sophie moved to position herself at the window as she heard Nash ordering people to step back from the door. At the same time he kicked in the door, Sophie jumped. She launched herself through the window, tackling the man who had hit her.

"You asshole!" Sophie yelled as she jabbed a knee into his groin. The man let go of her hair and Sophie let loose with a right cross. "You will never get me. Tell Ares he can kiss my ass."

The other man was stuck between helping his partner or getting caught as Nash leapt through the window and the sound of people running toward them was clearly heard. Sophie felt Nash behind her but she couldn't stop. She was frightened for her life. And she was more pissed that she was frightened.

"Tell Ares," she yelled to the man darting back to his van, "to crawl back into the hole he came out of or face me like a man if he wants me. Unless he's too much of a coward to come himself."

The man slammed the door as Nash took hold of the groaning man who had attacked Sophie. The van tore out of the parking lot as Cody, Ahmed, Nabi, and half the town fired off rounds at the speeding van.

"Let him go," Nash called out. "He'll deliver Sophie's message, and we'll get this over with one way or another. As for you," Nash smiled so menacingly Sophie shivered as he looked down at the man on the ground, "we're going to have a little talk."

"Oh no, I'm going to have a talk with him," her mother said as she came to a stop with her gun drawn. The man looked between them and her mother's eyes turned to ice. "Trust me, you're gonna wish Nash had talked to you after I'm done with you. Nobody hurts my baby. Ahmed, Bridget, can we take him out to your kennels? I think the dogs would like to meet him."

"It doesn't matter what you do. The future is unchanged. Ares is coming for her, and Ares always gets what he wants." The man smirked a moment before Annie's fist connected to his chin, sending him into temporary unconsciousness.

"Damn, that felt good," Annie said cheerfully.

"Great punch, honey," Cade said, kissing his wife's forehead.

"What did we miss?" the Rose sisters and their husbands asked as Pam Gilbert and her sister, Morgan Davies, helped them out the back door of the café. Morgan's husband, Miles, was already offering to help Ahmed escort their prisoner to his farm.

"Wait, shouldn't we be taking him to the jail?" Cody asked.

"Bless your heart, you're still new here. Just close your eyes for a moment," Miss Lily said as she reached back through the door and got her broom. "A couple whacks with this and he'll be talkin'."

"Stand back! I got this!" Aniyah yelled as she ran on her tippy toes in her stilettos around the building with a gun in hand. Everyone screamed and dove for cover as she teetered on her heels, which had gotten stuck in the gravel. Her arms pinwheeled and Nash leapt on top of Sophie, covering her body as they fell to the ground. A shot rang out and someone screamed. Everyone looked up to see which poor soul took the hit.

The previously unconscious man Miles and Ahmed had hold of was jumping on one foot. "The bitch shot my foot!"

Everyone let out a sigh of relief as they stood back up.

"I guess getting shot wakes you up. Your aim's getting better, Aniyah." Riley smiled as she walked over to Aniyah, who was sprawled on the ground. "You hit the right person this time."

"I've been practicing," Aniyah said proudly. Sophie was pretty sure she saw Ahmed roll his eyes, but when she looked again his face was a blank mask.

"How about I take that from you while you get up," Riley said, holding out her hand for the gun. Everyone's breath stopped until Riley had the gun in her possession. "This must be a new one. I haven't seen it before."

"DeAndre keeps taking them away from me, but I'm an independent woman, and I need my protection."

The man who was shot screamed as Dr. Emma looked at his foot. "Oh, please, it's just your pinky toe," Dr. Emma said as she pulled off his sock.

Sophie moved toward the man, but Nash held her back. "What are you doing?" Nash asked softly.

"I want a word with him," Sophie whispered back.

Nash nodded and followed her toward the man Ryan was handcuffing as Ahmed and Miles kept a tight hold on him.

"See, these are personal cuffs and can't be traced back to the FBI," he explained to Cody. "I've learned it's good to have a spare set of everything for these incidents that can't be reported." Cody stood, nodding his head.

"What's your name?" Sophie asked as she stood in front of him.

The man spat at her and before Nash could move, she slammed her heel onto his wounded toe. His scream pierced the air.

"See, you keep your head down, and you can't file a report since you didn't see what happened," Ryan calmly continued to instruct Cody.

"Name?" Sophie asked again.

"Dryas," the man spat.

"That's not his real name if you couldn't figure that out," Miss Daisy called out as she held a wooden spoon menacingly. When Sophie raised her eyebrow, asking silently for more information, Miss Daisy continued. "Dryas is a son of Ares, the god of war in Greek mythology. Doesn't anyone study Greek mythology any more? Surely you all still read *The Odyssey* and *The Iliad*."

Sophie shook her head. She made a note to read both since this group was so tied to the myth of Ares that the soldiers were named after his children.

"We'll call you Dryas for now," Sophie said, focusing back on the man. "What does Ares want with me?"

"You'll find out soon. He'll come for you. He'll

force you to spill all your secrets about the missile and how it's made. He'll break you." The man laughed. Sophie stood strong. She refused to give him the satisfaction of seeing her afraid.

"He can try, but he'll be too late. The missile is complete," she said, ignoring the questioned whispers about a missile coming from the gathering crowd.

"That's a lie and Ares knows it. He knows everything the second it happens when it comes to you and your project." The man smiled again and sang, "He's coming for you."

"Can I please?" Nash asked exasperated.

With a nod of her head, Nash delivered a right cross of his own that sent the man back into oblivion.

"He has a better cross than I do," Annie said sadly.

"I'm sure he'll teach you if you want," Cade said reassuringly to his wife as Sophie began to pace.

"What was that about a missile, dear?" Miss Violet asked.

Sophie looked to Nash who shrugged his shoulders. The cat was out of the bag.

"She is developing a smart missile for the government," John Wolfe said at the same time as newly arrived DeAndre. The two looked at each other questioningly as all heads swiveled from John and then over to DeAndre and back to John. No one ever got the scoop on John.

"And Ares wants to know how to make it?"

Cade asked.

Sophie nodded as residents whispered such curses under their breath that Father James made the sign of the cross.

"What can we do?" Deacon asked as he put his arm protectively around Sydney.

Sophie looked to confirm that the man was still unconscious. "The only thing holding up the missile from being tested for a final time and then handed over to the government was a glitch in the guidance system software. But I figured it out tonight." Sophie reached into her bra and pulled out the folded sheets of paper. "I was going to email them, but from what he said, Ares would know instantly. He either has someone in my lab or he's hacked our computers."

"So, what happens when you fix the glitch?" Piper asked.

"The missile will go into a formal testing phase and will be handed over to the government after our internal testing is passed. A whole new team will start producing prototypes and the Air Force will start testing them. If all goes well, then it will go into mass production," Sophie explained.

Piper looked at the papers in Sophie's hands and thought for a minute. "Then we need to get those to someone you trust at your lab."

"Yes. And I know just the person—my boss. I trust him completely. The problem is that my email or my boss's email may have been compromised. Ares knows too much about my plans and whereabouts."

"I can fly it on our jet to your lab. Where is it?" Ariana Ali Rahman suggested.

"Thanks, Ari," Sophie said to the new college graduate. "My lab is in Maryland, and we have a testing facility in New Mexico. My boss should be arriving at his home in Maryland, just outside of DC, from London tomorrow morning right before noon. It would be best to meet him at home. But since Ares has contacts, he'll know I'm with Nash. I would think anything to do with the royal family will be tracked immediately."

"I'll take it. I can drive out tonight and meet him at his home tomorrow. It's only eight hours away, right?"

Sophie turned to see who had spoken. Andy pushed his way forward. Andy was the opposite of Nash in every way, although when Nash had arrived in Keeneston so many years ago they had been very similar—short, skinny, and unsure about themselves. Nash had grown out of it. Andy was still finding his way.

He stood only five feet seven inches and his shocking carrot-orange red hair added a couple of inches. He'd been invisible in high school as the mascot but had always been like a kid brother to the Davies family since he was Sophie's younger cousin. His mom and her mom were cousins and were now as close as sisters.

"No one ever pays attention to me. I could walk right up to your boss and give him the papers. I even drive a nondescript truck," Andy said, pointing to the tan truck that was neither new nor old. He had a point.

Sophie looked down at the papers clutched in her hands and up to Andy's freckled face. His parents, Deputy Sheriff Dinky and Chrystal, stood proudly behind him. Sophie had a decision to make. She could send the papers under armed guard in a massive convoy or slip them through off the grid with a cousin no one noticed. But he was also a cousin who couldn't hurt a fly and was thus unable to defend himself or the papers.

"Okay, Andy. Here's where I need you to go and what I need you to say." Sophie handed the papers to Andy and gave him her instructions while Zinnia hurried back into the café to prepare some food for the trip. No one left Keeneston hungry.

Chapter Seventeen

Nash watched as folks began to filter back into the café. Ahmed, Miles, and Annie left with the man Sophie captured. If anyone could learn anything, it would be those three. Zinnia handed Andy a basket filled with food for his trip as his parents kissed him goodbye. It was a big step for Andy to risk his life like this. The odds of being found out were minimal. But if he were, then the chance of him ending up dead was almost guaranteed.

Andy closed the door to his truck and started it. He rolled the window down when Nash knocked. "Do you know how to use a gun?"

Andy nodded, his red hair bouncing. "Dad taught me."

"Good. Do you have one in the truck?"

"No. Do I need one?"

"Only if Ares or his men find you." Nash handed Andy his gun as Andy audibly gulped. "They probably won't, but it's better to be prepared."

"Thanks, Nash. I won't let you down."

Nash stepped back and Andy rolled up his window and pulled out of the small parking lot with a billion-dollar formula stuffed in the glove box. Nash turned to check on Sophie only to find a man around their age holding her hands. He leaned close, his head bowed as Sophie gripped his hands. What the hell?

Nash strode forward trying to rein in his temper. Maybe it wasn't what it looked like. Maybe the attractive man in a tight workout shirt and athletic pants, who had obviously been out running, wasn't hitting on the woman he'd just made love to an hour before.

"I'm always here for you," Nash heard the man say quietly. "Day or night. You can come to my place tonight like you have before—"

Nash didn't wait to hear anymore as he strode past Sienna, Sydney, Piper, and the rest of Sophie's girl group and spun the man around.

Sophie's eyes went wide. "Nash, wait!" But all Nash saw was her hand still holding his.

"You sleep with me but you go to him at night?" Nash spat as he shoved the man back. The man dropped Sophie's hand as he righted himself and held up his hands indicating he didn't want to fight.

"Come on," Nash challenged.

"I know we haven't met," the man said. "When Sophie is with me at night she comes—" Nash didn't let the man finish. His fist did his talking as he slammed it into the man's hard stomach. The man was definitely in shape, Nash would give him that.

That didn't stop the air from being forced out of his lungs, causing the man to bend over to catch his breath.

"We need to talk," Nash growled to a shocked Sophie.

"Oh my word! Father Ben, are you injured?" Father James called out as he hobbled over as fast as he could.

Nash looked to Sophie where she was cringing, to her cousins who were shaking their heads and trying very hard not to laugh, then to the man with his hands braced on his knees drawing in as much air as he could. "I'm sorry, did you say *Father* Ben?"

Sophie winced, "I made the same mistake when I first met him."

"But you see him at his place at night," Nash stuttered, looking from person to person for someone to tell him he didn't just punch a priest.

"To counsel her," Father Ben said as he slowly righted himself. "My door is always open to the people of Keeneston."

"Oh God, I'm so sorry," Nash apologized and then winced again as Father James rolled his eyes at the whole taking the name in vain thing. "Jesus . . . I mean, shit." Nash stumbled over himself trying to find the right words.

"Just 'sorry' is good," Father Ben said, holding out his hand. "I'm Ben Jacobs."

"Nash Dagher," Nash said, holding out his hand and shaking Father Ben's.

"The town must be excited to have you back. I

can tell you that you haven't been forgotten during your absence. And may I compliment you on quite the punch. We should spar sometime." Ben smiled as his breath fully returned to him.

"Spar?" Nash asked. Could priests do that?

"Yes. I was on the boxing team at seminary. DeAndre and I usually get in the ring together a couple times a month. You should join us next time." Father Ben smiled as if Nash hadn't just punched him. "Be safe, you two. If you ever need anything, either of you, my door at the rectory is always open."

Nash watched Father Ben hold out his arm to assist Father James from the parking lot. As soon as they were out of sight, the cousins lost their battle against laughter.

Nash buried his face in his hands. "I can't believe he's a priest."

"Don't worry," Layne reassured. "We all made that mistake."

"Some worse than others," Piper giggled.

"Someday when you and Sophie are married, we'll tell you another story." Syd smiled as Sophie turned red and the rest of the girls had to lean on each other to keep from falling down laughing.

"Married?" Nash tried to say as if playing the idea off as a joke.

"Nash, you announced to everyone you and Sophie made love and then punched a man you thought was coming between you. Yeah, I think the M-word can be mentioned when it's perfectly clear the two of you have loved each other for a very long time," Sienna said with her arms crossed and in a perfect shrink voice. "In fact, I'm guessing you were in love two years ago when you both left because you couldn't reconcile your feelings for each other."

"That's freaky," Sophie said quietly, but Sienna heard anyway.

"I'm at the top of my field, and it's mostly personal stuff that messes with football players' minds. I've gotten really good at getting to the root of an issue quickly. After all, they have an NFL game every week and don't have time to explore issues slowly. And Father Ben's door isn't the only one open if you need it." Sienna took a breath as her phone rang. "Speaking of clients."

Sienna walked off as she answered her phone, leaving the rest of Sophie's cousins staring at them. Nash had been interrogated before but nothing could compare to this.

"Now that this is over, let's get our dinner and head back to where we are staying," Nash said, trying to get away from the knowing smiles.

Nash placed his hand at the small of Sophie's back and escorted her through the back door. As they approached, there was a sharp whistle and then Poppy's sweet Alabama-accented voice filled the room. "We have to get confirmation!" she yelled as patrons grumbled.

All hell broke loose the second Nash and Sophie walked out of the small hallway and into the dinner area. Poppy put her fingers to her lips and the piercing whistle quieted the group.

"I'm sorry," Poppy said, turning to them. "But I can't close the betting books on you two being a couple without confirmation. We heard about the Father Ben incident, but sex isn't a relationship."

Nash froze like a deer in the headlights as he heard Cade not so subtly whispering threats from where he sat nearby with his sons while the entire restaurant crowd stared at them. Nash turned to an annoyed-looking Sophie, wrapped his arms around her, dipped her backwards, and planted a searing kiss on her lips. If he was going to die, he was going to die happy.

Sophie's fingers laced around his neck as she kissed him back. When he pulled his head back, she smiled up at him. "I'm so glad you cleared that up. You may have to remind me we're a couple back at the cabin. Maybe a couple of times. I don't want to forget." And then the saucy minx winked at him, and he felt his heart trip. Neither of them was running scared this time. This time they were partners and nothing could tear them apart.

The café cheered and Father Ben pumped his fist in the air. "I won! We can have the live Nativity this year!"

Sophie laced her hand in Nash's as folks began to sort out who won and who lost the bet. Zinnia hurried to make them dinner and brought out an entire chocolate pecan pie.

"To celebrate," the svelte cook said with a kind smile.

Nash looked across the table. Cade didn't look like he was going to be celebrating. "Just wait until Annie hears about this. It's a good thing you'll be in hiding or you'd be a dead man."

"Dad, really?" Sophie complained as they took a seat.

"We'll discuss it after Ares is caught," her father said as he dug into his dinner.

"Speaking of which, do you think Mom will get anything useful out of the man I caught?" Sophie asked.

"I doubt it. Ares trains his minions well. They're more afraid of turning on him than anything we can do to them. I would bet Ares is aware of what had happened and every word you said. He'll be sending more people after you now. Everyone needs to be on guard," Nash warned the café.

"Maybe we should leave. I don't want to put everyone at risk," Sophie said nervously.

"Nonsense," Miss Lily said as she and her sisters shuffled to the table.

"We're family. This is what we do," Miss Violet reassured her.

"Plus, it's gotten down right dull around here since everyone started having children. We could use some action," Miss Daisy told them.

"On that note, ladies, our ride is here," Charles, Miss Daisy's husband, said as he came to get the old women.

"We'll be right there, Charles." Miss Daisy smiled before turning a not-so-innocent look to

Sophie and Nash. "And May would be perfect for a wedding."

Cade looked as if he were going to have a stroke as Miss Daisy turned to leave after dropping that bomb on the table.

"I think we need to get back. It's a long trip," Nash said, shoving his chair back.

Sophie must have agreed because she placed a quick kiss on her dad's cheek, grabbed the pie, and the two of them hightailed it out of the café on the verge of laughter the entire way.

The next day Sophie sat looking at the water running over the stones in the stream. It was twelve-thirty. Andy would be waiting for her boss, Sam, at his house by now. Her mother had called on the disposable phone Uncle Cy had given them last night and told them all she could get out of the man was that the missile played heavily into some future plan Ares had. Ares would stop at nothing to get the technology Sophie had in her head.

Sophie had spent the night curled in Nash's protective embrace. They hadn't discussed marriage or even love. After they made love in the fire-lit cabin, she'd told him she loved him, but he didn't reply. Instead he kissed her forehead and pulled her into his arms to hold her. It had been a bit soon to say it, but had it really? Not when they had had these feelings for so long.

"Have you heard anything yet?" Nash asked as

he walked out of the cabin with some pumpkin spice bread Zinnia had made them.

"Not yet. Nash, what can I do to help catch Ares? Everyone is looking for him, but no one is going to find him. They've been looking for him for years. And now he's after me. He's not going to stop until he has me," Sophie said, agitated. She didn't like sitting, doing nothing.

"You did it last night. You taunted Ares. He's smart but just like the mythological Ares, he responds to any slight with outrage. There's a story of him being wounded in a shootout and him complaining constantly about his minor wound. One of his personal guards told Ares it wasn't that bad and Ares shot him dead. Your taunt will push him over the edge. He wants what he wants, and he wants it now. By defying him, you'll cause him to act recklessly. That's when I'll kill him," Nash explained as he sat on the ground next to her.

"You mean capture, right?"

Nash didn't respond, he handed her the plate of bread and looked over the stream. Sophie took a bite of bread and didn't push him. She trusted that he would do the right thing when the time came. His main priority was keeping her safe, and she knew that was one mission he'd never fail.

They were silent for what seemed to be days but were really only two hours. They sat, they tossed pebbles into the stream, and they walked the clearing. Then her phone finally rang. The unidentified number filled the screen as Sophie snatched to answer it.

"Hello?" she asked putting it on speaker.

"It's me," Andy said, not using his name as Nash instructed and calling from a burner phone he'd bought with cash on his way to DC.

"How did it go?" Sophie asked impatiently.

"Just as planned."

Sophie let out the breath she was holding.

"Were there any messages?"

"It will be personally handled today and your services are no longer needed."

Sophie grinned. Sam would see that the code was programmed personally and with that working piece, the missile was complete and her job on the contract was complete. She had done it. She had finished the missile and now she could stay in Keeneston forever.

"Thank you."

"Anytime. I'll see you soon."

Sophie hung up the phone that would be destroyed and pitched before Andy headed back home.

"You did it. I'm so proud of you," Nash said, pulling her against him for a tight hug.

"I would celebrate if I didn't have to worry about Ares."

"We can celebrate starting right now, and I guarantee you won't be thinking of Ares," Nash said, his voice deepening as he lowered his lips to hers.

Chapter Eighteen

The café was quieter that night as Miss Lily took a seat at the reserved table with her sisters. Their husbands were hosting a card game at the bed and breakfast and the café was about to close for the night. There were only fifteen or so people grabbing a late-night dessert before heading home.

"I made some of that mint tea y'all like," Zinnia said as she brought three mugs to the table.

"Thank you, dear," Vi said as their cousin filled the cups.

"Have a seat, Zinnia," Daisy said, patting the empty chair at the table.

It was about time they had a talk with them about their past. Zinnia and her sister, Poppy, had come to Keeneston from Alabama seven years before. In those past years, they hadn't breathed one word of their life there. They'd also never gone back.

"Dear, we wanted to discuss something with you," Lily started. "Do you ever miss your home? You came here to take care of three old cousins you never met. We feel horrible for monopolizing you and Poppy."

Zinnia sloshed the tea she was pouring. "Oh no, Miss Lily. We're so happy in Keeneston. We had nothing at home to go back to. This is our home now, and we're so grateful that you reached out to us." Zinnia smiled at them and then jumped up. "I forgot I have one last pan to wash out before we close. I'll just be a moment and then I can drive you home if you'd like."

The sisters watched Zinnia head back to the kitchen.

"Something definitely happened," Daisy said, stating the obvious.

"Maybe we can ask Nabi to look into it," Violet suggested.

"Good idea. We'll talk to him tomorrow." Lily turned to the door as the bell chimed, indicating it had opened. A man with a shaved head and thick neck strode in. He wore jeans and a gray sweater. By the way the sweater bulged at his waist, it was clear he had a gun attached to his hip.

"Well, hello, young man," Lily called out, gathering the café's attention. "You must be new here. Can we help you?"

Lily noticed her sisters turning as the man walked farther into the room, ignoring them while looking at all the patrons now staring at the newcomer.

"I'm sorry, sonny, but maybe you didn't hear my sister," Miss Daisy said, standing up and pulling a wooden spoon from her long sleeve. "She asked how we can help you."

The man spun to glare at her, his hand going to his hip and resting threateningly on the gun under his sweater. "It's none of your damn business."

Miss Daisy swatted his hand on his gun with the spoon and the man looked so surprised that he stood, just staring at her.

"Everything that happens in this town is our business," Miss Lily said as she and Violet moved to stand on each side of Daisy. "Everything like what kind of gun you have there," Lily said loud enough for the patrons of the café to hear.

"You want to find out, lady?" he snarled.

"Why, yes, we do," Violet said as she dug around her purse. "Here, Daisy, hold this," she said, passing off her spatula to her sister as she shoved things aside looking for something. "Because I would love to know how it compares to my Smith and Wesson," Violet finally said, pulling out her purple gun.

"Oh, is that a new one, Vi?" Lily asked.

"It was a birthday present from Anton." Vi smiled as she clicked off the safety.

In unison, chairs scraped the hardwood floor and when the man turned in a full circle, he saw guns drawn at every table. "Welcome to Keeneston," Zinnia said, swinging a skillet as she came up behind the man. The *thunk* of the skillet hitting the man's head reverberated through the café as he fell to the floor.

"So you went with the twelve inch? Nice. I always preferred the crepe pan personally," Violet said as she put away her gun and pulled out her phone to send a message out on the town text tree.

Zinnia shrugged and blew back an errant strand of hair falling in her face. "It was the only one I hadn't washed yet and I didn't want to use a clean one in case I got blood on it."

"Very practical. Now, does anyone have anything to tie him up with?" Miss Violet asked, sending the patrons into action.

Annie crawled into bed with a sigh. She was so frustrated. She'd learned nothing of substance from the man they had captured the day before. She'd even gone back that day and tried again. Ahmed had told her that in cases like, this the footmen have been so brainwashed to believe the leader in all that matters that they are very hard to crack. But she wouldn't give up.

Cade opened his arms, and she rested her head on her husband's bare chest. "I failed Sophie," Annie said, discouraged.

Her husband's arms came around her and gently stroked her back. "No, you didn't. She's safe and that's all that matters. Sienna is going to talk to him tomorrow. She said she's read up on the kind of psychology leaders of gangs like this use to guarantee complete obedience and she has some ideas she'd like to try to break him through mind games."

"I hope someone can get something from him.

We need to know more about Ares so we can defeat him before he can hurt our daughter," Annie said, frustrated.

Cade suddenly stilled and Annie opened her senses. The sliding glass door had just opened. "It looks like we may get a second chance," Cade whispered as he shoved the sheets down and reached for his gun.

Annie didn't hesitate, slipping from the bed. She still had two of her babies in the house to protect. It didn't matter to her they were twice as big as she was and probably three times as strong. They were her babies, and she'd kill anyone who tried to hurt them.

Annie quietly moved to the window as Cade went to the door. She unlatched it and pushed it open. It had been decades since she had fled this room via the old tree outside the window, but she wanted to cut off the intruder's escape.

She looked at her husband who blew her a kiss and then disappeared out the bedroom door. Annie reached the tree and had to stifle a groan as she lowered herself to the next branch. It was a hard realization that she wasn't thirty anymore. Shoot, she wasn't even fifty anymore. "I better get grandkids for this," she muttered as she nervously eyed the seven-foot drop to the ground. Great, now she was sounding like her mother-in-law, Marcy.

Letting out a worried breath, she dangled from the last branch and dropped the remaining couple of feet to the ground. She pulled her gun after checking to make sure she was still intact and silently slipped toward the open sliding glass door in the backyard.

She approached the back door on high alert and almost jumped when she heard two quick shots. Her family! Annie dashed inside with her gun held out in front of her, ready to take down anyone who hurt her family. Instead, she heard her sons' doors being thrown open and the sound of two men cursing.

When she rounded the living room, she found the men lying on the ground at the base of the stairs holding their shoulders and cursing. She kicked their guns aside and looked up as her husband walked down the stairs with a smile on his face.

"You shot them?"

Cade sent her a wink. "I couldn't let you have all the fun. Colton, Landon, tie them up."

Colton came downstairs with a lasso he used for horses. "I was woken up by a text from Miss Violet. They caught someone at the café, too."

"I guess you'll have a couple more chances at getting some information then." Cade grinned at her.

"Yes, I will. And I'm going to start right now," Annie said as she looked at the men.

Ryan Parker came into the dark house flat-out tired. He'd spent the day at the office working every contact he had to find out more about Ares. He walked through the dark hallway and into the bedroom where his wife was sitting up in bed.

Books and papers were all around her. Some were even resting against Hooch, who was snoring so loudly the television with the local news couldn't be heard.

Ryan unhooked his service gun and badge, setting them on his nightstand before leaning over Hooch and kissing Sienna. "What are you working on?"

"Ahmed approached me about talking to the man they captured yesterday," Sienna said as she wrote down a quick note.

"I don't think I want to hear about this. Do you have any idea how many laws I'm breaking by not taking him into custody?" Ryan asked as he slipped out of his sports coat and started to unbutton his shirt.

"It's really fascinating, actually, the way these top-tier gangs work. It's drilled into them that the head of the organization is all that matters, and they must do everything possible to protect him and the rest of the organization. It's almost cult-like. I've read some research on how to chip away at that mentality to get a subject to open up. I'm going to try it tomorrow," Sienna told him before turning back to her computer.

"I don't think so. You're not going to interview someone who would kill you in a second if he got free," Ryan protested over Hooch's snores.

"Hmm," his wife hummed as she ignored him and went back to her notes. He'd been married long enough to know what that sound meant—she wasn't going to listen to him.

Ryan let out a resigned sigh. "Fine, but I'll come with you."

Sienna looked up from her computer and smiled victoriously. "Thank you. You're the greatest husband a woman could ever have."

"Really? I can think of a way for you to show me how great I am." Ryan grinned as he shoved down his pants and walked naked to the bed. Sienna laughed and then licked her lips in anticipation.

"I'd be happy to," she said in a sexy voice that turned Ryan on as much today as it did when they were first together. He watched as she set her computer aside and shoved the papers onto the floor. She tried to shove Hooch but didn't have much success moving him.

"I need to take a quick shower, how about you join me?" Ryan asked, leaning over and kissing her again before she could answer.

"Hmm," she murmured against his lips before her hand ran down his stomach and straight to his — *GRRRRRR.*

"Not now, Hooch," Ryan said against Sienna's lips.

GRRRRRR.

This time both Ryan and Sienna froze. That deep, almost silent growl caught their attention. The big dog's hair was on end and his eyes focused on the hallway.

"Hide in the closet," Ryan ordered as he yanked her from the bed. "There's a taser on the top shelf.

Turn it on and don't come out unless you know it's me."

Ryan shoved her into the walk-in closet as he strode across the room to get his gun. "Come on, Hooch," Ryan whispered as the two silently exited the room.

Hooch kept his side against Ryan's leg as they crept down the hall. Ryan felt the big dog's silent growls as they neared the kitchen. Before Ryan could react, Hooch let out a fearsome snarl and launched himself into the air. A gun with a hand attached to it was coming around the corner and Hooch latched onto the arm, taking the man down. The gun fell to the floor and Ryan calmly picked it up.

"Why, hello there. I see you've met my dog," Ryan said as he stood looking at the man currently howling more than Hooch. "If you move a muscle, he'll tear your throat out. Look at him drooling for the chance." Hooch thumped his tail happily, rattling a picture on the wall.

"Let me cover up, and we'll have a little chat," Ryan said pleasantly as he grabbed a blanket from the living room and wrapped it around his waist. He pulled a kitchen chair out and set it over the man's throat.

"Hooch, release," Ryan ordered the big dog. Hooch let go of the man's arm and came to stand over his head. Hooch, with his big jowls flopping open, looked down at the man and drooled on his face.

"Are you comfortable? Good. Let's talk," Ryan said as he straddled the chair, pinning the man by the throat to the floor.

"I'm telling you, Sugar Bear, I heard something outside," Aniyah said as she shook DeAndre awake.

"Baby, I just got off a double shift. I'm sure it's nothing," DeAndre mumbled into his pillow.

"It's not nothing. I hear someone outside," Aniyah hissed.

"Fine. I'll take a look. Will that calm you so I can get some sleep?" DeAndre groaned as he hauled himself out of bed.

"Be careful," Aniyah cautioned.

DeAndre sighed and headed downstairs. This business with the man Sophie caught at the café yesterday had his baby on edge. DeAndre looked around the house and didn't see any signs of someone trying to break in. He opened the back door and looked outside at the farmland. Nothing. He made his way back to the front door and flipped the deadbolt.

DeAndre didn't know who was more surprised when he flung open the door. Himself or the man pulling out a lock-pick set from his jacket. DeAndre and the man stared at each other for a split second and then DeAndre hauled back his arm and smashed his fist into the man's face. The man dropped the lock-pick set and stumbled off the stoop.

"Baby, bring me my gun!" DeAndre yelled up the stairs.

"See, I *told* you someone was outside. I got you, Sugar!" Aniyah called from the bedroom.

DeAndre looked up from where the man was sprawled on the ground. The guy staggered up, swaying when he finally was upright. DeAndre wasn't worried, though. He was very handy with his fists and could easily take him. However, there was something he knew that the man didn't. Behind the man now staggering up was a contingent of Rahmi guards armed to the teeth. Little red dots from their laser scopes lit up the intruder like a Christmas tree.

"I got the gun, Sugar!" Aniyah yelled as he heard her run down the stairs. The Rahmi guards heard it, too. They froze and looked around nervously. They'd unfortunately learned all too well that his Baby couldn't shoot worth a darn. He'd tried and tried to teach Aniyah, but nothing had worked.

The man lunged at the same time Aniyah tripped as she came out the door. A gun fired and the man went down screaming.

DeAndre reached down to help his girlfriend up and saw her cringe. "Did I shoot him?"

"No, your safety is on. I shot him," Ahmed said calmly as he walked toward them. "Good thing, too. You were aiming at Nabi. And I really wanted to shoot him. It's been a while since I shot anyone."

"Men, take him to the holding cell," Nabi

ordered as Ahmed grabbed the gun from the man's hip.

DeAndre was in awe. Ahmed was his hero. A couple of times DeAndre had been lucky enough to be working out in the gym while Ahmed sparred with the young guards and had been instantly struck with respect for the man.

"Nice punch, DeAndre," Ahmed said seriously.

"Thanks," DeAndre replied seriously. He was trying not to freak out. Ahmed reached into his pocket, pulled out his phone and frowned.

"Nabi, have one of the barns ready for visitors. According to the town text tree, there's a man being held at the café. Send someone to get him. There are two at Cade and Annie's, and Ryan has one at his house. I'm telling Ryan and Cade to bring their men here," Ahmed ordered.

He may have been retired, but it didn't matter. Everyone listened to him.

"We need to get in touch with Nash," Nabi said quietly.

DeAndre looked around. "I can do that."

"Sorry, they're at an undisclosed location," Nabi said before turning back to Ahmed.

"I mean, I know where they are."

That got the two men's attention.

"How do you know where they are?" Ahmed asked in such a way it sent chills down DeAndre's spine.

"Um . . ." DeAndre sputtered under Ahmed's narrowed stare.

"Oh, my Sugar always knows things, but he'll never tell me how he knows," Aniyah smiled as she patted DeAndre's arm, completely unaware that Ahmed might strike him down at any second.

DeAndre gulped as Ahmed stepped closer. "Have you been talking to John Wolfe?"

DeAndre shook his head.

"Then how do you know where Sophie and Nash are?"

DeAndre gulped again. "I have my ways, but I can't tell."

"Do aliens talk to you?"

DeAndre's eyes went wide. "No, sir."

"Well, you can't say that for sure," Aniyah countered as Nabi and Ahmed turned to look at her. "There could very well be aliens among us. Let's be scientific here, aliens aren't little green creatures. I'm sure they're very advanced and can change their appearance to fit in so they can learn more about us to take back to their mother ship."

Ahmed and Nabi shared a look, and DeAndre saw his chance of fitting into their select group closing. "But I can help. Just tell me what to do. Do I need to get them? Warn them? Move them?"

Ahmed looked at him and DeAndre felt his soul freeze under the penetrating stare. Then Ahmed relaxed and gave the slightest nod of his head. "Bring them to the interrogation room."

"Yes, sir!" DeAndre said, taking off down the sidewalk.

"DeAndre," Nabi called, stopping him.

"Yes?"

"Why don't you put on some clothes first? Unless you really want to make the trip in a pair of cheetah boxers and no shoes."

"Yes, sir," DeAndre chuckled. In his excitement to be part of the team, he hadn't even realized he was without clothes.

"You like those?" Aniyah asked. "I can get you a pair for Christmas. I see you more as a zebra print and Mr. Ahmed as a tiger."

"Roar," Ahmed said stone-faced before turning to leave.

DeAndre ran inside to get dressed and grab his gun from Aniyah. He had a mission from Ahmed and he wasn't going to fail. And he certainly wasn't going to picture Ahmed in tiger print boxers.

Chapter Nineteen

Nash lay in the dark with the woman of his dreams in his arms and thought of murder. Sophie had thought he'd turn Ares over to the police to answer for his crimes. That scenario had never entered his mind. Not even once. Why? Because men like Ares didn't deserve to live.

At the military academy, Nash had learned about the Battle of the Crown. He had learned that King Emir had beaten his cousin Sarif at swords and could have ended his life right on the palace grounds surrounded by the entire military. Instead, he handed Sarif over to be tried by a court. That was the same battle for which Ahmed had earned the Golden Oryx Award for his bravery against Sergi. Sergi was very much like Ares. They had shown mercy, but Nash had seen too much of what Ares was capable of to show mercy. So Nash plotted Ares's death.

Ares would come for Sophie and when he did, Nash would be there to cut the head from the serpent. He'd brought down Red Shadow, and he'd do whatever it took to bring down Ares.

Nash tried to close his eyes, but the sound of a muffled curse and a quick yelp had him on high alert. Someone was in his trap. Nash slid from the bed and turned on his phone. Text messages filled the screen as soon as he got service. Ignoring them, he looked at the feed from the wireless cameras. There was a person hanging upside down from a tree limb.

He sat his phone down and grabbed his gun and a knife. He slipped silently from the cabin and hugged the shadows of the woods as he drew nearer the man hanging by his foot.

"Nash," the man whispered loudly. "Are you out there? It's me, DeAndre Drews."

Nash slid his gun into his waistband and stepped from behind a tree. "I'm here. But what are you doing here?"

Nash didn't make a move to cut DeAndre down as he waited for an answer. "Ahmed and Nabi sent me to get you. There were coordinated attacks across town tonight as Ares's men searched for Sophie. They hit the café, her house, Sienna's house, and my house. I guess they hadn't heard I moved in, and it wasn't your place anymore."

The information was a blow to Nash. "Is anyone hurt?"

"No. All the men were captured. Ahmed wants you to come to the interrogation room," DeAndre told him. "Um, can you cut me down now?"

Nash walked over and helped DeAndre down. "Sorry about that. I just had to make sure, you know?"

"I understand. I just don't want to mess up the first thing Ahmed asked me to do. I really look up to him."

Nash smiled at the young trooper. "I do, too. Come up to the porch and have a seat. I'll get Sophie, and we'll head over to the security building."

Sophie stood on the other side of the two-way mirror and watched her best friend question the man Hooch had taken down. Ahmed, Nash, and her parents were working on the others. Sienna was sure she'd be able to uncover some information and insisted on being in the room alone with him. Ryan had not been happy but agreed only if the man was shackled and he was watching from the attached room.

Sienna looked the part of a powerful professional even at four in the morning. She sat across from the man chained to the table and talked. They had been talking about movies, travel, and family for the past two hours. At first, it was just her talking and the man not even looking at her. Then slowly he started engaging with her. He told her which movies he liked and soon Sienna had him talking about travel. She discovered he was from Canada and had traveled the world with Ares.

Instead of pushing for details, Sienna talked about restaurants in London, the best hotels to stay at in Paris, and wine in Italy. Then she talked about the understated values of places like Croatia and how she thought more people should visit there. Through it, she learned that Ares tended to avoid countries with heavy surveillance, instead staying in countries like Turkey, Romania, Hungary, and Taiwan that were noted for their high Internet crime rates.

Ryan shook his head. "I can't believe it. She's narrowed down his bases of operations by finding out which restaurants he likes to eat at and attractions he sees the most."

"My father is the head of the family, like Ares is," Sienna said pleasantly. "When we traveled, everything had to be a certain way. Bags packed just so, we'd only fly a certain airline, and we'd better rent a certain kind of car so we could all fit in it."

Ryan snorted. "Yeah, Will's the real dictator."

"I'm pretty sure Kenna does all of his packing or Will would travel anywhere in the world with just two pairs of jeans and a couple of football polos," Sophie smirked.

"But the worst was the constant harping on travel conditions and sticking to the game plan," Sienna chuckled.

"I know what you mean. I think the worst is the private jet we fly on. Ares insists on using it, but there's not enough room for all of us and all the luggage so whoever is the last person on the plane has to get off and transport all the guards' luggage on the cheapest, fastest transport since Ares won't pay for it," said the man who went by Phobos, another name of a mythological child of Ares.

"My dad once left my brother at a rest stop since he didn't want to wait for him," Sienna joked immediately afterward, preventing Phobos from realizing he'd started giving up detailed information.

Nash opened the door and came to stand by Sophie, slipping his hand around her as he stood looking into the two-way mirror. "Has Sienna learned anything?"

"Quite a lot actually," Ryan said, tearing a sheet of paper from his notepad and handing it over.

Nash scanned it and Sophie saw his eyebrows rise in surprise. "Wow. This is a lot to go on. I'm impressed. We got that Ares is in the United States, and he'll be coming for Sophie soon. Apparently there's one thing he has to do first before he can come for a visit," Nash said sarcastically.

"Did you learn what that one thing is?" Ryan asked.

Nash shook his head. "No. Maybe Sienna can."

Sophie looked down at her phone when she felt it vibrate. It was her boss, Sam. "It's Sam. He wouldn't be calling on this number unless it was an emergency."

"Put it on speaker," Nash said as Sophie answered the call.

"What's wrong?" Sophie asked immediately.

"It's gone," Sam's panicked voice said over the

line.

"This is Nash Dagher, security for the Ali Rahman royal family. I'm here with FBI Agent Ryan Parker," Nash said calmly and clearly. "What is gone, Mr. McMillan?"

"The missile. It's gone," Sam said neither calmly nor clearly.

"Sam, slow down," Sophie ordered. "Start with when Andy met you at your house."

Sam took a deep breath. "I arrived home and found Andy in the kitchen with my housekeeper. She left and Andy handed over the papers with all your notes. As soon as I saw them, I knew it would work. I went to the lab and programmed the fix for the software myself. I ran a simulation, and it was perfect."

"What then?" Nash asked.

"I contacted the government liaison and let them know we were ready for testing. We agreed the safest way to transport the missile to our New Mexico testing facility was with a small contingent of guards in a disguised tractor-trailer. It looked like we were shipping oranges. Who would know it held a missile?" Sam asked, his voice rising in panic.

"What happened?" Ryan asked as the three shared a look that said they knew what had happened but didn't want to admit it until they heard the words.

"We don't really know. We found the soldiers dead on the side of the road in the mountains of West Virginia, the missile gone, and the tractor-trailer on fire," Sam's voice squeaked between shallow breaths.

"How did they find out?" Sophie asked in shock. All her work, all her team's work, a deadly weapon, all gone.

"I don't know. I did it all myself. I entered the coding myself, Sophie!"

"Mr. McMillan, Special Agent Parker here. Was there anyone who heard you make the phone call to the government?"

"No. I was in my office alone."

"Wait," Sophie gasped. "Did you dial the phone yourself?" Sophie held her breath. She thought she might have found the mole. The one person who sat quietly right outside Sam's door, which he usually kept open every single day.

"Well, no. Amy dialed the phone for me like she always does," he replied about his assistant. "You don't think — ?"

"What's her last name?" Nash asked quickly.

"Woodly," Sam said slowly. "It can't be."

"It makes sense," Sophie said gently as Nash and Ryan rushed to run her name through their computers. "She made all of your calls and could probably listen to them if she wanted. She knew your schedule, she filed the updated reports we all sent you, she heard us talking about problems with the project, and I bet she was there when you fixed it. She had all the access you did. Plus, she was in London and knew about the meeting with Mr. Storme."

"But Amy's been with me for fifteen years. She has the highest security clearance levels," Sam protested.

"Who else could it be? The liaison for the government?" Sophie asked.

"No, it was Amy," Nash said, walking back into the room with an open laptop.

"I can't find anything," Ryan said, looking up from his computer.

"That's because you're playing nice. I'm not. I went straight to her bank records. She was in massive credit card debt and her house was in foreclosure," Nash told them as he continued to work on the laptop.

"She didn't say anything, and we would have found it out at our random review," Sam said.

"If she was still planning on being there," Ryan pointed out as he looked over Nash's shoulder. "She got paid well for her services, and I have a feeling she will be stepping down from her position real soon."

"When did she get paid?" Sophie asked.

"A wire transfer is currently being processed into a brand-new account for $5,000,000," Nash told them.

"She was paid as soon as they had the missile," Sam said, recognizing the truth. "Who do we even trust to call to report a stolen missile? I called you first."

"I'll take care of it, Mr. McMillan," Ryan told him reassuringly. "I know people I'd trust with my life that can help handle this."

"I trusted Amy," Sam said sadly.

"Well, my brother knows I can still kick his ass if he messes up," Ryan said, trying to lighten the mood. Sophie snorted. Ryan was no slouch, but his brother, Jackson, was only getting bigger and stronger with age.

"We'll call you back shortly, Mr. McMillan," Ryan said before nodding to Sophie to turn off the phone.

"It was Ares, wasn't it?" Sophie asked as soon as the phone was off.

"It has to be. We need backup. He has the weapon he wanted. All he needs is you to tell him how to build more and use them," Nash said, pulling out his phone and sending a message.

Whoever he and Ryan were contacting, they better be ready for a battle because Ares sure was. For the first time, Sophie became truly worried. Ares wouldn't care about hurting everyone she cared about to get to her and now he was coming for her himself.

Chapter Twenty

Sophie was constantly surrounded by people now. It had been hours since Ryan and Nash took over the Ares situation. Sophie was now locked away just like Ares's soldiers were. Her brothers never left her side. Either her mother or father was in the room with her as well, along with six Rahmi guards.

"Do you have the gun I gave you?" her mom asked for the sixth time.

"Yes," Sophie sighed and lifted her shirt again to show the gun secured in the corset.

"Just checking," her mom said, causing even the guards to snicker.

"Lovely," Veronica, Zain's all-around right hand, sang as she strolled into the room in her pencil skirt and silk blouse. Her hair was pulled back into some sort of fancy twist and her red lipstick matched the red soles of her four-inch heels. The guards straightened to attention for the bombshell even though Veronica didn't even see them. She cared more about women than men, which was why she was currently checking out Sophie's uplifted shirt.

"Thanks," Sophie said, dropping her shirt. "You here to get us all in line?"

Veronica was hell on heels. Ares didn't stand a chance against the woman's vast network of informants, her crazy ability to foresee all outcomes, and her abilities to prepare for each.

"Of course." Veronica smiled. "Jackson Parker just arrived with his entire FBI Hostage Rescue team. Dylan Davies is en route from somewhere unknown. And Abby," Veronica sighed at the name of her not-so-secret crush, "will be here any minute."

Sophie loved Veronica. They all did. She took a no-nonsense approach and was great at her job. She lived in Lexington and her social life was as secret as Dylan's job. However, that didn't stop her from being the Rose sisters' next matchmaking project. Sophie wondered though if Veronica was as happy as the perpetual half smile she wore. She'd never seen Veronica with her hair down, so to speak.

"You do know that Abby's not gay, right?" Sophie whispered.

"Of course," Veronica grinned, "But that doesn't mean I don't enjoy the show."

"You lead some wild secret life, don't you?" Sophie asked.

Veronica just winked and looked down at her phone. "Ah," she said before turning and opening the door for Abigail Mueez, Ahmed and Bridget's daughter. Everyone in Keeneston called her Abby.

Abby was twenty-six with shoulder-length, dark

brown hair currently in a ponytail with shaggy bangs, and bright, Caribbean-blue eyes. She was also deadly. There had to be no fewer than ten weapons on her body at any time, although Sophie couldn't see a single one. Abby told everyone she was starting a private security firm in DC, and that could be true, but Sophie thought there was more to the story — much more. However, Abby wasn't talking about it and Sophie wasn't asking.

"Abby!" Sophie cried as she rushed to hug her friend. "Thank you so much for coming."

"Of course. I brought help, too." Abby smiled.

Sophie looked behind her friend to see four very intimidating men standing at attention. One was holding a briefcase. "And toys," Abby said happily as she motioned for the briefcase to be placed on the table in the room.

Sophie, her mother, and Veronica looked down at the briefcase Abby opened. Her mother gasped in such a way it could be borderline orgasmic. The briefcase held toys all right. Guns only Sophie had seen at tradeshows described as "guns of the future," knives, switchblades, needles filled with unidentifiable liquids — the list went on.

"I love when you come home to visit from your *private security* job," Annie said, using air quotes when she said *private security*. Apparently Sophie wasn't the only one who didn't believe Abby's whole story.

"Thanks, Mrs. D," Abby said. "Now, let's get you armed."

"You want me to put all that on my body?" Sophie asked, eyeing the case suspiciously.

"Yup. Guards, out. We need some privacy," Abby ordered as the guards filed out to stand by the door in the hallway. "This way if you're caught, you have more options available to aid in escape. Strip."

Veronica's grin widened and Sophie rolled her eyes. No chit-chat for Abby. She got right down to business. Sophie pulled off her shirt and Abby eyed the corset.

"We're twinsies," Abby winked as she pulled up her shirt to expose the same corset filled with weapons. "Now, let's use all those little pockets. Gun," Abby said, handing over a gun to go along with the one her mom had given her. Sophie put one under each arm and moved the gun she designed to the pocket at the small of her back.

"Knives, here and here. And then this one will strap to your calf," Abby said and handed over the next set of gear.

"And then these are the good stuff," Abby told her, carefully pulling out one of the needles. "Stab someone anywhere on the body, just get through the first layer of skin, and you inject this and the effect is immediate. The person goes down for ten hours. This one keeps the person awake, but they are completely paralyzed for a couple of hours. Put them in the slim slips between your breasts," Abby instructed.

Sophie examined her corset, looking for where to put the needles. It worried her a little to have them on her like this. What if they broke?

"Need some help?" Veronica winked.

There was a knock at the door and Veronica went to answer it as Sophie slid the needles into the foam-protected pockets on her sternum. She heard a deep voice and looked up at the door. She couldn't see who was there, but she knew who it was. Dylan Davies was back.

Sophie put on her shirt as the door opened and her cousin walked in. Dylan was Tammy and Pierce's oldest son. He was the same age as Abby. However, Abby was a clone of her parents. Dylan was the exact opposite. Sophie's Uncle Pierce was a farmer and an inventor. Dylan's older sister, Piper, fell into that mold. Aunt Tammy was a small pixie of a carefree woman while Dylan was over six feet three inches of solid muscle. His dark brown hair was cut short and his hazel eyes revealed nothing. There was nothing carefree about him. If he moved just right, the end of a tattoo could be seen under his collar. Dylan Davies was a walking billboard for a bad boy.

"I thought I was the only one in the family who got into trouble," Dylan teased as he walked into the room and picked her up for a tight hug before turning to greet Abby. "Hey, Abs. Long time, no see," he said, his lips showing no sign of a grin. Dylan didn't grin. He was too bad to grin. Instead, if he was highly amused, his lip might twitch. All the girl cousins teased him relentlessly about this.

"I know. The wedding the other week, it was

forever ago," Abby deadpanned back. Dylan's lip might have twitched but Sophie was pretty sure he just blinked instead.

"Ryan filled me in. You develop missiles? Where the hell have I been?" Dylan asked.

"Good question, where have you been?" Sophie smirked.

Dylan sent her a wink. "Around. I just met with Jackson and his FBI team. And I see Abby brought some friends, too. Nash is meeting us in a couple minutes to set out a plan until this Ares character is caught."

Abby handed Sophie the knife to attach to her leg. Sophie shook her head in disbelief of the situation but took the knife anyway. She felt as if she were a metal detector's worst nightmare. She attached the knife and her mother hugged her nephew and began talking guns. She wouldn't trade her family for anything, but sometimes she wondered what Sienna's professional opinion of them would be.

"Ready? May I escort you ladies?" Dylan asked so smoothly with his deep husky voice that even Veronica blushed. They walked into the hallway and she saw her cousin, Jackson Parker, heading toward them.

"Your cousins are so sexy they could sway even me," Veronica whispered as Sophie cringed. Eww. She didn't want to think about that.

"I agree completely with that statement, except for the swaying part. They're fair game in my book,"

Abby whispered from Sophie's other side.

Jackson was one of the few Jake Davies grandchildren who hadn't inherited the famous Davies hazel eyes. Instead, Jackson had inherited his father Cole's silver eyes and quiet confidence.

"Well, I didn't think I'd be able to be back in Keeneston so soon." Jackson walked up to the group. "Hey, cuz," Jackson said, giving Sophie a hug and shaking Dylan's hand. "I have a bet with my men that you have no fewer than six weapons on. Don't make me lose this bet," Jackson teased Abby.

"You know me," Abby grinned back. "I have seven."

"Atta girl." Jackson winked before turning to hug Sophie's mom. "Nash said to bring you all over to the main house. He and Ahmed have two plans of action to run by everyone."

Nash was deep in discussion when the ballroom in Dani and Mo's mansion began to fill. He thought it would be all guards and police, but when he turned to look, it was filled with Keeneston residents as well. The three Rose sisters and their husbands were already in the front row along with half the town scattered among Rahmi security, FBI, Keeneston sheriff's department, and DeAndre with five state troopers.

Nash's heart pounded as he watched Sophie walk toward him surrounded by Abby, Jackson, and Dylan. She was his everything and right now someone was trying to take her from him. The idea of something happening to her would send him over the edge so he refused to believe Ares could get to her.

"What's going on?" Sophie asked as her cousins joined the rest of the town and greeted friends and family.

"We have two options, and we need to decide which one to choose," Nash told her, taking her hand into his. He couldn't lose her. He wouldn't lose her.

"What are they? And why is everyone here?" Sophie asked.

"I have no idea why everyone is here. It was just for security but somehow it went out on the town text," he said as he shot a stare to Miss Lily, who blinked innocently back at him. Innocent as a teenager who said nothing was going on, that is. "As for our options for tonight, we can either stay under guard here or we can go back to the cabin by ourselves."

He saw Sophie thinking it over as she nibbled on her bottom lip. "If we stay here, we have guards protecting me, but we saw what Ares can do to guards. If we go to the cabin, we're on our own, but also not where Ares thinks we'd be."

Nash nodded. "I was thinking of setting up a heavy contingent of guards at one of the spare houses on the property. It'll look like we're there when we're not."

"You want to set a trap," Sophie said. "But

shouldn't we be here for it?"

"We can't risk you being found, and I'm not willing to let you out of my sight. Ares already has the missile. If he has you, too," Nash said, shaking his head, "I can't risk it. I'm the last thing between you and a madman. If that means we miss the takedown, then so be it."

"I don't like it, but I understand it. Let's set the trap," Sophie admitted.

"Nash, you're on," Ryan interrupted. Sophie gave his hand a squeeze and went to take a seat next to a very tired-looking Sienna.

For the next twenty minutes, Nash told the group his plan for watching the town for anyone new coming in. Two men were posted on the only two roads into town around the clock. Jackson's team took control of the fake Sophie location on the farm, Dylan would be staying in town, Abby was at Cade and Annie's house, and Ryan had some of his FBI agents at his house while he sent Sienna to stay at her parents. DeAndre and the state troopers were all over the county while the Keeneston Sheriff's Department, along with various Davies cousins, uncles, and aunts, were to spread throughout the town and at various houses.

With the plan in place, the ballroom emptied out as everyone drove into Keeneston. It was time Sophie was seen. They would have dinner at the café, hang out with the townspeople, and then everyone would leave at once driving off in different directions. Nash and Sophie would head to the farm. En route, Piper and Gabe would slip into Nash's car and drive to the house Jackson and the FBI had surrounded. They would enter the house once again dressed as Sophie and Nash while Sophie and Nash slipped into the woods at the side of the road and headed to their cabin. It would be an extra couple of miles to walk, but it would be near impossible for Ares's men to see the switch.

In the meantime, Nash was going to enjoy some bread pudding. They were safe, and while he knew he couldn't relax in his guard, it comforted him to know he had the entire town for backup.

Sienna's cousins surrounded her without being asked as they started to walk from the ballroom. Nash went to follow, but a perfectly manicured hand with bright red nails closed around his arm.

"Nash, wait," Veronica ordered. She had taken notes and would be running communications with all the groups. When it came to organization and timing, Veronica was unbeatable. She stood behind Nash along with Piper.

"What is it?" Nash asked as he kept one eye on Sophie's retreating figure.

"I know you're a big tough man, but I want you to wear this. It's just smart," Piper said.

Nash turned his entire attention to the ladies as Veronica handed him a white rectangular box with a pink cheetah print bow on it. "Yeah, I know. I ran out of ribbon and had to borrow some from Aniyah," Veronica admitted.

Nash hid a laugh as he yanked the bow off the

box and opened it. He pushed aside the tissue paper and looked down at a black hooded jacket. The material was tightly woven, yet smooth. "A jacket?"

"A Piper Davies nanotech jacket that is supposed to be bullet- and stab-proof. This is Piper's prototype," Veronica said, nodding to where Piper stood, looking nervous beside her.

"Really?" Nash asked as he slipped into the jacket. It weighed no more than a sweatshirt.

"Well, that's the idea anyway," Piper said shyly. "Do you like it?"

"It's great. Lightweight and not obvious at all. Did you make this at the lab in Rahmi?" Nash asked of the international nanotechnology lab Zain and Piper had just finished building in Rahmi.

"No, I made it in my lab here, but I had the other scientists help with some of the areas I was stuck on. I tested it out at my parents' farm. I want you to have it. You're the one most likely to be shot at," Piper said with a shrug.

"True." Nash laughed even though the thought was sobering. "Thank you," he said, kissing her cheek. "It's a brilliant invention."

Piper blushed. For as smart as she was, she was still surprised anyone ever thought so.

"Now, may I escort you ladies to your cars?"

Veronica and Piper walked with Nash outside to where Jackson, Abby, Dylan, and Sophie waited for him in his car. He thanked Piper again and slid into the driver's seat. If all went well, Ares would be caught and Sophie would be safe by tomorrow morning.

Chapter Twenty-One

The café was already full by the time Nash arrived. A space had been saved for them out front, along with a table inside. As they walked up the sidewalk to the front door, they saw Cody and a state trooper in regular clothing sitting outside.

"Hey, man," Cody said to Nash. "We have two men out back, too."

"Good. Thank you," Nash said as he followed the group inside.

"Nash!" an ear splitting shriek rang out.

"I'm outta here," Dylan muttered as he sidestepped out of the way.

"Cowards," Nash hissed as both Jackson and Dylan practically dived out of Nikki's oncoming path.

Sophie and Abby were already at a table with the girls and didn't see the imminent threat. Nash didn't feel any better when Father Ben crossed himself as Nikki teetered by him in her five-inch-heeled, thigh-high boots and mini sweater dress that barely covered her ass.

"I was so worried about you. I heard all about

those horrible men who were captured. You're *so* brave," Nikki purred, well, that is if she could move her lips to form an *r*, instead it came out slurred as if she'd had a pitcher of the Rose sisters' special iced tea.

The trouble with Nikki was she was a beautiful woman—in a train wreck sort of way. You couldn't help but look at her lips when she licked them seductively. You never knew if this was the time they'd explode. You also couldn't help staring at her tits on full display and wonder how skin could stretch that far. The trouble really set in once you started staring. You couldn't really stop. That's when she had you trapped. Nikki took it as sexual interest instead of wondering if she belonged in a circus. And once Nikki thought she had your interest, you were screwed—and not in a good way.

Nash shuddered and refused to let his eyes travel south of her spidery fake eyelashes. They were the stuff of childhood nightmares. "Thank you, Nikki, but we're all okay," Nash said, looking at the ceiling after having a sudden urge to see if she had spiders all over her face.

Nikki moved closer and Nash cringed when he felt her breasts press like two boulders into his chest. "Do you have something in your eye? Let me take a look," she slurred.

"Down," Poppy ordered as she shot Nikki with a squirt bottle. "I told you no hitting on my patrons." *Squirt squirt.*

Nikki shrieked. When she spun around to face

Poppy, her butt implants knocked into Nash, sending him careening onto Miss Lily's table.

"Don't you just love it?" Miss Violet whispered to Nash, spread out on her table.

"Addison giving Poppy the squirt bottle she used to try to break her father of horrible pick-up lines was a great idea," Miss Lily smiled down at him.

"Just a shame it didn't work on Henry, bless his heart," Miss Daisy sighed as they all watched the defense attorney in the shiny silver suit rock back on his heels in front of Nikki and smile.

"There're so many things I want to say right now about you being wet," Henry grinned before Poppy squirted him, too.

"Bad!" Poppy yelled and squirted again.

"Daaaaad," Addison groaned from the table next to the Rose sisters.

Henry ignored his daughter. "You know Halloween is coming up," Henry began as he lost the battle and let his eyes drop down to Nikki's body. "Are you dressed as a supermodel? Because you're the most boo-titty-full woman I've seen."

The Rose sisters groaned. Neely Grace, Henry's wife, leaned over and tapped Miss Daisy's shoulder and asked, "Can I borrow that?"

Miss Daisy nodded and handed Neely Grace the wooden spoon. Neely Grace smacked her husband on the side of his head.

"For $500 an hour, I'll get you off," Henry quipped to his wife.

"Oh my gosh, Dad. Mom, not again," Addison cried as she covered her ears with her hands.

"Should we move on to oral arguments?" Neely whispered not quietly enough into her husband's ear.

"You had me at *pro bono*," Henry growled as he grabbed his wife and kissed her while Nikki stood looking confused.

"Remember," Neely Grace warned, "I'm the only one looking at your briefs. Addison, you can get home on your own, right?"

Addison didn't lift her head from the table. "I don't want to witness your *ex parte* communications," she groaned.

Neely Grace and Henry smiled at their daughter. "I knew she had it in her."

"You know what your mother will have in—" Henry started to say before Addison yanked the water bottle from a stunned Poppy and squirted her father.

"Out!" Addison ordered as her parents stumbled from the café, kissing. "I'm so embarrassed. Their foreplay is so wrong."

"I thought you could use this," Gabe said, setting a large glass of iced tea in front of her.

Addison looked up at Gabe. "I don't think iced tea will get me to forget what we all just witnessed."

"Then it's a good thing it's ninety percent bourbon." Gabe winked before rejoining Nash who had stood up. "Poor kid. And I thought it was embarrassing when my parents did that royal wave to the crowds back in Rahmi."

Nash looked down at his watch. It was only six o'clock. Nothing would happen until the middle of the night. That's when Ares would think he had the advantage of darkness. For a little while, they could sit back and relax, though it was hard to, knowing they had a chance to catch Ares that night. It would be hell waiting to hear if Jackson's team had captured the elusive, sadistic Ares.

Nash and Gabe made their way to their table and took a seat.

"Let me ask you a question," Matt said as he waited for his to-go order. Nash raised an eyebrow to indicate that Matt should ask. "If you and Sophie took two years to get together, kind of like Riley and I did, then you wouldn't wait that long to pop the question, right?"

"Are you serious?" Nash asked, his face not revealing a thing.

Matt smiled. "I gotta tell you, it's nice being on the other side of the bets once again."

"Really?" Nash challenged. "So, when are you going to become a dad?"

Matt froze in horror. "Shit," he cursed, realizing he was still in the betting pool.

The men snickered, but Zain, Ryan, and Deacon looked as scared as Matt while casting glances toward the Rose sisters and Poppy with her betting book.

"You have to keep your voice down," Zain whispered. "They're always listening."

"Yeah," Deacon said, leaning in close to the group. "It's like they know if you're even thinking about it."

Ryan nodded. "We wake up to baby blankets and booties on our doorstep."

"We do, too," Zain and Deacon said together.

"Yeah, you're not making a strong case for marriage," Nash told them as he sat back with his coffee.

"We don't need to make a case for it. Too much time alone with Sophie and Uncle Cade will demand a shotgun wedding." Ryan smiled.

"That's so antiquated—" Nash began but got cut off as the guys laughed.

"If you feel that way, then Ares isn't who you need to fear the most. It's our parents. Even my father said he and my mom didn't wait all that long to have my brother and me. Last month he said it was my duty to secure the line," Zain told them with a roll of his eyes.

"Cy thinks Riley and I don't have sex," Matt said, making everyone laugh.

"Yet Aunt Gemma told my mom she foresaw a grandchild by her birthday," Ryan gleefully told him.

Matt blinked. "Shit," he cursed again.

"We need to go on a baby strike. No babies until they back off," Deacon suggested. Nash heard it before he saw it. A spatula flew through the air and hit Deacon on the head.

"Oops, it slipped," Deacon's mother-in-law, Katelyn, said innocently from where she stood at the

Rose sisters' table.

The men turned white and suddenly broke from the table to hide behind their wives, leaving Nash and Gabe alone. Gabe shook his head. "If you never settle down long enough to have a girlfriend, you can keep out of the betting pool. But you already put a label on your relationship. You're a goner," Gabe teased.

The idea didn't bother Nash too badly. Sure, it was annoying to think that every aspect of your relationship—if you're dating, if you're going to propose, when the wedding will be, and the birth of children—were all wagers, but it was what made Keeneston great. He wasn't going to change his feelings just for the betting pool. The fact that the citizens cared enough to bet on him was also the reason they were all here tonight armed with everything from guns to wooden spoons to help one of their own. And it was worth it if it meant Sophie was his.

Nash looked at Sophie trying to pretend she was fine. She laughed, but it wasn't real. He could tell she was nervous as her cousins and friends tried to preoccupy her. Instead, all he wanted to do was take her back to the cabin and think of other ways to make her forget about Ares.

"Noooo," Gabe whined. "Not you, too."

"Me too what?" Nash asked, turning his attention back to Gabe.

"You've got that I'm-in-love look on your face. I'm not ready to have another married friend. Do you have any idea how annoying newlyweds are?

Why do you think I traveled for six months after Zain and Mila got married?

"Don't get ahead of yourself. It's been days. Not months," Nash reminded Gabe.

"It doesn't matter. You have the look. She has the look. Then you two keep looking at each other . . . it's a done deal. See, even Annie is over there with the moms, and they are looking at you two as if measuring you for your tux and her for her gown."

Nash looked at Annie and shrugged when he looked back to Gabe. "They don't want me to marry their daughter. I'm sure it's more like they can't wait to get Sophie back in their house. I'm just a soon-to-be-out-of-work soldier. What good am I to someone like Sophie?"

Gabe shook his head. "You know you're not out of work. And you know everyone in town loves you."

"That's different from letting me marry into the most popular family in town."

"Nash Dagher," Gabe sighed, "not afraid of the deadliest men in the world but taken down by fear of rejection."

"You would be too if you were rejected the last time you shared your feelings," Nash murmured.

"I'm not one to give relationship advice," Gabe said more seriously this time. "But at some point, you just need to pick yourself up and take a leap of faith. I have a feeling this time Sophie will be waiting to catch you."

"What do you think they talk about?" Zinnia asked as she set down a large slice of chocolate cake smothered in bourbon caramel sauce in front of Sophie.

"Different ways to kill people?" Layne suggested.

"Nah," Zinnia said, shaking her head. "Gabe is too much of a diplomat to kill anyone."

"You obviously haven't seen him and Zain sparring," Mila whispered to the group.

Zinnia's eyes got big. "I want details."

The ladies laughed, but Sophie didn't feel like laughing. She forced her lips into a smile and only half listened. Instead, she watched Nash. She'd told him she loved him, but he'd never answered. Before the others joined the table, she'd talked to Sienna, who had a love-hate relationship with Ryan for a number of years before they finally got together. Her professional opinion was Nash was scared of rejection. But as Sophie numbly ate the cake, she watched Nash eat his dinner and thought about him. Nash wasn't scared of anything. He went into the darkest, most dangerous locations in the world to fight evil. And he won. How hard could it be to tell her how he felt?

Sophie set her water down so hard it sloshed over the rim. She made up her mind. If there was a chance she was going to die at the hands of Ares tonight, she was done playing games. She was going to find out Nash's feelings. How hard could it be?

Chapter Twenty-Two

N ash and the others made a scene about leaving the café. Gabe and Piper left twenty minutes before to change into similar clothing that Sophie and Nash were wearing. Now Nash and Sophie stood outside the café with the entire Davies family, pretending to talk. Nash was sure they said something to him, but he was too busy looking out for Ares or his men to really pay attention. He smiled and nodded mostly.

In position was the text he finally got from Gabe. It was go time.

"Come on, Sophie. Let's get back to the farm," Nash said loud enough to be heard over the Davies family.

Sophie hugged and kissed her parents and brothers. Her parents clasped her tightly, and Nash felt the full weight of the trust they were placing in him. They were trusting him with their daughter's life.

"Take care of my baby," Annie whispered, her voice tight with emotion as she hugged Nash.

"We'll get Ares, don't worry. Just keep Sophie

safe," Cade said, shaking his hand. Nash nodded to them both and opened the door for Sophie. She climbed in and soon they were driving out of the small downtown surrounded by a line of vehicles.

"Sophie, you know I'll do everything I can to protect you, right?" Nash asked as some of the cars peeled toward their farms. Nash tried to express his feelings. Surely she would know he loved her if he was willing to give his life for hers.

"I know, Nash. And I love you, you know that right?" Sophie asked as she slipped her hand onto his leg as he drove.

Nash looked at Sophie. Her face was lit only by the glow of lights on the dashboard of his vehicle. It was time. "Get ready, we're here," Nash said, turning his attention back to the curving country road lined on one side with woods and the other side with a large cow pasture. The cars in front and behind him slowed for the turn and as soon as they were around the curve and out of sight of anyone following behind them, he slammed on the brakes, put the car in park, and was out the door.

Gabe and Piper leapt into the car and in seconds the line of three cars were heading toward the farm while Nash and Sophie were sitting quietly in the woods looking out for any tails.

"Do you think they're even here? Maybe they gave up after their failed attempt to find me?" Sophie asked hopefully.

"They're here all right. I just don't know where. Ares has all he needs except you, and he's not someone to sit back and wait. Come on. Let's hike back to the cabin. It'll take a while from here," Nash said, forgetting about his feelings and focusing entirely on keeping Sophie alive.

Sophie was cold, tired, and damp. A light rain had begun to fall halfway through their trek to the cabin. The trees no longer had their leaves, so they didn't keep them dry. Left with her thoughts as they walked the miles in the dark to the cabin, Sophie thought about the kind of person Ares was. From all the reports she'd listened to, there was little known about the man akin to a cult leader. It was estimated he had close to twenty thousand men around the world who did everything from extortion, bribery, racketeering, fraud, counterfeiting, robbery, money laundering, arson, illegal gambling, smuggling, piracy, prostitution, cyber theft, identity theft, and good old-fashioned murder for hire.

With twenty thousand men loyal to the death to him, Ares still remained a mystery. When addressing his minions, he was dressed in a mask, holding a spear as if he were the Greek god himself. No one knew his real name except Poseidon, who'd held to a criminal's code and refused to give it to anyone prior to his death.

Sienna and the others involved in the investigation believed the group would collapse under a power vacuum if Ares were taken out. And according to the information that had been gathered, Ares kept such a tight hold on the group there wasn't a clear second-in-command. It was Ares, then everyone else.

"Watch your step," Nash said, catching her arm as she stumbled on a downed branch hidden under leaves.

"Thanks," Sophie said, coming back to the now. She slipped her hand down Nash's arm and into his hand.

She smiled to herself when his grip tightened instead of pulling away. He loved her. She knew it. He just needed to know she was putting them first now.

"I've been thinking about what's next," Sophie said as they moved through the dark woods.

"If Ares isn't caught tonight—" Nash started.

"No, I mean for me *after* Ares is caught. I'm moving back to Keeneston, and I want to find a house that has some property to it so I can build my own lab. I don't want to stop working. I have so many ideas I want to explore with biometrics that have nothing to do with weapons."

"That's really great, Sophie. You're so smart, and you have so much to give. I'm proud of you," Nash said so sincerely Sophie thought her heart might burst.

"What about you? Do you want to stay in Keeneston?" Sophie asked.

"Yes. There was a time I worked hard to do everything I could to leave Keeneston. I served the king and did my duty as a soldier. While Rahmi will always be my birth country, Keeneston is my home.

I just hope Mo can convince the king to reassign me. For all Mo said about hiring me privately, to be dishonorably discharged for failing to take orders . . . well, I don't know if I can do it. I might have to do what my king orders even if I don't like it. That's the life of a soldier, after all," Nash told her as he helped her climb over a fallen tree.

That's what was worrying him. She didn't have a solution to that before, but she did now. "Well, I've always wanted to go to Rahmi. I'll have a reason to go if you're stationed there."

Nash turned quickly back to look at her. Sophie smiled at him and almost laughed as she saw him processing the intentions of her words. "We're here," Nash said instead of a declaration of love.

Nash led them down a narrow path, and after a minute of walking, they were in the clearing with the little cabin blending into the shadows of the rainy night. "Stay here," he ordered, leaving her in the trees as he pulled his gun and went to make sure the cabin was secure.

"Stupid man," Sophie muttered as she worriedly watched him disappear into the cabin. That was it. She had thought she'd been clear, but she was going to lay it out straight. She wanted to be with him. Not just now, but in the future as well. The one thing having Ares after her had taught her: Sophie didn't want to wait until later to say something that was on her mind at that moment.

Nash appeared a moment later and waved her forward. Sophie crossed the clearing and met Nash on the porch. He was holding a towel as he ushered her inside and turned on a battery-operated lantern.

"I'm sorry, we can't risk a fire or the noise from the generator," he told her as he stripped out of his clothing and dried off.

Sophie understood. She'd tolerate being cold for a couple hours if it meant Ares were captured. Following Nash's lead, she stripped down and used the towel to bring some heat back to her skin. She pulled on a pair of royal blue fleece pants and reached for a sweatshirt when Nash stopped her.

"As much as I hate seeing you covered up, it would be better if you stayed armed. Just in case," Nash said, pulling on a new pair of jeans and the rest of his clothes.

Sophie reached instead for her ten-pound corset and then slipped her oversized sweatshirt on over it. "So, what do you want to do for the rest of the night?" Sophie tried to say lightly, but it fell flat.

Nash took pity on her and stepped away from his lookout at the window to put his arms loosely around her waist. Sophie's head fell back, her damp hair hanging down her back as she looked into Nash's face. Worry lines creased around his eyes and on his brow. His dark brown eyes seemed black in the low light of the cabin.

"Sophie," he said softly as his fingers speared her hair and brushed it from her face. "There's so much we need to talk about."

"I know," Sophie said, leaning her cheek into the warm palm of his hand. "I've learned that no matter how well you know someone, it's better not to guess at what they are feeling, but to simply ask. I know you've been feeling out my reactions to things, like if you're stationed in Rahmi. Let's be truthful with each other and stop trying to hint at our feelings. I love you, Nash. I tried to replace that feeling with anger when you left, but it was really anger with myself for letting you go."

Nash's fingers fisted into her hair as he pulled her to him, his lips covered hers. He used his hands to angle her head so he could deepen the kiss. Everything about it was perfect, and the knowledge that Nash was the only man for her was as clear as day. And this time she was seeing it for what it was.

Nash pulled back and looked at her, feathering her face with light brushes of his lips as he whispered endearments.

"I'll follow you anywhere, Nash. I don't want to spend a single day without you. I never stopped loving you," Sophie declared as she placed her head on his shoulder and clung to him.

She felt Nash shaking his head. "I never should have walked away. You deserved my support and understanding. I admire you so much for what you've accomplished. I always checked on you, you know?"

"Matt told me you asked about me," Sophie admitted.

"I could only get away from other Red Shadow members occasionally. As soon as I did, I got a burner phone and called Matt before I even called the king. I followed your career. I made sure you were safe and protected even if I couldn't be with you as I desired. I never thought I would get another chance with you," Nash whispered as he placed a finger under her chin and dipped his lips to meet hers in a gentle kiss full of hope for the future.

"Nash, I love you so much," Sophie said, passionately willing him to feel the depth of her love for him.

Nash brushed back her hair and in his eyes she saw it. She saw the love he had for her. "Sophie, I've waited so long to tell you —" Nash stiffened in her embrace.

"Is everything okay?" Sophie asked as Nash pushed her against the back wall and down to the ground.

"Stay here," he ordered, not answering her. The abrupt change in him startled Sophie as she crouched against the wall and looked over the length of the bed at the front door.

Nash had his gun in hand as he slowly inched toward the window. It was then Sophie heard it. A sound that was quiet, but not natural. There was some kind of disturbance in the woods. Sophie pulled her gun and another from the corset and used the bed to steady her arms.

All the classes in self-defense, all the hours at the shooting range, all the knowledge she had of weapons never prepared her for the reality of the situation. She had to be ready to use all her knowledge to handle whatever was going to come through that door.

"Is it Ares?" Sophie whispered as she hoped against hope it was just DeAndre coming to offer them reinforcements.

"I'm sure it is. Sophie, I have to tell you. I—" The sound that had been muffled became clear. Light flooded the clearing, blinding Nash through the window as loud sounds came from the roof of the cabin. In a split second, the reality of the situation set in. The noise she had heard was helicopter blades and the loud sounds were of men landing on the roof.

"Get down!" Nash yelled as he fired at the shadows of men sliding down ropes from the helicopter and landing outside the cabin.

Men fell, orders were yelled, glass broke as a canister careened into the cabin. It flew past Nash, who didn't take his eyes off the men trying to storm the porch and landed three feet in front of Sophie.

Sophie didn't hesitate. She dropped her gun and lunged for the device. It was black and cylindrical and could either be tear gas or a flash grenade. Not wanting to find out which, Sophie picked it up and hurled it with all her strength back out the shattered window.

It made it to the porch before exploding midair. The sound stole her breath and the flash of light blinded her. Sophie fell to the floor in agony. The light burned her eyes, and her ears rang from the blast. She tried to remain calm, knowing it would eventually pass but also knowing that until it did, she was completely vulnerable.

"Sophie!"

She heard her name being called from what seemed to be a very long tunnel.

"Sophie! Answer me!"

At the command, Sophie struggled to force herself to open her eyes. She had thought Nash was far away, but in reality he was right in front of her, grabbing her to see if she was injured.

"Are you hurt?" he yelled. Too stunned to answer, Sophie shook her head. But those seconds to come back to reality were all Sophie had to realize they'd lost. Ares was here, and they wouldn't be able to stop him.

"I'm sorry, Sophie. I failed you. Try to hide. I'll keep them out for as long as I can. If you see a way to escape, take it," Nash said, his voice coming into focus through her damaged eardrums before he leapt up, guns firing as figures moved past the windows and battered against the door.

Sophie grabbed her discarded gun and ignored his order to hide. There was no place to hide, and she sure as hell wasn't going to sit back and wait to be taken. She fired at the figures in black, which were highlighted by the glare from the helicopter. She wasn't sure she was even breathing as the men kept appearing no matter how many she hit. They were grossly outnumbered.

Her body trembled as she lined up her sights and fired. A man dropped. Her gun emptied. Nash moved closer to the door, reloading as he went.

Sophie reached into her corset and pulled out a magazine clip for the gun she'd designed and tossed the empty pistol her mother had given her to the ground.

Was it hours or was it seconds? Sophie didn't know as she guarded Nash's back. It could have been both for all she knew. What Sophie did know was this was the end. She saw her parents crying at her funeral. She saw her friends and family mourning her and Nash's lives. And she briefly wondered if they could be buried next to each other. Would she be able to spend death with the man she loved and whom she didn't get a chance to spend life with? Fear of the end, anger at not being able to fulfill her future, and sadness of their lost future coursed through her.

Sophie let the rage take control as she rose from her position behind the bed. She relentlessly fired at the men outside. She saw some fall, but like ants pouring from an anthill, they kept coming, dressed in their black tactical gear.

"Why aren't they firing?" Sophie yelled.

Nash fired his gun and took the time to toss her a quick look. "Because they want you alive. Sophie, you have to try to get out of here. Promise me no matter what happens you'll run, and you won't look back."

"Nash," Sophie said as panic filled her voice. They were out of time. She heard the sounds of boots by the door and someone scraping the inside walls of the chimney as he was lowered down it.

"Promise me," Nash begged as he pulled a grenade from a duffel bag at his feet.

"I promise," Sophie choked out.

Nash pulled the pin and waited. At the last second, he threw the grenade and pressed himself against the wall. Sophie fell to the floor as it exploded on the porch. The remaining glass windows were blown into the cabin. When she opened her eyes, she found Nash back at the window firing up at a helicopter. It was then she noticed not one, but two lights pointed at the cabin. There was more than one helicopter. No wonder there were so many of men.

"Get ready!" Nash yelled, motioning for her to come to him.

Sophie ran to him as he pulled another grenade from the duffel bag. "Hold this. I'm going to take out their lights. The second this explodes, we leap through the window and run for the woods. Head straight for the main house. I hope by now our people will have heard the noise and be racing to help us."

Sophie nodded her understanding.

"Cover me," Nash told her as he lined up the shot at the helicopter. The grenade had done more than shatter the windows. It had also ripped off a chunk from the patio roof, allowing Nash a view of the helicopters.

Sophie ducked under the windowsills. In five crouched steps, she was against the wall, shooting out the second window. It took Nash six shots to take out the lights and plunge the clearing into darkness.

"Get ready," Nash ordered. He pulled the pin, counted, and tossed it at the door right as Sophie shot the man who had suddenly appeared in the fireplace.

The grenade blew the door in and sent men flying. Sophie didn't wait, she hopped through the window, and with jagged glass tearing into her hand, she vaulted outside.

Nash grabbed her then. "Run!"

He shoved her forward, and she made a dash across the clearing with him right behind her, firing to provide them cover. The safety of the trees was only ten yards away when Ares's men converged on them.

"Don't stop and don't look back," Nash ordered.

Sophie pumped her arms and legs as she kept her eyes glued to the safety of the nearing trees. Shots rang out. She felt some of the bullets fly by and hit the trees. Some bullets caused the earth near her feet to spray up, but she didn't deviate. She pushed herself harder, knowing she could not allow them a chance to prevent her escape. Sophie was only a few strides away from the woods. There was yelling, gun fire, and then she was in the shadows.

"We did it," she gasped as she dared a glance back at Nash. "Nash?"

Sophie wrapped her arms around a small tree as she spun around and saw that Nash was no longer behind her. Instead, when the bullets had gotten too close, he'd stopped and charged Ares's men who were closing in on them. He ran straight at them firing guns from both hands.

"Run!" He yelled the moment before the first bullet slammed into him.

"Nash!" Sophie screamed as if she'd been hit with the bullet herself.

But then they kept coming. Nash went down on one knee as he struggled to keep the men away from the woods long enough to give Sophie a chance to escape. But then he was hit again, and again, and again.

With one last Herculean effort, Nash fired before wavering and collapsing face first onto the ground.

"No, no, no," Sophie chanted as she almost ran for him. She stopped herself, knowing that Nash had just died to save her and this time Sophie wouldn't let him down. So she turned away from the inert body of the man she loved and ran.

Chapter Twenty-Three

Sophie ran as branches slapped her face and her hair was ripped from her scalp by bushes. No matter how hard she pushed herself, she still heard them coming.

She caught glimpses of the helicopter following her from above and pushed herself deeper into the woods in hope of the men losing sight of her. It didn't work. The foot soldiers were relentless in their pursuit. Her lungs burned, but she was running high on adrenaline and didn't feel it.

The worst part wasn't that she was likely to be caught. The worst part was knowing Nash was probably dead. Part of her wanted to just quit. Without Nash—no, Nash wouldn't want her to quit. He would want her to fight for her life and that was exactly what she intended to do.

With renewed determination, Sophie ran. She ran for Nash. She ran for her family. She would never let Ares win, and she would kill him for taking Nash from her. Through the sound of her heavy breathing and pounding feet, through the sound of the two helicopters flying above, and through the sound of her pursuers, she heard it. Loud engines.

Distant lights broke through the woods as she realized she was almost out of the dark. Her friends had come to save her. "Help!" Sophie screamed as she burst through the woods and stumbled out into the pasture belonging to Desert Sun Farm.

Hope soared. Across the large pasture was an army of Rahmi solders and FBI agents. They were coming for her. Sophie wanted to cry with relief. Instead, she kept running. One of the helicopters from above opened fire, and Sophie almost fell as she looked before it raced straight at her rescuers with guns blazing. The other helicopter was landing directly in her path.

Sophie veered, but it was too late. Ares's men reached through the trees like fingers from a grave. They poured through sections of the trees for tens of yards. Sophie ran like a trapped deer, trying to avoid her capturers while the helicopter and her rescuers battled it out.

A massive explosion rocked the night sky as the helicopter blew to shreds. The blades went flying and slammed into the ground. Sophie hoped it would be a distraction. Rather than running from it, she continued straight for the fireball plummeting to the ground.

"Enough. Take her down," a deep voice yelled from the second helicopter now grounded near her.

Sophie darted around her shrinking enclosure. Her friends were so close. She heard them coming.

She just needed to hold them off . . . then the world tilted and blurred. Sophie looked to the helicopter and at the man who had yelled. Next to him was a man with a rifle. She looked down at herself. Was she shot? She stumbled to the ground, no longer having control of her legs.

As she fell, she saw it. A dart was impaled in her upper left shoulder that matched the dart her father had found. She struggled to fight off the tranquilizer. The world was nothing more than blurred shadows as Sophie clung to her gun. A shadow moved, and while she couldn't make it out, she fired. The shadow cursed, but it sounded as if it were in slow motion.

"Nash," Sophie whispered as the darkness came.

"Is dead," the voice from the helicopter said. "And you have a date with Ares." And then nothing. Sophie was neither alive nor dead. She was neither here nor there. She was nothingness.

"Sophie!" Jackson shouted from the back of the pickup truck flying toward the helicopter as it lifted off. He raised his sniper rifle to shoot it down so he could clear a path toward his cousin trapped in the field as men swarmed from the woods.

"Do you see her?" Nabi asked next to him.

"Let me get rid of the helicopter first," Jackson said as he put his eye to the scope. It didn't matter that the truck was bouncing across the pasture. He held his gun steady and looked through the scope. His finger flexed against the side of the rifle as he moved it to the trigger.

He took a slow breath as Nabi moved to steady him. He looked for the sweet spot right under the blades. A hit would take them down in seconds. As the scope traveled from the pilots to the open door, he saw who he figured was a manager of some kind. He could even be Ares for all they knew, but it was clear he was in charge. Jackson moved his rifle looking for the blades. When he saw golden hair piled on the backbench of the helicopter, he swung his scope back down for a better look inside.

What he saw sent shivers down his back. "Sophie," he gasped.

"What is it?" Nabi asked.

"Sophie's in the helicopter." Jackson cursed loudly and harshly. "Ares has her."

Nabi picked up his phone and spoke rapidly into it before turning to Jackson. "We'll try to track it," Nabi told him as he rested his elbows on the truck roof and began to fire at the few men who hadn't been able to make it onto the helicopter before it took off.

"Take them out," Jackson said into his coms. His team and Nabi's team opened fire as the men fired at them.

It took less than two minutes. Jackson slung his rifle over his shoulder and hauled up one of the men they had left alive. Ahmed marched toward them.

"Where's Nash?" He hadn't seen his friend on the helicopter.

Jackson shook the man he held by the collar. "Tell me where our man is, and I won't turn you over to Ahmed." Ahmed may be retired, but that didn't mean his name still didn't carry weight in the darkest corners of the world.

"At the cabin. We killed him," he spat.

Ahmed and Nabi shot each other a look and ran for the nearest pair of ATVs. Without saying another word, they tore off into the woods.

"Now that it's just us," Jackson said, his normally sparkling silver eyes turning cold as steel, "tell me where Sophie is headed."

The man shook his head. Jackson placed his gun muzzle to the man's knee and fired. He knew his team would be shocked. He knew he'd be reported. But he didn't care. They had his cousin.

"Davies," his friend and right-hand man, Talon Bainbridge, said, placing his hand on Jackson's shoulder.

"They took my cousin," was all Jackson had to say. Bainbridge was covered head to toe in FBI swat gear and only nodded his understanding.

"Men, let's go. This is Rahmi land, and we'll let them clean up. We'll rendezvous back at their security headquarters," Bainbridge ordered in his mix of Australian and American accents. The men shot Jackson a nervous look. "Misfire," Bainbridge said taking the gun from Jackson and handing him his. "I'll look it over to see if it needs to be scrapped."

"Thank you," Jackson said quietly as Rahmi guards quickly took over looking for survivors.

Bainbridge gave him a nod. "If you need me off the books, I'm here."

"Thanks," Jackson said to his best friend.

Jackson waited as his FBI team loaded up and then moved out. He smiled menacingly down at the man he'd shot. "It's just you and me now." Jackson put his gun to the other knee. "Where did they take Sophie?"

"I don't know," the man stammered as he shook his head wildly. "I swear!"

"Then what do you know? And let me tell you this, the amount of information you give me will determine if you live or die. So you better spill everything."

Nabi hadn't waited for Ahmed. He charged blindly ahead through the woods toward the cabin. He knew Ahmed would catch up. Within a quarter of a mile, Ahmed was directly behind him.

Nash couldn't be dead. Nash was a little brother, or more like a son, to him. Nabi had spent every day training him. Every week Nash sat at his kitchen table making his wife and daughter laugh. Nabi pressed the ATV to go faster, mindless of the dangers to himself.

Nabi tried to control his fear. This was part of the job and Nash knew that. He'd put his life before

Sophie's, and she'd had a chance to escape. That much was clear. Nash would have died a hero, but it didn't comfort Nabi as he barely kept the ATV under control.

The clearing was ahead. Nabi dreaded the arrival as much as he was eager to get to Nash. He didn't want to come face to face with his biggest fear in that moment—Nash dead. Nabi slowed as he approached the tree line. He could see the clearing and the small cabin blown apart as flames cast an eerie glow on the trees. As he got off the ATV, he could see Nash's body lying on the ground.

Nabi must have sucked in a horrified breath because the next thing he knew Ahmed had his hand clasped on his shoulder in a silent show of support. Nabi looked to his mentor and saw the unshed tears in Ahmed's eye that mirrored Nabi's.

"He got her out, and she's still alive," Ahmed said solemnly. "Let's bring him home."

Nabi swiped at his eyes. He was a soldier, and he wasn't going to leave a man behind. Side by side, Ahmed and Nabi moved to Nash's prone body. Nabi drew in a breath to calm himself as he reached for Nash's shoulder to turn him over. Fear of the way Nash's face would be frozen in death was worse than facing a hundred killers.

Ahmed moved to the other side and together they turned Nash's body over. Nabi stared at Nash and shook his head. "I just can't believe it."

"I can't either," Ahmed said, staring at Nash. "*Sssophie*."

Nabi almost fell back and he thought he heard a small yip from Ahmed before he concealed his surprise and placed two fingers on Nash's neck.

"He's alive," Ahmed said with disbelief as he ran his hands over Nash's body and then showed them to Nabi.

"No blood," Nabi gasped. "I thought since he was wearing black we just couldn't see it."

Nabi shook Nash. "Get up! They took Sophie. Ares has Sophie!" Nabi held his breath as Nash's eyelashes fluttered and then finally opened.

"Motherfu—," Nash moaned before rolling over and vomiting next to Ahmed.

"How the hell are you alive?" Ahmed asked as Nash groaned in pain.

"Piper's invention worked," Nash said, trying to take deep breaths to control the pain and come back to reality.

"What invention?" Ahmed and Nabi asked together.

"She used nanotechnology to develop this bulletproof jacket. Tell me about Sophie," Nash ordered.

Nabi explained and was relieved as he saw the color coming back to Nash's face. When Nabi concluded, Nash struggled to sit up. He pulled up his jacket and shirt and Nabi felt his eyes go round. Nash hadn't just been shot. He'd been pummeled with bullets. His entire chest and abdomen were nothing but black and blue.

"How many times were you shot?" Ahmed asked in wonder.

"I lost count after fourteen," Nash said, lowering his shirt after making sure there was no blood. "I fell to the ground after I lost my breath. There were a couple of particularly tough shots to my lungs. I was struggling to breathe when the men passed by me. One of them kicked me in the head and I went out."

"Come on. Let's get you back to the farm," Nabi said, helping Nash up while Ahmed called in an update.

"What?" Ahmed almost yelled and Ahmed never yelled. "We'll be right there, Bridget. Send everyone in to help."

"Is it Sophie?" Nash asked, moving to stand on his own.

"No, Ares sent his men to punish the town for taking out his men. Keeneston is under attack!" Ahmed cursed.

"Let's go to Ryan's. It's closest, and we can take one of their cars," Nash said as the three headed for the ATVs. "I have to find Sophie."

"Jackson was interrogating a man when we left. Maybe he'll have found something," Nabi said, tossing a phone to Nash. "Call him. Have him and his men meet us in Keeneston."

What had taken so long to walk was traversed quickly on the ATV. Nabi could feel Nash gripping him in pain as he tore through the woods, but Nabi figured Nash didn't care about the pain. The pain of losing a loved one was much more than any physical pain could ever be. And right now it wasn't just Sophie in danger. It was everyone they loved.

Chapter Twenty-Four

Nash gritted his teeth through the pain and soon enough was dragging himself over the fence onto Ryan and Sienna's property. The back door flung open and Hooch bounded out, followed by Sienna carrying a shotgun.

"Don't move!" Sienna called into the night as Hooch thundered toward them, his teeth bright white in the night.

"It's Nash!" Nash called out. Hooch recognized his voice and let out a happy *woof* as he bounded over to the group.

"What's happening?" Sienna asked, racing out the back door.

"They took Sophie," Nash said. "I failed her, Sienna."

"He took twenty odd bullets to the chest, giving her time to escape, but they got her anyway. We are the ones who failed. We weren't prepared for two helicopters and fifty men," Nabi told her.

"It doesn't matter," Ahmed said. "We need every weapon Ryan has, your car, and you need to lock yourself in the house with that beast."

Sienna looked to Nash questioningly. "Ares sent his men into Keeneston," Nash answered the silent question.

Sienna didn't say anything. Instead she tossed Ahmed the shotgun and raced into the house. The men looked at each other and followed. Sienna was already pulling guns, knives, and everything else Ryan had out and piling them up in the kitchen.

"I have my sports car. Start putting it all in the trunk. Not much room so wear as much as possible," Sienna ordered, her voice cold and emotionless.

They worked quietly and quickly, loading up the sports car. When Sienna came out pulling a sweatshirt over a bulletproof vest with FBI on the front, Nash and the others looked at her confused. "What are you doing?"

"I'm driving. My car, my dog, my rules," Sienna said, hitting the garage button and walking over to the car.

"You're not going," Ahmed said simply.

In reply Sienna opened the door and slid her seat forward. Hooch lumbered over and jumped into the back seat. "If you're coming, you'd better get in. I'm leaving with or without you. I've been looking up interrogation techniques. I can help find Sophie."

"I'm injured, I need the front seat," Nash said, trying not to laugh because it would hurt too much. Hooch sat in the middle of the minuscule backseat with a string of drool growing longer by the second.

Ahmed said something that was likely a curse in Rahmi. Nabi nodded and Nash let a snicker escape as Nabi climbed into the back and maneuvered around Hooch. By the time Nash took his seat, Nabi, Hooch, and Ahmed were crammed into the back and only one of them was smiling.

Nash didn't want to show it, but he was scared. Ares's men were one thing, Sienna driving at over a hundred miles per hour on small country roads was something else. The only noise that filled the small car was the sound of Hooch's panting. None of them knew what to expect as they approached Keeneston. Ares's solders were well trained and Keeneston was mostly filled with civilians.

Sienna took the sharp corner so fast that Nabi slid into Hooch, who slid into Ahmed, pressing him against the small window. But no one complained since they were looking down Main Street now. Cars were lined in front of the café as Ares's men tried to break through to get the people.

"Look," Nash said, pointing to the roof of the courthouse across the street. "Abby and Cade are up there."

Striding confidently from the café was none other than Dylan Davies looking not at all concerned that there was a gunfight going on as he shouted orders and moved townspeople behind the makeshift barrier. Cade and Abby were picking the ones off from the roof across the street who dared to try to break out of the ambush the town had trapped them in. Marshall, Cody, and Ryan were firing, along with half of the café, at anyone trying to break the car barrier. Then from the far side of town, Miles, Bridget, and Annie moved in. Miles's wife, Morgan, stood behind them, holding at least twelve police dogs.

Sienna stopped her car right behind Dinky and Noodle, who had been partners in the sheriff's department before Noodle retired. They were accompanied by Colton and Landon and were working behind Noodle's old truck, slowly moving forward, pinning Ares's men in further.

Nash leapt from the car. "What's the status?"

Noodle turned to him. "Our guys watching the road saw them coming and called it in. We were ready for them. They thought it would be easy to waltz into town and pick us off. Instead we ambushed them. They pulled up to the café, and we closed 'em in," Noodle said in his thick country accent. "Dylan orchestrated the whole thing."

Another pair of headlights came into view and Nash reached for his gun.

"It's Pierce Davies. He had to cut through some farms to get here, but he has something to help," Dinky told them.

Colton nodded. "Uncle Pierce said he had something that will give us a chance to take them alive in hopes of finding Sophie."

Pierce, the youngest of the Davies uncles, was an inventor. However, his inventions usually had to do with farming and nothing to do with warfare.

The old pickup truck slid to a stop as Pierce and his wife, Tammy, stepped out. A large device filled the entire bed of the truck.

"Oh my gosh, is that my baby?" Tammy cried as she pointed at Dylan striding from one group of people to the next as bullets pinged off the ground near his feet and shattered car windows. Without missing a beat, Dylan pulled out his gun while giving orders to another group of townspeople and shot an Ares soldier who was firing in the direction of the Rose sisters.

"Dylan's organized everything. We wouldn't have been able to hold out as long as we have without him," Noodle told her.

"What's this thing?" Ahmed asked Pierce.

"I originally intended for it to be a natural way to discourage animals and insects from bothering crops. It was supposed to emit a sound that humans can't hear along with a pulse wave that pests, whether underground or in the air, don't care for. The idea being that they leave the crops alone. I discovered it was a disaster for its intended purposes. When the pulse and sound mix together, people are incapacitated for a short time. It disorients them. Thank goodness Cassidy had her headphones on when she found me testing it. I was on the ground holding my head, physically incapable of getting up. It made Cassidy sick to her stomach, but she was able to turn it off. I recovered a minute later," Pierce explained. Cassidy, now nineteen, was away at college and wouldn't be helping anyone today.

"How's the best way for us to use it?" Nash asked.

"Tammy and I have ear buds to pass out to prevent us from becoming completely debilitated. We'll pass them out and crank this baby up. Don't be surprised if you're physically affected. Since you won't be hearing the higher frequency as much, you'll recover in seconds as opposed to a minute," Pierce explained. "I was told they wanted the men alive to question so we're going old-school. Disable them, take the guns, and then knock out anyone who gives us trouble."

"Couldn't we just shoot them all in the leg?" Ahmed asked.

Nash had to admit he liked that idea better, too.

"It'll work," Pierce said in such a way that Nash wasn't so sure it would.

"Here you go." Tammy smiled up at him. Her blonde hair was cut short and colored pink. Nash took the ear buds, and with a shrug, slipped them into his pocket.

"I'll take these to Dylan and pass them out for you, Mrs. Davies," Nash said, taking the large bag from her. He gave this plan next to zero chance of working.

Five minutes later, all the ear buds had been issued and people were ready to go. The second they could move, they'd break through the barrier and snag every gun and tie up every man they could before

Ares's soldiers recovered.

"How many men?" Nash asked Dylan.

"Around fifty. Not too bad at all. We have close to seventy-five people here," Dylan relayed. "And the dogs are ready to be released as soon as they're recovered. I've never seen dogs with ear buds in before," Dylan said as he tilted his head and looked up the street at Bridget and Morgan holding the dogs.

"Pam, you ready?" Dylan called out a second later.

"I gotcha covered!" Pam Gilbert called back, dressed in khaki pants with the perfect crease down the middle and powder-blue pea coat. Her penny loafers gleamed in the streetlight as she climbed into her minivan.

"Carter, Wyatt, ready?" Dylan asked. Nash didn't like being out of command, but he was also smart enough to know that when a capable leader was in charge, you didn't mess it up.

They held up rope and a group of men Nash recognized from the various farms stood behind them ready to leap into action.

"Everyone else ready?" Dylan called back to the café army.

Miss Lily tapped her broom on the ground. Miss Daisy slapped her wooden spoon in her palm, and Miss Violet looked as if she'd do damage with her spatula. Poppy and Zinnia, white-faced with fear, were armed with pans. Others had tasers, a rolling pin, a purse that looked as if it were a wrecking ball, baseball bats, and John Wolfe wore a smile.

"Runners, get ready," Dylan ordered as kids from the high school sports teams spread out.

Everyone looked as if they knew what they were doing so Ahmed, Nabi, and Nash plugged the buds into their ears and went with it. Dylan waved to his father and the device was turned on. Nash didn't hear anything, but he sure felt it. His stomach churned as if he were on the largest roller coaster in history. It turned, it flipped, and it sent him to one knee.

Nash was sure he was going to be sick. His head swirled, his stomach revolted, his vision blurred, and then it was over. He blinked his eyes open and found everyone similarly bent over or lying on the ground.

"Runners, go! Pam, go! Ropers, go!" Dylan bellowed as he leapt over the gate of cars.

Cars were moved as Pam raced into the kill zone with the side doors and tailgate to her minivan open. Ares's men writhed in pain on the ground as the runners picked up guns as easily as taking candy from a baby. They tossed them into Pam's minivan as she drove with the runners, primarily trying to avoid the downed men. The ropers, all farmers led by vet Wyatt Davies and Ashton Farm manager Carter Ashton, bound the hands of the enemy.

Nash didn't need to wait to see more. He jumped in, grabbing guns along with the rest of Keeneston. The seconds ticked by, and with every one, the men became more and more alert. The first punch was thrown as Pam zoomed out and cars were moved back to block everyone in.

Some people were dragging bound soldiers to one corner and holding them hostage at gunpoint while others wrestled to tie the rest up. Ares's soldiers recovered as Nash made it to the middle of the enclosed block. Those men had been trained — well trained — and they weren't going down without a fight. Nash slammed his fist into a masked face. "Where's Ares?" Nash shouted as the man went down.

Carter appeared out of nowhere and hog-tied the prisoner faster than Nash could blink. Grace, Nabi's wife and local kindergarten teacher, hauled him to the holding area and Nash was left facing another solder.

Dylan plowed through them, the Rose sisters beat them into submission, and if their wooden spoon or broom didn't work, Poppy or Zinnia bashed them in the head with a pan. Nash heard a cheer and looked up to find Jackson and his FBI team joining the melee. A large mountain of an FBI agent leveled a man who got too close to Zinnia with a punch. His partner, a tall but leaner man, spun Poppy out of the way and fought with another man until the agent finally took him down with the help of a pan-wielding Poppy.

"Nash, look out!"

Nash spun from where he'd laid out another soldier after trading a few hits and was met with a fist to the face. His head snapped back with the force, but he didn't think he'd been hit hard enough to be seeing things. But he had to be, right?

Father Ben, dressed with his Roman collar on, spun the man who had hit Nash and delivered a fierce uppercut to the chin. The man crumpled to the ground and a ranch hand from Cy Davies's farm had him tied in seconds. Father Ben made the sign of the cross, murmured an apology to God for using violence, and then offered a smile to Nash before delivering a wicked jab on another of Ares's soldiers.

Nash looked around. Ares's men were falling left and right. They were no match for Keeneston now. Nash turned to face another challenger armed with a knife when he heard Nikki purr from behind, "Hey, handsome."

"This is not the time," Nash yelled as the man became momentarily distracted and Nash quickly disarmed him. When he looked up to Nikki, she was pulling her shirt back down over her bare breasts.

"You're welcome," she said with a wink before heading over and flashing another soldier, rendering him temporarily stunned long enough for Aniyah to take him down with her purse.

Nash looked to see Father Ben making another sign of the cross after witnessing Nikki's form of help. "Come on, Father, I bet I can take more of the remaining soldiers out than you can."

"I'll put twenty on Ben," Layne called out from twenty feet away where she fought side by side with her father, Miles.

"*Stellen!*" Bridget gave a dog the attack command before reaching for the next dog Morgan had. "No way, twenty on Nash. Sorry, Father. *Stellen!*"

Bridget's dog sprinted across the street and latched onto the arm of a man with a knife approaching the huddle of Keeneston Belles fighting people off with a surprising amount of skill.

"You're on," Father Ben said, flashing Nash a grin.

Chapter Twenty-Five

N ash was sweating by the time he reached the cars forming a barricade in front of the courthouse. His fists were scraped, his chin was bruised, and he found Father Ben looking similar ten feet away.

"Thirteen," Father Ben panted.

"Sixteen," Nash tossed back.

"Rats! We needed new candlestick holders."

"You got them," Nash said and held out his hand. Father Ben shook it. "Thank you."

"Performing your wedding ceremony to Sophie will be thanks enough. Go get her," Father Ben said as Sienna stepped up to him.

"I've been watching the men as they were tied up and hauled over to the makeshift holding area. I see three that are the weakest. They are who you should ask where Ares is."

Nash turned to the bound men surrounded by the town. Dylan hauled the last freshly bound man over. "Which do you think is the weakest?" Nash asked Sienna.

"The one right in the middle. The one all the rest

are trying to block. They're doing it because they know he's weak," Sienna said as she turned her back to the group.

"Bridget!" Nash called out. "Can I borrow you and one of your dogs for a moment?"

"What can I do?" Dylan asked, having clearly handed off the next phase to Nash.

"Bring me that man," Nash said, pointing to the man looking nervously around as his men tried to shield him.

When Dylan went off to drag the man from the group, Sophie's family joined them along with Jackson and the two agents who helped out Poppy and Zinnia.

"Talon Bainbridge and Lucas Sharpe," Jackson introduced quickly.

"What's the plan now?" Annie asked as she gripped her husband's hand.

"I'm going to break the weak link. Hopefully, he'll know where Ares is," Nash told them.

"The crew out at the farm didn't," Jackson put in. "I tried to get something out of them, but they said they had no idea where Ares was."

"Someone knows," Nash swore as Dylan dragged the man toward them.

"Where do you want him?" Dylan asked.

"The café," Nash said, and they all followed Dylan into the café now unrecognizable with destruction. "Make sure no one can see in."

"I won't talk," the man said defiantly.

"You'll talk," Nash said, sounding completely

unconcerned. "Do you want to know why?"

The man looked to the group lining the shattered windows of the café and shook his head.

"You'll talk because I won't kill you," Nash said, picking up a plate with an uneaten slice of pie on it. He took his time picking up a fork and taking a bite. "See, death is easy. What I will do to you is not. It'll be slow, excruciating pain."

With a slight nod of his head, Bridget brought her sleek Belgian Malinois closer. The dog snarled and the man blanched. "How attached are you to your balls?" Nash asked as the dog barked.

The man kicked out in fear at the dog. Bridget pulled her back to avoid the contact, but the man's foot connected to her muzzle. A deep rumble from the gates of hell made Nash's hair stand on end. Hooch, in a rage of snarling jowls laced with drool, charged forward from his place, peeking through the bodies lining the front of the café.

"This is his girlfriend, Lucy," Bridget told him as they all watched in horror as loose skin rolled across his massive body, teeth gnashed in fierce determination, and chairs went flying as he lumbered like a locomotive at the man who had dared threatened the pretty Malinois.

"I can stop him if you tell me where Ares is keeping Sophie," Nash said, taking another bite of his pie as a chair went crashing.

"A barn!" the man yelled as Hooch lunged. Drool flew. The man screamed. The Malinois wagged her tail.

Nash grabbed for Hooch's collar but came up with a handful of loose skin instead. It was just enough to stop the dog from biting. "Which barn?" Nash asked calmly.

"A black one," the man answered quickly.

"They're all black around here. I'm losing my grip on him," Nash said casually, and a glop of drool fell onto the man's face. When the man looked up, all he could see were jowls and teeth.

"I don't know. It has some colorful design over the door that looks like an old blanket my grandma had. Please, he'll kill me," the man begged.

So quickly most people didn't even see it, Nash stabbed his fork into the man's leg. "I'll make you wish I'd let him kill you. Remember that. Where's the barn?"

"I don't know. I swear," the man cried.

"How far away is it from here?"

"Twenty minutes or so," the man answered.

"Near Lexington?" Nash asked.

The man shook his head. "No, we came from the other way."

"Have you heard of Ahmed?" Nash asked as he saw everyone trying to think of every farm within twenty minutes and one hundred eighty degrees from downtown.

The man's eyes widened and Nash had his answer. Ahmed stepped quietly forward. The look was one of pure menace. The man pissed himself, and Hooch wrinkled his nose in disgust as he moved to lick the Malinois on the face.

"He's my mentor," Nash stated. "He's old-school in his interrogation techniques. No coddling or calm conversation like we're having. He's going to take you now. If you don't want to experience what Ahmed is famous for, then I suggest you tell him everything and everyone who can help us locate Ares and Sophie."

Ahmed reached down and hauled the man up by his collar as if he weighed nothing. Dylan's lips twitched in amusement. "Let me help you with that," he offered as they headed out back.

The moment the back door closed, Annie released a breath. "Someone get a map," she ordered.

"I have my phone," Jackson offered.

"No, we need something we can spread out," Annie told him.

"The property office at the courthouse will have it," Marshall said, pulling out a key. "Um, I guess I'll have to give this back eventually. But it'll work now. I'll be right back."

"What are you thinking, Aunt Annie?" Jackson asked.

"We divide up the map and split up. We look for any barn, no matter how far off the beaten path, that is black with a wooden Amish quilt over the door."

The sound of sirens reached the door and Ryan pushed his head through the space where one of the front windows had been. "FBI prisoner transport is here. Do we have everyone?" Ryan looked around to try to find the man Nash had questioned.

"Yes," everyone answered at once.

Ryan raised an eyebrow but didn't press. "Hooch, not again. It's embarrassing." Ryan shook his head at his dog who was currently rolled over on his back showing off for Lucy.

Ryan turned to leave and Marshall hopped through where one of the large glass windows had been. "I've got it!"

The group crowded around as he spread a large aerial map onto a table. Cade picked up a pencil from Poppy's stash near the cash register and studied the map.

"I say we investigate everything that takes us ten to twenty minutes to get to. Ares, for all intents and purposes, is a tourist, and you know how slow they drive on these roads."

"There," Annie said, pointing to the map, "to there."

In minutes they had the map divided up and everyone had an assignment and a partner. Soon after, they were piling into cars that were still operable—everyone except Nash. He was still studying the map.

"What are you looking at, son?" John Wolfe asked as he shook his head at the sight of the café in shambles.

"Ares has Sophie in a barn with a wooden Amish quilt over it somewhere between ten and twenty minutes from here, away from Lexington. Annie and Cade divided the area up and people are searching, but I have to pick the right place. I can't risk not finding her."

"I have an idea," John said, but it wasn't just John. DeAndre stood with Aniyah next to them. She was still rocking her five-inch heels even through a siege. DeAndre and John stared at each other. At once, they both narrowed their eyes.

"I know where she is," they both said together, looking horribly confused.

"How?" John asked.

"You first," DeAndre replied.

Nash slammed his hand onto the table. "I don't care if you have the town bugged, you're telepathic, aliens speak to you, or what. Just tell me where Sophie is!"

"There," they both pointed to a place on the map.

"It's the old Haney place," John said, shooting a triumphant look to DeAndre.

DeAndre rolled his eyes. "It's been abandoned for over a year since the heirs live in Texas, and there are several large barns on the property. It has easy access if you travel over the property to this state highway."

"Thank you," Nash called as he ran out the door and straight for Sienna's sports car. Fear and hope battled within him as he slid into the low seat. He'd apologize to Sienna later for taking her car. Nash slammed on the gas, the engine roared as all five hundred seventy-five horses were unleashed.

"Hang on, Sophie, I'm coming."

Chapter Twenty-Six

Sophie's first thought was that she had a hangover. Had she been drinking at the Blossom Café all night? When she went to rub her throbbing temples, she realized her hands couldn't move. It was then several things became apparent concurrently. She wasn't at home, hers hands and legs were tied to a chair, she was cold, and there were people all around her.

Sophie heard them talking, she felt the cold draft against her face, and she sensed when someone came to stand directly in front of her.

"Hello, Miss Davies," the completely average voice laced with a slight Boston accent said. "I know you're awake. Open your eyes."

Sophie didn't want to. Although the voice was only mildly threatening, there was something in his voice that made her break out in chills. It might be that the voice was completely devoid of any emotion. She didn't have time to think of it further when the palm of a hand slammed into her cheek.

Pain bloomed, her cheek pulsated at the contact, and her eyes shot open as tears involuntarily filled the eye next to the slapped cheek. What Sophie saw wasn't what she expected. She saw a man in a mask with soldiers in black lined up behind him. She had always envisioned Ares as the devil himself, or at least a mighty warrior akin to the Greek god of his namesake, and the mask certainly conveyed that. However, that's not who stood before her.

The figure before her was an average man of average height and average shape. Physically, he looked like every man you passed on the street in Boston. Nothing about him stuck out except the warrior mask he wore in the image of the god Ares. He was five feet nine inches or so, around one hundred and eighty pounds with a slight beer belly. Beyond the mask, Sophie saw he had brown hair and a brown beard. Take off his mask, throw a knit sports hat on him, and probably the only thing that would make him stand out was his suit. It was expensive and shiny, just like Henry Rooney's suits. Everyone in Keeneston always did say those suits made Henry look like a mob boss. And essentially, that's what Ares was.

"You need to learn that when I give an order it's to be executed immediately or else you pay," Ares said in his completely boring voice. It was hard to take the threats seriously, but the throbbing of her cheek reminded her he was more than he appeared to be.

"Didn't anyone teach you to treat your guests with manners?" Sophie snarled back, suddenly thinking she sounded a little too much like her mother as she took a backhand to the other cheek.

"Anything else to say?" Ares asked as he glared impassively down at her.

Sophie took a deep breath and let it out, trying to maintain control. "I guess I should expect it from a Yankee."

This time it was a punch to the stomach. She saw it coming and exhaled fast, allowing her to keep her breath. But she could not diminish the pain of the punch. No matter what, she could take it. She would stay defiant until the end because Ares wouldn't expect that. If she was going to die, then she was going to die on her terms while giving Ares a big middle finger.

"Oh, you're so tough, hitting a tied-up girl," Sophie wheezed as she struggled to sit back up.

"Enough pleasantries," Ares told her as he motioned for a man to come forward.

The man tilted back her chair and spun it around. The seconds it took to turn her chair gave Sophie a chance to look around. She was in an old tobacco barn. It appeared abandoned since the wooden grids were missing. A breeze drifted through the wooden slats on the walls, which were spaced slightly apart to help with the drying of the tobacco leaves. The dirt floor was compact, but it was what she was now facing that scared her more than anything.

"It's beautiful, isn't it?" Ares asked. Sophie felt him stand behind her and place his thick hands on her shoulders, squeezing painfully as she stared in shock at the missile she'd developed. It now rested on a launcher.

"You made it small and portable. Genius. I really am quite in awe of your talents, Miss Davies," Ares said, placing one meaty hand around the back of her neck. His fingers stroked her pulse point, and he chuckled as he felt her pulse kick up in fear.

"You have the missile. You don't need me anymore. Let me go," Sophie demanded.

Ares's fingers squeezed and Sophie's vision was covered in spots as he stopped the flow in her carotid artery. "You think these things come with instruction manuals? You are my instruction manual. I don't want to destroy it. I want to replicate it."

Sophie shook her head. "I'll never tell you. You might as well kill me." Sophie felt it in the pit of her stomach. She had never been so certain of anything in her life. She was going to die.

Ares chuckled again and resumed his stroking of her neck as he bent his head down to her ear. Sophie felt the smoothness of his mask against the side of her face. "I heard your boyfriend is dead. Did you know that I knew him? Oh, he never knew it was me, but I befriended him while pretending to be an embassy worker and fed him information on Poseidon. It was easy for me to make him do my bidding without him even realizing it."

Ares laughed softly in her ear. "Your boyfriend thought he was playing hero. He thought he was rescuing those women and children. But really he took them from Poseidon and put them on my ship and straight into my employ."

Sophie felt sick. Nash's work had been nothing but a manipulation by Ares. "All of them?" Sophie whispered.

"No, Nash won one round. He'd found the official I was bribing in Rahmi, and he suddenly disappeared. Nash put the Rahmi people on boats under his direct control. The boats he put the previous workers on were made to see the light of delivering them to my people or else," Ares said with a smile under his mask.

"Where are they?" Sophie asked.

"All over the world. See, I'm a leader of my own country. My country just happens to span the world as little pockets inside of towns. And the only person who knows everything is me. I maintain absolute control, and you're about to find out how I utilize that control," Ares bragged.

Sophie had to keep him talking. She knew Nash was dead, but Jackson had seen her. There had been help on the way. She just needed to give them time to find her. Tears threatened as she realized nothing would stop her parents from coming for her. Sophie only hoped her parents brought an entire army with them or they might end up victims of Ares's deviousness.

"How do you keep track of everything if you don't trust anyone enough to help you run things?" Sophie asked.

"Talkative, aren't you?" Ares trailed his fingers

down the back of her neck and over to her shoulder as he kept his head near hers.

"I think you're lying. I don't think you have dens of iniquity all over the world. Sure, you may have one or two, but there's no way one person can keep track of all that you supposedly do," Sophie said with a huff of disbelief. "I mean, come on. Only you know the locations of your entire drug, human, and weapons trafficking rings. Only you know all the people you're extorting or bribing, and all the people your group has killed? Please. I call that delusions of grandeur."

He was in front of her in one second, his fingers digging into her cheeks as he yanked her head up to look at him. "You think it's all made up? Then how did I get this?"

Sophie felt her face torqued to the right to look at the missile. "I didn't say you don't have the men to do it. I'm just saying you don't have absolute control."

"Or I'm just that superior to you," Ares said, shoving his masked face in hers.

Sophie refused to be cowed. She knew it would hurt. She knew she'd bleed, but she laughed anyway.

This time it wasn't his palm that landed on her face—it was his fist. She saw stars and felt her nose break. Fighting against all instincts to cry out in pain, she sucked a breath through her mouth and looked at Ares. Drops of her blood were scarlet against the smooth ivory of the mask. She smiled, tasting the blood in her mouth, and laughed again.

"There's the big tough man hitting a tied-up woman. Now I know you're lying."

Ares was in her face again as she felt the warmth of her blood flowing over her chin and down her throat. "I'll tell you something since I appreciate your courage, however misguided it is. I control everything from my laptop. I'm meticulous in my record keeping as I am in getting what I want. Now, Miss Davies, our chat is over. Tell me how your missile works."

"Bless your heart," Sophie replied with a hard smile. She enjoyed the way Ares temporarily froze as if trying to figure out what she meant.

Ares took a deep breath and with a quick flick of his finger a minion quickly approached. "It's getting cold out and Miss Davies is overdressed."

The soldier nodded and pulled a blade. Sophie kept her eyes locked on Ares as the man cut her sweatshirt from her and then her pants. Her shoes and socks were next. Sophie fought her body's natural tendency to shiver when faced with cold as Ares eyed her. He stepped forward and pulled her gun from her corset followed by the rest of her weapons.

"You are an interesting lady, Miss Davies," Ares said as he examined her gun. "Very interesting."

Sophie shivered as she sat in her corset and underwear. The damp cold air was already penetrating her muscles. She curled her head down to shrink into herself as she tried to control her shivering. For a split second, her breath caught as she looked down at her breasts. Hidden between them were the two needles Abby had given her. Hope brought a rush of heat to her body. She just needed to get a hand free.

Ares looked at her gun and found it loaded. He stepped forward and pressed the gun to her head. "Let's play a game. I give you an order and you obey. If you don't answer, then I'll shoot you."

Sophie smirked up at him. "Okay. Let's play."

"Give me the programming guide for the missile."

"No."

Ares was still behind the mask. "Fine. I'll figure it out without you."

"No, you won't. You're not smart enough," she said loudly. Ares's minions sucked in their breaths.

"I told you I'd extract payment," Ares said softly as he moved the gun to her shoulder and pulled the trigger.

Nothing.

He pulled the trigger again.

Nothing.

Sophie smiled up at him. "My gun, my rules. If you can't even figure out how to use my gun, then you're never going to figure out my missile."

Ares threw her gun to the ground and flexed his hands into fists. He went to the old water pump and grabbed one of the pails hanging from the wall and ordered others to grab the remaining two. Sophie had to give him credit. He kept his temper. She shivered as she watched him fill the pail. It wasn't freezing out, but it was close. It was certainly cold enough to send her into hypothermia if kept in these cool damp conditions for any length of time. Growing up in the country, she knew that any temperature lower than her body temperature could throw her into hyperthermia, but it would take longer the warmer it was. The two factors to speed hyperthermia up were wind chill and wetness. And by the way Ares was carrying the bucket of water toward her, she knew her chances for hypothermia were about to dramatically increase.

The water hit her like a cement truck. It was so cold it stole her breath. The second she recovered from the shock, a second wave hit her. She was no longer just damp—she was soaked. Her body began to violently shake to keep her warm. There was no fighting it this time. Instead, she let it happen. When her shaking finally subsided some, a third bucket of cold water was dumped on her.

Ares knelt in front of her with his masked face tilted to one side and his fingers loosely clasped between his knees. "I know that I can enter biometric information into the missile, and it'll target that individual. Tell me how to enter that information," Ares requested calmly. There wasn't a hint of worry or anxiety in his voice. He was in full control of Sophie, and he knew it.

"G-g-g-g-go t-t-t-t-to hell," she stuttered through her shivers.

Ares cocked his head to the other side as she felt

his eyes taking her in. Her hair was straight and wet, hanging down her face and dripping down her back. Her skin was ice cold. Her corset was soaked and coldly clinging to her.

"Physical pain doesn't scare you, does it?" Ares asked, pulling out a knife and slicing her thigh.

The wound wasn't deep. It was more of a scrape than anything. Sophie watched as the blood welled up and then mixed with drops of water to run off her leg.

"No, I'm too cold to feel it. Thanks," Sophie smirked.

"You know, I take great pleasure in finding people's weaknesses and exploiting them. It's a fascinating study in psychology and human behavior. I've actually written a book on it. One I revise after each person I break," Ares said, running a thick finger down her cheek to grab her chin and forcing Sophie to look at him.

"Let me guess, it's on your laptop, and you won't let anyone read it because you're not brave enough to have anyone critique your work," Sophie challenged.

Ares smiled under his mask and then stood up. He walked to a bag leaning against the wall and opened it, revealing a laptop. He pulled it out and turned it on as he walked back to her.

"You're right. I've never let anyone read it before. Because I respect you, I'd love your opinion. Here, read this page and tell me what you think," Ares said, turning his laptop for her to see.

As water dripped from her hair over her eyes, Sophie read the work of a clearly sociopathic killer. He described psychological and physical torture of the likes of which Sophie had never heard before. She hid her shivers of fear in her shivers for warmth.

"So, what do you think?" Ares asked, closing the laptop and setting it on the ground next to her gun.

"I think you need a ghostwriter," Sophie said. The punch came so fast this time she didn't have time to exhale. She coughed and wheezed for air as her stomach revolted. Nausea and panic rolled over her as she closed her eyes and forced her brain and body to relax. She sucked in air. When her heart slowed and the panic receded, she looked into Ares's eyes under the mask. She had hit a nerve. He was worried about what others would think.

"I'm sorry, but obviously you never learned there was more to writing than using the word *I* five times in each sentence," Sophie rasped out, preparing for another hit.

"I've figured you out, Miss Davies. I can't hurt you. But I know what will." With another wave to another underling, the doors to the barn opened to reveal a second missile launcher bolted onto the back of a converted Hummer. "Isn't technology amazing? It used to be you had to have massive tanks to launch missiles. Of course, those are still viable. But when you want to take out a small area, say a couple blocks of a small town where everyone is gathering, you don't need much anymore. This one missile will do it for you now," Ares said with pleasure. "An area about the size of downtown Keeneston, for example. Poof. Gone with just one shot."

Sophie's heart was pounding so hard she was worried she'd have a heart attack. She knew better than to react, but it was hard not to. From what she read of Ares's book, she knew he took great pleasure in torturing victims through their loved ones. The part she read was about a man who had been pinned and forced to watch his whole family die very slowly through the old Chinese torture of cutting. It was known as death by a thousand cuts. It was slow, painful, and sick. The man had cracked after watching his wife be tortured to death. Even after the man gave up the information, Ares had still killed the man's children. No matter what, her town, her loved ones, were dead. Unless . . . unless she could get free and kill Ares herself.

"Stop!" Sophie cried out. "You win. You win," she said softly, letting the tears she had been holding back flow freely.

Ares smiled under the mask as he knelt once again in front of her, this time gently putting his hands on her thighs as he spoke to her. "Good. Good girl. I knew you were special. Now, will you tell me everything I need to know? Will you answer all my questions?"

"Yes," Sophie said, letting her voice break with emotion as she hung her head.

"Good. Now tell me about your missile," Ares

said as he patted her leg.

Sophie launched into an explanation that didn't involve many words less than four syllables. Some she even made up. When she felt Ares's hands tighten on her legs, she stopped talking and looked at him. "Would it help if I wrote it down? It's almost easier to explain with pictures."

Sophie held her breath as her body continued to shake as hypothermia began to take hold. Ares studied her, and Sophie purposely looked fearfully at the missile outside the barn. With a snap of his fingers, a soldier retrieved a notebook and pen from Ares's bag. Sophie kept her head down for fear Ares would see her look of triumph. Ares didn't know it yet, but Sophie's parents had taught her to never give up. And she wasn't about to start now.

Chapter Twenty-Seven

Nash didn't let up on the sports car's gas pedal as he headed out of Keeneston. He ignored the FBI agents who were busy loading up prisoners. He ignored the groups of his friends and Sophie's family as they drove out in different directions to search for her. His entire focus was on getting to the deserted farm as quickly as possible. Sophie's fate rested in the uncanny connection John and DeAndre had of knowing all things going on around them. Nash didn't have time to wonder how they knew the things they did. Any intelligence that came from John was worth its weight in gold, and it appeared that applied to DeAndre as well.

The rolling hills were nothing more than shadows in the dark night as he flew by them. Cows and horses were nothing but blurs at his speed. Soon houses gave way to farms that gave way to wide open pastures and woods. For once in his life, Nash didn't think about his plan of attack. Normally he planned every move he made, but this time it was all instinct. All he thought about was getting to Sophie. He would be outmanned and outgunned, but he didn't care. He was going to rescue Sophie or die trying.

Sophie held her breath as a faceless subordinate came forward with the pen and paper. She kept up a steady talk of overly complicated explanations of quantum physics, causing Ares's eyes to glaze.

"Shut up," Ares groaned as he placed his knife at the ropes on her wrists and sawed through them.

Blood rushed back into Sophie's hands as they burned and prickled with renewed sensation. Sophie opened and closed her hands, bringing strength back to them. The other man handed her the pen and paper. Ares watched her hesitantly, waiting for her to make a move. As tempting as it was to stab him with the pen, Sophie was biding her time.

Talking fast and drawing unrecognizable parts of what could be a missile as if she were five years old and making one up, Sophie worked continually. She smiled on the inside as Ares and his minions looked on with thorough confusion.

"Wait, what's that?" Ares asked, pointing to something that could be a control panel or an abstract painting by Picasso.

"The panel I was telling you about," Sophie said patronizingly.

"And where is that panel again?" Ares asked, trying to play it off as if he understood but just forgot.

Sophie made a move to stand up but fell back

down into the chair. "Um," she said, not complaining of her ankles being tied to the chair. "You remove that panel there, and then under the wires there's an interior panel. But make sure you get the right one or you could cause the missile to self-destruct."

"On the left or —" Ares started.

"Right," Sophie nodded and almost laughed as she imagined Ares's brow knit in confusion under his mask.

"Wait, the left is right or the right is right?"

Sophie let out a breath. "Would you pay attention? You have to get this right or we're all dead," she warned.

Ares looked at the missile. "There's a self-destruct?"

"Five of them," Sophie smiled. "I didn't want anyone getting the technology if they happened to steal a missile."

"Five?" Ares asked, concern evident in his voice.

"If you don't follow all of my instructions to the letter then . . . well, then we'll go out together," Sophie said seriously. She kept her eyes locked with Ares's and held his gaze until he broke it to look at the missile. His men were standing by with computers, wires, and tools to take control of the missile. But they all looked decidedly less confident than they had when she first woke up.

Ares pulled his knife and sawed the ropes from her ankles. Sophie groaned in a mixture of relief and pain. She couldn't help it as it felt as if she were walking across hot knives. Ares gestured with his chin, and she was instantly dragged out of the chair and onto her feet. Her knees buckled, and she let out a hiss of pain as her full weight came down on her feet. The man put his arm around her as she took her time hobbling to the missile, surrounded by bright workshop lights. She went slowly, allowing feeling to return to her feet. She would need them soon.

"Can I have that?" Sophie asked a minion with an electric screwdriver. The minion was about to hand it over to her when Ares smacked him.

"No tools. You can tell him what to do," Ares told them.

Sophie nodded in understanding. Ares thought she'd use anything she could as a weapon, what he didn't realize was the weapon was just a breath away.

"Here, hold this," Sophie ordered as she shoved the pen and paper into the man's hands that had helped her over to the missile. Ares looked at the pen and back to her. She saw him visibly relax and begin to radiate smug power. He thought he hand broken her. Well, he was in for a surprise.

Sophie started talking the man with the electric screwdriver into removing the panel. She kept her back turned to Ares as she worked with the man to open up her missile.

Nash cut his lights as soon as he saw the small dirt road that seemingly led to nowhere. He drove past the drive and parked in front of an old molding roll of hay. He left the car running in case he and Sophie actually got away. The field was overgrown and the dirt road headed straight back to a stretch of trees running parallel to the road. According to where DeAndre and John pointed on the map, the barn would be through the trees. It wasn't a dense line of trees, but it was enough to hide the barn from the road.

Moving through the overgrown field in a crouched position, Nash took his time making his way through the field, avoiding any potential detection by sentries. The closer he got to the trees, the more he was able to see through them. He couldn't make out the barn in the rainy night, but he could see slivers of light coming through the boards of the barn. This was it. DeAndre and John had been right. He had found Sophie.

Sophie watched as the man slowly removed the control panel. It took some work. The panel was hard to open for a reason. Sophie tried not to smile as every second it took was a second longer she had to develop a plan.

"Okay, you take it from here," Ares ordered as the man stepped back, allowing Sophie to pry the cover off.

The mass of wires underneath did exactly what she hoped they'd do. They made everyone very glad they weren't the one trying to program the missile.

"Tell me what everything is and how to connect it to our computer," Ares ordered as he stepped next to Sophie and looked at the guts of the missile.

"Each missile is set up to only respond to one computer through a secure network. Each missile has its own portable Wi-Fi that communicates with its master computer, which is programmed before the shell of the missile is put on," Sophie explained.

"I have to hook up your computer directly to the missile's software to reprogram it. It'll take a while since you don't have the software, and I'll basically have to re-create it," Sophie said as she carefully moved wires around. "That's the second panel and the one that's near the self-destruct."

Ares bent forward on her right side to watch her. Everyone around her sucked in air and nervously held it. Sophie let out a shaky breath. "Here we go," Sophie whispered as she hid her hand under the cover of the missile's outer shell and pulled a set of wires to disable the missile.

"I found the panel," Sophie said with relief and saw Ares relax. She moved to replace her right hand with her left. "I just have to —" The second Ares turned to see what she was doing was when Sophie made her move.

As Sophie had worked inside the missile, she'd slowly moved to get her right hand between her breasts. The whole time she felt the needles there but she didn't want to make a move to grab them and lose her element of surprise so she had waited, drawing everyone into a sense of trust.

In one move, she grabbed the first needle she could, ripped the cap off with her teeth, and stabbed it into Ares's chest before he turned to see what she was doing. The soldiers made their move to grab her and Sophie leapt back. The minions froze as Ares blinked and collapsed to the ground. His eye blinked, but he didn't move. He was trapped in his body.

"I should mention that I set the self-destruct button. The missile will blow in two minutes," Sophie warned, causing the men in black to pause. She sold the bluff well. It gave her time to make a mad dash across the hard-packed dirt floor to get her gun.

Sophie versus twenty bad guys fully armed. She might get a couple of shots off but at least she disabled the weapon. Her hand closed around the gun as she voice-activated it and began to fire. Unfortunately, the only place to hide in the barn was behind the missile, and she wasn't about to have bullets hitting it. It probably wouldn't go off, right? Her eyes narrowed on the open door with the missile launcher bolted to the Hummer. There was her escape, if only she had cover to make it there.

Nash closed in on the barn. He saw a black Hummer sitting outside the barn doors with the light from within highlighting the small missile launcher that had been bolted to the back where seats normally would have been. Nash narrowed his eyes and recognized the missile that sat loaded and pointing back toward Keeneston. It was military grade, but not Sophie's.

Suddenly shouting arose from inside the barn. The men guarding the missile on the Hummer reached for their guns and ran toward the barn. Sophie!

Nash sprinted to the front of the barn and went down on one knee. Inside, gunfire erupted, and from the shadows of the doorway, Nash saw Sophie glance at the Hummer as she fired off shots. Nash aimed and scanned the situation. Some men were running out the back of the barn closest to the missile that had to be Sophie's. Wires were exposed and a man in a mask lay still on the ground, a needle sticking from his chest. Ares.

"Turn it off!" a man yelled as he pointed a gun at Sophie who was moving backward, all while trying to keep her gun raised.

Off? That meant that the missile was armed! Nash aimed his gun and fired. The man closest to Sophie dropped. Sophie looked back in surprise, but still didn't see him as others now opened fire in Nash's direction. Sure, shoot toward the missile, great idea.

Nash fired three times in rapid succession and three more men dropped. Sophie didn't wait for an invitation. She hauled herself up and ran.

Sophie's feet hurt, and she was pretty sure she'd forgotten to breathe for minutes, but she kept her eye on that Hummer and prayed Jackson could get her out. From the shadows, she saw more men in black move toward the barn. Panic filled her as a

mountain of a man raised the meanest rifle she'd
seen and fired straight at her.

Sophie dropped to the ground and covered her
head with her hands. A second later, she opened her
eyes and breathed for the first time. She was alive,
but the gunfire had intensified. She was trapped in
the middle.

More gunfire sounded from behind. Sophie
twisted her head to look over her shoulder and let
out a cry of relief. Dylan strode forward with Abby
and Ahmed flanking him as they took out man after
man.

Sophie wanted to scream, but she didn't want to
distract them. When she turned to see if Dylan's
group had stopped the advance, a body in jeans and
a black jacket leapt on top of her. Sophie screamed
as the body landed heavily on her and then groaned
as she felt a bullet slam into him. The large figure
was closing in on them as the man covering her took
another bullet to his back. Sophie felt the vibration
of the impact reverberating through his body. Oh
god, she hoped Jackson was wearing a bulletproof
vest. Panic clawed at her. She had to know he was
still alive.

"Jackson!" Sophie yelled. "Answer me!"

He groaned and Sophie sighed with relief. He
was alive. There was one final gunshot and then
quiet. Nothing. The loud constant sound of shots
being fired still echoed in her ears. But it wasn't
over. Fear gripped her as the large man materialized
before her. Sophie struggled to reach for her gun

trapped under her stomach.

"Sophie!"

"Jackson?" Sophie said with confusion as she turned her head away from the man to see her cousin appear next to him.

"Shit, Nash," Jackson cursed, ignoring her.

As Abby, Dylan, and Ahmed came into view in front of her, the tears finally flowed. "I know, he's dead," Sophie broke down. "I saw him get shot. He saved me," Sophie sobbed, finally allowing herself to mourn.

"You can't get rid of me that easily," the pained voice from the body lying over her said.

"Nash? Oh my god! Someone help him!" Sophie screamed wildly. The huge man along with Jackson bent down to help him up. They each took a side and let Nash lean against them.

Dylan reached down and helped Sophie up to her feet. Nash looked as if he had trouble breathing and blood was spreading through one jean-clad leg. "I thought you were dead!" Sophie launched herself at him. Jackson and the large man holding Nash's other side braced for impact.

Nash let out a groan but lowered his head to rest in the crook of her neck as she sobbed. Tears of relief, tears of love, tears of the sheer exhaustion of what they'd been through ran down Nash's coat.

"We have to get you to a doctor," Sophie finally sniffed as she pulled back.

"It's just a leg wound. Are you hurt? Oh damn, Sophie. I'm sorry I didn't get here sooner. Look at your face," Nash said as he stumbled out of Jackson's hold and gently touched her swollen face.

"You came. It was you who got here first, wasn't it?" Sophie asked, sniffling.

"I told you. You're worth fighting for."

"Okay, tough guy. Let's get you patched up," Dylan said. "Bainbridge, hold him up for me."

Sophie held her breath as Nash turned. Her eyes went as wide as they were able. There were no bullet holes in his back. "You were shot more than once," she stammered.

"Piper," they all said together.

"She developed this bulletproof jacket using nanotechnology," Nash hissed as Dylan tied off Nash's leg right above the bullet hole.

"He probably has some broken ribs," Ahmed told her in his typical matter-of-fact way. Abby rolled her eyes.

"Dad. A little compassion, please," Abby said, shaking her head before lashing out with an axe kick and sending the minion next to her back into unconsciousness.

"Sorry, but I'm pissed. I thought it would be a better fight. I'm highly disappointed after hearing so much about Ares. His men were running like scared babies," Ahmed huffed.

Sophie smiled, but immediately stopped when her face instantly began to throb. "I told them the missile was about to self-destruct."

"Is it?" Gabe asked, strolling in with the haughtiness of the prince he truly was. It was hard for Sophie, or any of the people from Keeneston, she supposed, to think of Gabe as a prince. But every now and then, he would surprise them. He seemed completely in charge even with strong men like Nash, Ahmed, Dylan, and Jackson standing there. Gabe stopped and looked down at Ares lying motionless on the floor.

"No. I disabled it," Sophie told them. "However, the missile out there is targeting Keeneston."

"Can you disarm it?" Gabe asked.

"Yes. With some help."

"I gotcha," the man she heard called Bainbridge said with an accent that seemed to be Australian.

"Me too," the man standing to Bainbridge's right said with an unidentifiable, general-type accent. "Besides, I have a feeling we shouldn't see what's going to happen next."

"Who are you?" Sophie asked, too tired to politely handle the introductions.

Jackson cleared his throat. "Sorry, cuz. These are my two friends, Agent Lucas Sharpe," Jackson said, indicating the tall, lean man on the far side of the human mountain. "And Agent Talon Bainbridge."

"Right this way, ma'am," Agent Sharpe said politely, holding out his bare arm for her to hold.

"Aren't you cold?" Sophie asked, placing her hand onto his arm and not liking the way she had to use it for support.

"Cold? This is a heat wave back from where I'm from," Sharpe laughed.

"Soph," Nash called, preventing them from

leaving. He struggled to take off his coat, and as he lifted it over his head, Sophie sucked in her breath. His body was solid black and blue. "Speaking of cold," he said, handing her his jacket.

"I told you it was a great corset," Abby smiled as Sophie looked down and realized she was half naked.

"How many guns does that hold?" Ahmed asked as he finally got a good look.

"Easily three, but up to six," Abby told him as if they were checking out the newest in tactical gear.

Sophie hurried to slip on Nash's jacket as Gabe handed over her shoes. "Thank you."

"You're welcome. I'm glad you're both safe." Gabe bent and placed a gentle kiss on her swollen cheek. "I expect to be a godfather," he said.

"Sophie, wait," Ahmed called out. "One more thing."

"What?" Sophie asked, standing up after putting on her shoes.

Ahmed reached for her, and she thought he was going to kiss her cheek as well, but he put his thumbs on her nose and before she could react, there was a *crunch*.

Sophie swore colorfully, causing eyebrows to raise and Abby to give her a high-five. However, she quickly discovered she could breathe again. "You could have warned me."

Ahmed's lips twitched in amusement. "But then you would have flinched."

"Well, thank you. Now, I can breathe while I

disarm a missile."

Bainbridge and Sharpe escorted her to the modified Hummer. Behind her, Jackson and Dylan set a couple portable lights outside and slid the doors to the barn closed. As she approached the missile, she saw that it had indeed already been armed. No matter what she had given Ares, he would have destroyed her town.

Chapter Twenty-Eight

N ash stared down at Ares. The group huddled around the criminal mastermind were realizing there was so much more at stake than just killing him and getting it over with. Nash really did want to kill him. But there was no way he could do it when Ares was defenseless.

"What's wrong with him?" Jackson asked.

"See that needle," Abby said, pointing to the needle plunged in Ares's chest. "It'll paralyze him for a couple hours. It's the drug that basically traps him in his body. He's fully conscious. He just can't move."

Nash bent down and looked Ares in the face. "I bet you didn't envision this as your downfall. Your men who attacked the town were defeated by broom-wielding grannies. A scientist took you out. And now your men have either been captured or killed. You went after the wrong town and the wrong woman."

The barn door opened, but Nash didn't look back as Sharpe ran in shielding his eyes from where Ares was lying. "I'm not looking. Carry on. Can't

report what I don't see. Sophie said Ares kept
everything on his laptop, just getting it to keep it
safe while she tries to disarm the missile
programmed to hit Keeneston."

"Dylan," Nash said, looking up at the hard face
across from him. "Evacuate the town."

Dylan gave one curt nod of his head and pulled
out his phone. He sent a text on the town loop and
then dialed all the numbers he could to warn them
to evacuate downtown.

"Nash, the FBI will want jurisdiction. They'll
want an investigation into the gunfight, and they'll
want you to hand over Ares," Jackson said softly.

"Only if they can find him," Gabe said harshly.
He pulled out his phone and waited a brief second
for the person to pick up. "Nabi, I need to make a
man disappear." Gabe looked down at Ares. "Yeah,
they got him."

Gabe watched Sharpe leave the barn before
speaking. "Rahmi will handle it."

"Damn right we will," Mo said, striding into the
barn from the opposite door Sharpe had exited.

Nash looked from Gabe to Mo, who was
followed by Zain, and shook his head. Like father,
like sons. You'd never know they were royalty until
they wanted you to. And then it was a sight you'd
never forget.

"Dad," Gabe said before looking at his brother.
In some strange twin-speak, they said all they
needed to without opening their mouths.

"What's your plan?" Mo asked as he used the

toe of his Italian loafer to nudge Ares.

"I know Uncle Dirar wants Ares. I'm happy to have Nash deliver him after we've had a go at him."

Mo gave a regal nod of approval. "Who is he?"

The group stared down at the man blinking behind the mask. Nash bent down and placed his hand under the chin of the smooth ivory mask shaped to look like the Greek god Ares. Would the devil be behind it?

When Nash pulled the mask off, it wasn't the devil he found, but someone he'd worked with. "You? You're Ares?" Nash growled. He'd been played a fool, and he wasn't about to pretend it wasn't a big deal.

The man rapidly blinked in all his plainness. Nash remembered him. He went by the name Poe and always talked with a heavy Boston accent. He had talked sports with Nash all the while weaving a story of being stationed at the American embassy in Taiwan. When Nash investigated him, he found that Jonathan Poe worked for the embassy, just as he claimed to. And all at once, Nash realized the extent of the manipulation. The information Nash had acted on that Poe had given him was actually straight from Ares.

"You took the people I rescued, didn't you?" Nash growled as he fisted the man's shirt and lifted him limply.

Ares blinked rapidly again, and Nash saw the flash of victory there. "Don't think you've won. I found them once, and I'll find them again. You know what happens when you die, right? Your organization goes with you. Just like Red Shadow died with Poseidon. But don't worry. We'll make sure we ruin you, your organization, and your legacy before you're quietly killed and your body tossed out to sea."

Sirens sounded in the distance. Nash pursed his lips in agitation. He wouldn't get anything out of Ares in this state. One thing he did have to do was get Ares into the diplomatic protection of the royal family.

"Abby, can you and Dylan accompany Mo and Gabe to the farm? We need to get Ares there quickly."

"My pleasure," Abby smiled as Dylan reached over and slung Ares over his shoulder.

"Ahmed, it might be good for you to go, too. I don't want any connection to Rahmi when the police ask about Ares's whereabouts," Nash said as he shook his mentor's hand.

"You did well, Nash. I couldn't be more proud of you," Ahmed whispered as he pulled Nash in for a thump on the back. Nash bit back his groan for it wasn't every day his hero complimented him.

Nash watched as his princes and his friends walked from the barn with Ares dangling down Dylan's back. Nash wasn't done with Ares. Until Nash was able to talk to Ares, he felt the man would keep haunting him. The feelings would probably last until he was dead and gone from their lives.

"Sophie," Nash said out loud as he thought of

her life having been so entwined with his these past days. What would their future hold now the threat to her was gone?

Sophie cursed and Bainbridge chuckled. "Damn, I don't even know some of those words," he said as he casually handed her the tools she asked for.

"Ares programmed the guidance system via the GPS location of the Blossom Café. If he thinks he'll get the last word when this missile fires, he's dreaming," Sophie told them as she worked to open the nose of the missile to get to the guidance system to disable it.

"How do you know all this?" Sharpe asked curiously.

"I'm a weapons developer. At least I was. I think I'll send in my resignation when I get home," Sophie said while slowly sliding the shell of the nose from the missile, exposing the guidance system. Most missiles were set up with a guidance system, a warhead, a fuel section, and the propulsion section. Where they fell on the missile depended on the type of missile. Sophie could take out either the guidance or the propulsion sections, but with Keeneston being the target, she wanted to take them both out.

Sophie shook with cold and took a step back. She had to warm up before she could go on. She looked over at Lucas Sharpe and shook her head. He was in a short-sleeved T-shirt under his bulletproof vest and didn't even look cold.

"What?" Lucas asked.

"I have to warm up or my hands won't be steady to work. I still can't believe you're not cold."

"Here, take my jacket," Bainbridge said, slipping it off and handing it up to her. The second layer brought immediate relief. Now it was just her legs that were freezing.

"Want my pants?" Sharpe asked. Sophie couldn't tell if he was serious or not, so she stared at him, trying to figure it out when Sharpe suddenly yanked down his pants.

"What are you doing?" Sophie exclaimed as she got an eyeful of dark blue boxers covered with polar bears.

"We need to warm you up. Your pants are shredded, so take mine. We don't want you shaking and accidentally setting off the missile, now, do we?" Sharpe told her as he bounced on one leg trying to pull his pants over his boots.

"Who are you?" Sophie asked wide-eyed.

"Don't mind him," Bainbridge told her, apparently used to his younger partner's antics. "He's from northern Alaska and thinks it's summer anytime the temperature is above freezing."

A second later, Sharpe handed her his pants. Well, the man had stripped for her. She couldn't just decline the pants. Sophie held onto the launcher as she stepped into the pants. They were so long she could have worn them like a dress, but that didn't matter when they provided so much warmth.

"Do I hear sirens?" Sophie asked as she examined the guidance system.

"You'll have company soon. And if I know my teammates, they're going to want to take over disabling that," Bainbridge warned her.

Sophie rolled her eyes. She was used to dealing with men like that, and she didn't have time to give them a lecture on feminism.

"I'll slow them down," Sharpe said happily as he strutted off down the dirt road in his FBI vest, polar bear boxers, and combat boots.

"Come up here, Talon," Sophie ordered as she worked carefully to disable the system. "Hold this," she said, handing him a small flashlight. She looked at the power distribution unit, the guidance computer, and the set control before deciding the best approach to disarm the system.

Sophie saw the flash of lights from the FBI and God knows how many other government agencies. But they weren't alone. It seemed as though someone had spread the word on the town text where they were. A solid line of headlights followed behind the government vehicles.

"How are you doing, Soph?" Nash asked quietly so as to not startle her.

Sophie didn't answer as she took a deep breath and went for it. For all her training, she had to admit even she closed her eyes for a second. But there was no explosion and Bainbridge and Nash were still looking at her. She let out her breath. "Good. The guidance system is disabled. I'll just finish taking apart the engine to reduce the chance of explosion, and I'll be all done."

"Um, why is Sharpe standing in the middle of the road wearing his boxers?" Jackson asked.

"I was cold and he didn't want my shaking hands to blow us all up," Sophie responded, moving quicker now that the bomb was no longer a threat to Keeneston.

"Okay," Nash said slowly. "First, can you do us all a favor?"

"As if saving the entire town isn't a big enough favor?" Sophie asked as she grabbed a tool from Bainbridge.

"Good point," Nash conceded. "But we need you to tell the government that you never saw Ares. It was only his soldiers who captured you."

"And why would I do that?" Sophie asked as she removed an engine component controlled propulsion and handed it to Nash.

"Because Rahmi has requested the right to deal with Ares. If the FBI knows he's here, they'll take him. I'll question him further to try to find his entire operation and then he'll be transported to King Dirar for trial."

"Trial?" Sophie snorted, handing down more pieces of the missile.

"Yes, a real trial. It just won't be televised and covered by the media 24/7 like it would be here."

"Fine," Sophie agreed as the first car pulled to a stop. "The things I do for the man I love."

Nash smiled at her, and Sophie almost fell off the launcher. Nash hadn't said his feelings yet, but the look on his face was full of love. He raised his arms and his hands enclosed her waist before lifting her down. She saw the pain etched on his face, but he didn't complain when he pulled her against his bruised and battered body to kiss her.

"Sophie!"

Sophie turned to see her parents running toward her. Good thing she had clothes on now. The fact that they weren't her clothes and the fact that Nash stood shirtless and Lucas strutted around without pants was not lost on her parents. Neither was the fact that she had just been lip-locked to the shirtless man.

Within seconds, the government agents who had been moving to surround her had been shoved aside as her friends, family, and townspeople rushed to the group now standing outside the barn. Jackson had closed the doors to the barn, and he was guarding the entrance.

Sophie and Nash were hugged and pulled in every direction, but Nash never let go of her hand. At some point, someone tossed a jacket to Nash as she told her friends and family what had happened, leaving out Ares, as a group of particular dour-looking government agents tried to push past the group surrounding her.

"Oh, I need a phone!" Sophie said suddenly. She needed to get in touch with her boss to tell him the missile had been located.

"Miss Davies!" the head agent yelled over the crowd. The Rose sisters were currently cutting him off as they stood shoulder to shoulder with their husbands.

"Yes?" as all the unmarried Davies women turned to the man, causing his thick brow to furrow.

Her mother shoved a cell phone into her hand and Sophie quickly called her boss.

"Don't let anyone see that missile!" Sam yelled into the phone so loudly that everyone around Sophie heard it.

"Missile?" Piper asked. "I want to see it."

The dour-faced agent finally pushed past the crowd and bore down on Sophie. Nash and her father were suddenly in front of her and Sophie saw some of the agents trying to get past Jackson, Bainbridge, and Sharpe, who were guarding the doors to the barn.

"I need blankets, tarps, or anything to cover something large—now!" Sophie yelled into the crowd. People hurried off in different directions. Some into the fields where gray tarps covered the old rolls of moldy hay. Others rushed to their cars and produced blankets, tablecloths, and anything else they could find.

"That missile needs to be guarded by someone with top security clearance, way above some Homeland people," Sam told her.

"How did you know they were Homeland Security?"

"Because they think they should know everything. I'm afraid you'll have to stay with the missile until I get there. I'm heading to the airport now."

"Not a problem, there're plenty of people with that clearance level here." Sophie grinned as she looked at her father, Uncle Miles, and Uncle Marshall. "Your security clearances are still good, right?"

The three men nodded. No one seemed surprised by this. It was accepted that they had been and were probably still somewhat involved in the government. Sophie would ask John later what they did to keep that clearance level.

"Where are you from again?" Sam asked as she heard the plane engines roar to life.

"Keeneston, Kentucky," she smiled as she hung up. It wouldn't take more than an hour and a half for Sam to get to Keeneston.

"Miss Davies," the man said, pushing past her mom, who slammed her heel into his foot.

"Oops," her mom said, not even trying to pretend she was sorry.

The agent stared daggers at her mom, who just smiled in return.

"I'm Agent Rand of Homeland Security. We have reports of Ares being here and something about a stolen missile. I need you to come into the barn to answer some questions," he demanded.

"I'm sorry, but Miss Davies isn't answering any questions alone," Addison Rooney called out as she pushed forward with her father and mother, Henry and Neeley Grace, right behind her.

"And who are you?" Agent Rand demanded.

"We're her legal counsel," the Rooney family

said together.

"I'll have a judge—"

"Did someone say judge?" Kenna Ashton smiled. "I'm right here, and I believe I would rule that Miss Davies has a right to counsel. Would you like to file an appropriate motion? If so, the court opens on Monday at eight in the morning."

The man's face turned a deep red as he spun back to Sophie. "Where is Ares?"

Sophie shrugged. "I wouldn't know him if I saw him. Doesn't he always wear a mask?"

"Then what are you hiding in the barn?" Rand demanded.

"You can go into the barn to see the bodies of Ares's soldiers that Rahmi Special Agent Nash Dagher, FBI Agents Parker, Bainbridge, and Sharpe rescued me from." Agent Rand motioned for his men to move in. "*After* I cover up something that you don't have clearance to see."

The agent sputtered. Her father, Miles, and Marshall stepped forward to stand shoulder to shoulder behind her. To her, they'd just been pains in the ass as she and her cousins grew up. They had tapped their daughters' phones, followed them on dates, ran backgrounds on any boy who looked at them, and had generally driven Sophie and her cousins crazy. However, there had never been a moment when they didn't have her back. They were at every graduation, every sporting event, and she'd been consoled by them after boyfriends had run off in fear when her father answered the door armed.

And right now, she knew that not only her father and uncles had her back, the entire town did.

"What do you want us to do?" her dad asked, his eyes never leaving Agent Rand's.

"Collect all the blankets and tarps and cover the classified object. You'll know it when you see it," Sophie told them, giving them a grateful smile.

"You can't tell me these men have higher clearance levels than I do. I'm Homeland Security!" Agent Rand complained.

Miles smiled. And like Dylan, when Miles smiled, it was one of two smiles—the smile that made women giggle and blush, or the smile that turned a grown man to tears. This one was the tears type of smile. It was slow, confident, and intimidating.

Agent Rand sputtered and took a step back. Her father and uncles turned to start collecting items to cover her missile and quickly disappeared into the barn. Five minutes later, they came out talking animatedly in hushed whispers. Family dinner at Grandma and Grandpa Davies's house should be fun. She had a feeling they'd drag her away to ask a thousand questions about her missile. They liked anything that went *boom*.

Nash didn't leave Sophie's side. He felt her growing weary as Agent Rand kept her standing in the barn, telling her abduction story over and over again. Addison hadn't backed down the entire time and was now tapping her foot impatiently.

"That's enough, Agent Rand. My client has been more than accommodating after a terrifying ordeal. She needs medical treatment and rest. If you have any further questions, you can contact me and I'll set it up," Addison said, handing him her first business card as a newly sworn-in lawyer.

"But I'm not done. I have more questions about—"

Addison held up her hand. "We're done. You're done. You've asked the exact same questions three times in three different ways. If you're not smart enough to figure out the answers by now, that's not my client's fault."

Addison gave Nash a small nod of her head, and Nash turned Sophie to the door. Addison was still arguing with Agent Rand.

"I guess this means I don't get to drive the Hummer through downtown. I thought that would be badass," Sophie mumbled under a yawn.

"You don't need to do anything to be badass. You already are," Nash said, kissing the top of her head. "Come on, let me take you home."

The town had started to disperse. Paige and Cole set up rooms for their son's FBI team to stay at while Bridget was happily ushering Abby back to their home.

"Don't tell Homeland," Sophie whispered. "But I hid Ares's computer. He kept track of his entire operation on it. We'll need Kale to hack it. Do you think he'd come in this weekend for a chance to take down an international gang?"

"I think he'll be here by morning. I think everyone will be here by morning," Nash said, pulling an exhausted Sophie against his side before sending a text to Kale. He should tell Bridget and Ahmed their other child would be home soon, but he decided to let it be a surprise. This weekend, Keeneston would all be together again and he couldn't wait. He was finally home.

Chapter Twenty-Nine

N ash and Sophie arrived at Sophie's house in Sienna's sports car as the sun was beginning to rise. They took one look at the broken door and smashed windows and turned the car around.

Sophie was asleep by the time Nash pulled into the bed and breakfast. He'd had to take the long way around town and through farms to get to it since downtown was still blocked off. He was sure by lunch the entire town would be gathering to begin cleanup.

Nash turned off the car and tried to wake Sophie, who only mumbled something about taking the day off and didn't need to get up. Nash smiled as he looked down at her in pants a good foot too long and two oversized jackets, one bulletproof and one with FBI on the back. Her hair was tangled and had fallen across her bruised face. Her nose was swollen and a path of dried blood ran down her throat. Nash had never been so in love.

He reached down and pulled her out of the car just as another vehicle came into the small parking lot to the side of the house. Nash looked up as Lucas

Sharpe, still in his polar bear boxers, and Talon Bainbridge got out.

"Out of rooms at Jackson's parents' house," Bainbridge said softly as Sharpe hurried up the front steps of the B&B to open the door for Nash.

"Oh goodness," Zinnia exclaimed from inside.

"What is it?" Poppy's voice asked from inside the house.

"We appear to have guests," Zinnia answered as she hurried to open the door wider in nothing but an oversized T-shirt. "Oh, it's you!"

"Hi, ma'am," Bainbridge said respectfully.

"And you!" Poppy said as she reached for a blanket in the living room to wrap around her short pajamas.

"Nice to see you again, ma'am. I see we both like polar bears." Sharpe smiled at Poppy's pajamas with a smiling polar bear on the shirt. Unlike Poppy, Sharpe didn't seem embarrassed about standing there in a T-shirt and boxers.

"Is my room still available?" Nash asked as he held Sophie in his arms. "I'm afraid her house was damaged as well last night."

"Of course! Go right on up," Zinnia said, hurrying toward her office. "And do you guys each need a room?"

"Yes, ma'am," they answered together as Zinnia disappeared inside the office only to return a second later with three keys.

Nash was already halfway up the stairs when Zinnia caught up to him with the two FBI agents trailing. Zinnia opened the door for him and Sophie snored in response.

"I'm so glad you two are safe," Zinnia whispered. "And back home where you belong."

"Thank you. I'll be down at the café to help clean up when we wake. It's we who owe you and the rest of the town for defending us."

"I've never seen anything like it before," Bainbridge whispered. "You should have seen this woman swing a skillet."

"And her sister with that sauté pan! I thought my small town was interesting. This place is so cool." Sharpe smiled as a blushing Zinnia handed them each their keys and pointed them to their rooms.

They were still talking when Nash closed the door with his foot and gently set Sophie onto the bed. He turned up the heat in the room and began to undress her. Sophie mumbled something unintelligible in her sleep as he worked. He found the spot where she'd been tranquilized and frowned. It wasn't infected, but it was red from the impact of the needle.

Nash fetched a towel and a washcloth. He filled the ice bucket with hot water and gently began to clean the blood from Sophie's face. Her eyes fluttered open and slowly focused on his face.

"What? Where?" Sophie asked, blinking in confusion.

"Just cleaning you up for bed." Nash smiled gently. The pain it caused his heart to see her blood made him eager to get back to Ares. The need for retribution pulsed through him. "And we're at the B&B."

"Oh," Sophie said, her eyes fluttering to stay awake.

"Go to sleep, sweetheart," Nash quietly said as he wrung out the washcloth and continued to clean her face and neck.

"Mmm," Sophie agreed as her eyes drifted shut. "I love you, Nash," she whispered.

Nash barely heard her. He smiled at her lying in bed with the covers around her bare body. Her face was now clean but still showed signs of the traumatic night. It wasn't what he had planned but when he thought he'd lost her, he vowed to never hold back. "I love you, too."

Sophie responded with a soft snore.

Nash emptied the water from the ice bucket and rinsed off the washcloth. He was about to undress the rest of the way when his phone vibrated. It was a text message from Nabi. Ares was awake.

Veronica stood waiting for him at the front of the Mo and Dani's mansion. Their house served as their home but also as diplomatic offices for the royal family. He was sure Veronica, like the rest of the town, hadn't slept. But she showed no evidence of it with her hair in a perfect French twist and her suit without a single wrinkle in it.

"Good morning," she said cheerfully. "I have

clothes for you to change into and the family would like to see you after you're dressed. They're having breakfast."

"I'd like to see Ares first," Nash said, climbing the stairs up to meet her.

"Isn't it cute how you think you have a choice? It's an order. They want to see you immediately after you change," Veronica smiled while handing him the clothes.

Nash gave her an icy stare, but Veronica only winked at him before spinning on her stilettos and heading back into the house. Nash let out an annoyed breath and hurried inside.

Nash changed and walked with determined strides to the family dining room. They had a formal dining room for large functions, but when it was just the family they ate in a small, cozy room beside the kitchen.

He could hear the voices from the hallway. Nash pushed through the door and saw the Ali Rahman family sitting at their round table. Dani and Mo, Mila and Zain, and Gabe and Ariana all turned smiling faces to him.

"Nash!" Ariana cried out. She bounded from her seat and hurried around the table to wrap her arms around him. Her dark brown hair matched her dark brown eyes. She was only twenty-three but had maturity well beyond her years—a bit of mischief, too. Ariana was polite, quiet, and sweet. What that all told Nash was she was good at being sneaky. As a young girl, she could sneak in and out of rooms completely undetected.

Nash took the hug and pursed his lips to prevent a groan of pain from escaping. "Good morning, Ari," Nash told the young woman who had been like a little sister to him as she grew up.

"I was so worried!" Ariana rushed to talk as she grabbed his hand and pulled him to an empty seat at the table.

Nash turned to Mo. "You wanted to see me before I went to Ares?"

Mo nodded. "Ahmed found the computer Sophie hid and will turn it over to Kale as soon as he gets here, which should be around lunchtime."

"Good. Sophie said Ares kept information on all of his activities, crimes, and soldiers on there. If Kale can crack it, we can take down the entire operation," Nash said.

"I've talked to my brother." Mo put down his napkin and turned to face Nash, who didn't move. He stood at attention and awaited his judgment. He had disobeyed an order from his king and had refused to return to Rahmi in order to save Sophie. If that meant he could never return to Rahmi, then so be it.

"He wasn't pleased that you refused your order to return to Rahmi. However, after I told him the circumstances and promised you would escort Ares to Rahmi and hand him over to the king along with whatever information we find on the computer, he agreed you should not be punished. He was pleased that Rahmi would get credit for taking down the entire Red Shadow and Ares operations."

Nash took a deep breath. Relief washed through him until he thought of one more thing. "And after I hand over Ares . . . will I be stationed in Rahmi?"

Mo didn't answer.

"Nash," Dani said, drawing his attention away from her husband. "How's Sophie?"

"She's sleeping. She looks a little rough, but she'll recover soon enough. She's the bravest, strongest person I know," Nash said with pride.

Dani smiled at him as she reached to hold Mo's hand. "I hate to sound like our parents nosing around in our children's love life."

Zain, Gabe, and Ariana didn't bother hiding their disbelief. Dani and the rest of her friends loved to meddle.

"As I was saying," Dani said, ignoring her snickering children, "I think of you as a member of our family, and I want to see you happy. And I know Nabi and Grace feel the same. Have you found happiness, Nash? And more importantly, have you found love?"

"Yes, ma'am. I've found both and so much more with Sophie. If only she'll have me this time," Nash confessed.

Mo's serious look of worry disappeared and was replaced with a cautious smile. "Then your orders have changed. I told the king of Sophie and how she caught Ares after being abducted and how you rescued her, thus securing Ares. I also took a chance and told the king of your feelings for Sophie. If you are in love with her, he requests her presence as well and will present you with your next orders upon your return to Rahmi."

"Did he say what my orders were?" Nash asked.

"No. But I got the impression he was touched by your story. He knows my desire to have you returned to Keeneston and will weigh it along with your request to stay, what you've done for the crown, as well as the country's needs. I am hopeful the outcome will be beneficial for everyone since he didn't immediately order you back into service," Mo told him.

"I'll go with you," Zain announced.

"Me too," Mila smiled encouragingly.

"I'm not staying behind, even if it means getting a lecture from the king about not being married yet," Gabe said with a roll of his eyes.

"Ugh, me too. But it'll be worth it." Ariana sent Nash a smile.

"Excuse me?" Dani cut in. "What about you not being married?" she asked her daughter.

"In Uncle Dirar's words, 'Your eggs are dying every day you aren't married. How can we secure the line if no one is having babies?'" Arian mocked in her best impression of the king.

Nash took a deep breath to prevent laughing.

"No. No way. You're my baby girl. No man is good enough for you," Mo declared, slamming his napkin on the table.

"Didn't you just tell me I needed to secure the line?" Zain asked with a grin on his face.

"You—you're different. You're in your thirties and already married," Mo huffed as Mila buried her head in her hands.

"They're your parents. You deal with them," Mila whispered to Zain.

"And you," Dani said, pointing to Gabe. "If anyone needs to quit dawdling and get married, it's you. But no, you have to go sow your royal oats all over the freaking world. Can you stay off magazine covers long enough to find a nice girl? Definitely not the one you brought to that ball in Peru. What were you thinking with her?"

Nash looked around and found no one was looking at him anymore. Slowly he took a step back as Gabe defended his choice of revolving women. Nash quietly slipped through the door and the kitchen to the security center. Questioning Ares would be a snap compared to what Zain and Gabe were going through in the dining room.

Chapter Thirty

Nash was buzzed into the security building and found Nabi waiting for him outside the holding area. "How's Ares?"

"Defiant," Nabi said with a shrug.

"That's expected. I heard Kale was coming in this morning."

"That's right," Ahmed said, walking toward them. "So I'd appreciate it if you wrapped this up before I leave for the airport."

"Fine by me." Nash smirked.

"Ares is in room three," Nabi said as he and Ahmed headed into the viewing room to watch.

Nash walked down the hall. One of the guards stationed outside the room opened the door for him. Ares was chained to a metal table that was bolted to the floor. His feet were chained as well and anchored to the floor.

It still blew Nash's mind that the worst of the worst criminals didn't look anything like expected. Ares looked like someone you'd sit and have a beer with, not someone who had committed numerous unspeakable crimes.

"Hello, Poe. Let's talk," Nash said, walking into the room and taking a seat across from the man who had hurt Sophie. Nash would soon discover his real name and it would only be a matter of time until Kale unlocked all of the secrets he kept on his laptop. For all intents and purposes, Ares no longer existed.

Sophie woke up to the sounds of chatter from downstairs. She vaguely remembered Nash bringing her to the bed and breakfast. By the bright light streaming into the room, she'd slept the entire morning away.

She rolled to reach for Nash, hoping he'd been able to sleep as well only to find a note on the pillow instead of the man she loved. She read the quick note saying he was questioning Ares and then bringing back her clothes. Sophie decided to take a shower.

She turned on the hot water and turned to face the mirror. Looking up, she didn't recognize the person looking back. Her face was colorful, to say the least. It was swollen as well, making her look somewhere between an over-injected Nikki and a deranged raccoon. With a sigh of acceptance, she turned the hot water to cold to help with the swelling.

It didn't take long to wash her body and hair as she stood shivering. The second she was done, Sophie hopped out, wrapped herself in the fluffy towels to dry off, and buried herself under the warm covers of her bed. She used pillows to keep her head propped up and quickly fell back to sleep.

Sophie didn't know how long she had fallen asleep or if she really had. Time was something she wasn't able to track in her sleep-induced state. But she realized what had woken her—someone had come into the room. She opened her eyes and found Nash tiptoeing around the room.

"Hey," she said, smiling as he turned quickly in surprise.

"Hi. Sorry, I didn't mean to wake you. I went to your house and grabbed everything I could think of in terms of toiletries, clothing, and shoes," Nash told her as he came over to the bed with a bag of ice in hand. "For your face."

"How did it go with Ares?"

"As well as it can be expected. I'll know more after Kale finishes working on the laptop. I also heard from King Dirar."

Sophie pushed the ice off her eyes so she could see Nash. He looked nervous and that meant he'd been ordered back to Rahmi. "And?"

"He wants me to bring Ares and all the prisoners we are holding for trial. He also wants me to lead the takedown of any and all associates with an international team," Nash said taking a deep breath.

"So, you're headed back to Rahmi," Sophie tried to say cheerfully. She had things she needed to wrap up here while he ran the cleanup operation, and then she could head over to meet him.

"We're headed to Rahmi," Nash corrected. "The king has requested you come with me. I think he wants to thank you for your assistance. When we get there, he'll give me my final orders. I don't know what they are, but Mo said he's been lobbying for me to return to Keeneston."

"No matter what your orders are, I'll be with you," Sophie said, covering his hand with hers.

"You mean that?" Nash asked, looking deep into her eyes as if searching for the truth.

"Now that I've told you I love you, there's no getting rid of me." Sophie laughed. "You're worth fighting for, too, Nash."

Nash leaned forward as she dropped the bag of ice. With such gentleness, his lips met hers. "Sophie," Nash said as his hands ran down her arms, "I—"

Sophie almost cursed at the knock on the door. "Good afternoon!" Poppy called through the door.

Nash let out a sigh and smiled down at her. "I'll see what she wants."

Sophie put the ice back on her face and watched with one eye as Nash let Poppy in. "I brought some food. I went with things easy to eat just in case your face is hurting." Poppy smiled as she walked toward the bed, her eyes taking in the fact that Sophie was only covered by the sheets she was holding to her chest.

Sophie scooted up to sitting and Poppy put the

tray on her lap. "Thank you, Poppy. That's so nice of you."

"Of course. I also wanted to let you know that the town has already started work downtown if you want to join us. Oh, and Sienna wants her car back."

"Just for fun, can you tell her I wrecked it?" Nash chuckled as he pulled the keys from his jeans pocket.

"No way I'm pissing her off. She's armed with a hammer," Poppy teased. Sienna could get into a temper every now and then.

"We have to help with the cleanup," Sophie said before taking a sip of the iced coffee.

"Of course," Nash agreed. "We'll be down as soon as we eat."

"See you there," Poppy sang as she hurried out.

"She's probably rushing to tell everyone that I'm naked in bed while you're in the room. They'll be counting down the days to find out if we're engaged." Sophie laughed. Although when she looked up at Nash, her laughter died. He looked irritated.

"Sophie, I've been trying to tell you—" Nash cursed as there was another knock on the door.

"Is everything okay in there?" a voice asked.

Sophie looked in fear to Nash. "That's my mom," she whispered.

"So?"

"So?" Sophie panicked. "So, I'm naked!"

Nash pulled a sweater from the drawer and a pair of black yoga pants and hurried to Sophie as she put the tray beside her on the bed.

"Sophie?"

"That's my dad," Sophie cried in a hushed whisper as she frantically grabbed for the clothes. "Be right there!"

Sophie fumbled with the sweater as Nash started to put her legs in the pants. "You know this is ridiculous, right?" Nash asked as he pulled up her pants since Sophie had apparently forgotten how to dress herself. Right now she couldn't find the opening for her head to go through as the sweater trapped her.

She heard Nash sigh as he righted her sweater and pulled it over her head. "Thanks," she said sheepishly.

"I must admit I prefer to undress you than dress you," Nash whispered a second before opening the door. "Hello, Mr. and Mrs. Davies," he said, smiling.

Nash and Matt worked quietly, removing pieces of one of the shattered windows from the Blossom Café. Cy and his brother, Miles, worked on the other window. Marshall and Pierce were picking up two new windows and a new door. Gemma, Tammy, Katelyn, and Morgan worked at sweeping up inside the café while their children, Layne, Piper, Jace, Cassidy, and the rest of the Davies cousins swept the street or repaired bullet holes with the rest of the town.

Gone was the darkness of the night. Gone were

the rain and the fears. Today was a new day full of sunshine and promise. The cars had been moved to the courthouse parking lot so every inch of the ambush area could be cleaned. The Rose sisters had dusted off bistro tables and were issuing orders as if they were generals. No one minded, though. The look on their wrinkled faces as they saw the café in the light of day for the first time had everyone hurrying to bring it back to life.

"We survived another gunfight," Miss Lily said, putting on a strong face as Nash and Matt pried the entire window casing out and threw it in the dumpster.

"Another?" Talon Bainbridge asked while he and Lucas removed all the guns from Pam's minivan. They tagged each one as evidence and placed it in the FBI vehicle Ryan had brought. Ryan photographed each gun along with its tag number to be used as evidence against all the men currently in federal custody from the previous night.

"I daresay we've had a hand in taking down more bad guys than you have." Miss Daisy smiled sweetly and Nash snickered as he and Matt looked at each other.

"Oh, don't look so downtrodden. You're a very brave young man. Come here and give an old woman a hug," Miss Violet cooed as Bainbridge's head suddenly disappeared into Miss Violet's bosom.

"Vi!"

"Uh-oh, don't tell my husband." Miss Violet

winked as Bainbridge gasped for air. "Anton, my love!" Miss Violet turned to smile at her husband.

Nash felt at peace as the town talked and teased around him. His heart was another matter, though. He had been interrupted each time he'd tried to tell Sophie he loved her. He was determined to make that moment very special.

"Men with tools are definitely sexy," he heard Sophie whisper in his ear from behind him.

"I'll remember that." Nash winked. "Sophie, about Rahmi—"

Sophie shook her head as Nash turned to face her. "I told you, I don't care as long as we're together."

"Oh dear, are you two fighting?" Miss Lily asked.

Sophie shook her head. "No, I'm just telling Nash that nothing else matters but us. I don't care where we live. I don't care if y'all place bets on if we get married or if we're the panty droppers or anything else you can think of because I love him."

Nash bent his head and thoroughly kissed her for the entire town to see. "Sophie, I lo—"

"Well, then, if you're not fighting, get back to work," Cade ordered as Annie smacked his arm.

Nash let out a frustrated breath, but his frustration was forgotten when Sophie rose up and whispered in his ear to bring the tool belt home that night.

Chapter Thirty-One

*T*he Panty Dropper Strikes Again.

Sophie tossed the newspaper onto her kitchen table as Nash poured them both a cup of coffee.

"I can't believe people found a pair of panties halfway under the couch when they came to clean up the broken glass at my house," Sophie groaned.

"You did tell everyone that you didn't care if they thought you were the panty dropper," Nash chuckled.

"I guess I am a panty dropper of sorts," Sophie agreed. "With you now living with me, I wonder why I even wear them."

Sophie enjoyed the arrogant smile Nash gave her along with her coffee. "However, I am not *the* panty dropper."

"As long as you're mine, that's all that matters," Nash said, leaning over the island to kiss her.

"What's that?" Sophie asked at the sound of a large engine coming up the drive to her house.

"A present before we head off to Rahmi. It's been a long week since Ares was captured and most of it was spent going through a massive amount of data Kale got off the computer. So, I got you something to say thanks for putting up with my long nights," Nash said, moving to open the door.

"I'm pretty sure you thank me every night when you get home." Sophie smiled with satisfaction. She had enjoyed the week immensely. Sam had taken care of the missile. She would wrap up the sale of her gun with Mr. Storme after she got back from Rahmi. And then she and Nash would finally have time to spend alone. If she thought she had been in love with him two years before, she had been wrong. It was so much more than love now. It was love, friendship, mutual respect, and admiration. Nothing she thought about when she was younger. Now she was content with change, not fearful of it. She knew no matter what, they'd handle it together. She understood what her mother meant by saying she and her father were a great team.

"Close your eyes," Nash told her as he opened the door. "And don't open them until I tell you."

Sophie heard footsteps coming into the house. A couple of grunts, shuffling steps outside, and then they returned.

"Okay, you can open your eyes now," Nash said after the door closed.

Sophie opened her eyes and broke out laughing. Sitting in her living room was a brand new couch with a big red bow on it. "How did you know?"

"I noticed that you suddenly didn't sit on your couch anymore. So from now on, the only people having sex on our couch is us," Nash said with his voice dropping in such a way that had her rethinking the need for panties all together.

"It's perfect," Sophie said as she flung herself onto the new couch. The couch was long enough to stretch out on and deep enough that she didn't feel as if she were going to roll off. "Now get over here and kiss me. We have a couch we need to break in."

Nash shed his shirt. The deep purple bruises from the gunshots were still there, but healing. Sophie ran her hand over his chest and down to his pants. Maybe he wasn't the only one who should have the no-panty rule. But when Sophie unbuttoned his jeans and helped push them down, she realized he already followed that rule.

And as he placed gentle kisses on her neck, Sophie sighed with pleasure and passion. It didn't take fancy words or sonnets to tell of love. Nash showed it every day. He gave her the freedom she needed to be her own person and the support she needed to become a better person. He helped her up, lifted her, and held her close as only someone who truly loved her could.

Sophie leaned forward as Nash peeled her oversized sweater from her body, and she wiggled out of her leggings. They'd leave the next day for Rahmi to find what their future held. But as Nash kissed his way down her neck toward her breasts, she didn't waste time worrying about the what-ifs. And as his lips closed around her nipple and his hand dipped between her legs, she decided only the here and now was what was important. And the *here and now* was currently making love very thoroughly to her.

Nash waited with Sophie's hand on his arm for the large doors to the throne room to open. Zain, Mila, Gabe, Ariana, Dani, and Mo were already inside along with the rest of the royal family and all the Rahmi diplomats and advisors.

"Don't worry." Sophie smiled up at him. She was dressed in an elegant emerald green suit. Her strawberry-blonde hair, having turned more strawberry than blonde during the fall, framed her face, drawing attention to her perfectly plump nude lips. "We'll handle this together."

Nash covered her hand with his as the door opened. It was a long walk across the marble floor to where the king sat on his throne. They passed people they had never seen before until they finally reached the front. The Keeneston royals smiled at them as Nash and Sophie walked a few steps past them and came to a stop in front of the dais.

Nash bowed his head in respect as Sophie followed suit. King Dirar sat in the elaborately carved chair while Prince Jamal, his son and heir, stood next to him.

"Nash Dagher, I am thankful for your delivery of the man known as Ares and some of his soldiers," King Dirar said with plenty of pomp. "Tell us what you have learned while he was in your custody."

Nash had turned over all the evidence he'd collected, but he didn't expect the king to have read it already. Some assistant was probably doing that right this second.

"I learned that the man who went by the name of Ares was born Richard Dumney in Boston, Massachusetts. He is forty-six years of age and was a former accountant who joined Red Shadow after feeling bullied at the workplace. His first crime was embezzling from his clients. He left the firm after siphoning off millions and giving a good part of it to Red Shadow. After a year, he had become Poseidon's mentee.

"When he was captured, thanks to Miss Davies's grit and quick acting, he was in possession of a laptop. With the help of Kale Mueez, we were able to gain access to the laptop and now have a complete and detailed list of every member of his organization along with all assets, property, and victims. I believe that with help from numerous countries, I will be able to free any prisoners and close the operation within a week." Nash finished and felt Sophie gently squeeze his forearm in support.

The king was silent for a moment, looking between Nash and Sophie. "And what is your desire to serve Rahmi after you close down this operation?"

"I serve at your majesty's desire," Nash said humbly. And he did. He had thought about leaving the guards if he were ordered to stay in Rahmi. But after talking to Sophie, they had decided against it. Serving Rahmi was important to him, and Sophie wanted to support that.

"I had heard that you and Miss Davies were planning a future together," King Dirar said as he stroked his chin in thought. "Miss Davies, I must thank your family once again for coming to the aid of Rahmi. You cousin, Dr. Piper Davies, has been of great value to our small country, and I've read reports of other members of your family coming to the aid of my nephew, Prince Zain."

Sophie smiled softly at the king. "It's our pleasure. We think very highly of the Ali Rahman family. They're our friends, and we will do anything to help our friends."

"And you went and fell in love with a Rahmi citizen, didn't you?"

Nash saw Sophie blink in surprise at the king's bluntness. "Well, yes, I have." Sophie looked at Nash. When she smiled, he felt a warmth come over him. He was so lucky to have her by his side.

"Nash Dagher, I have settled on your orders. You are invaluable to the crown. You have served me well and will continue to do so from Keeneston."

Nash stood a little straighter as Sophie gripped his arm.

"You will complete the dismantling of Ares's criminal organization. Upon your return to Keeneston you will report directly to Prince Zain as his personal security advisor. Further, you will return to Rahmi twice a year for briefings and training. You will teach a winter and summer three-week class at the military academy. Meanwhile, Miss Davies, I have heard you are something of a scientist. You will have unlimited access to Rahmi International Laboratories should you decide to accompany Nash on his trips home."

Nash was filled with pride and gratitude. His king had promoted him to colonel with orders he'd happily accept. There was only one piece missing in his life now. Nash looked to where Sophie gave a polite and respectful nod to the king.

"I look forward to spending time here in the beautiful country of Rahmi."

"Now, Nash Dagher, come forward," the king said as he stood. An assistant hurried forward carrying a small box. Inside was the Medal of the Black Oryx, signifying his new rank.

Nash stepped forward and King Dirar pulled the pin from the box. "Congratulations. You have served Rahmi with honor," the king announced as he pinned the medal to his chest.

Nash bowed his head. "Thank you."

As the ceremony ended, music, food, and drink were brought out. The somber event turned lively. With Sophie in his arms, they danced into the night. However, come morning, he would have to leave her once more.

Sophie rolled paint on the wall of the café. Three days. She hadn't heard from Nash in three days.

Their last night in Rahmi had been magical — the palm trees, the stars, the dancing. There had never been a more romantic moment than when Nash escorted her from the party and out onto the beach. She could still hear the strains of music as he held her close and they danced on the sand.

It seemed as if it were a lifetime ago. Now he was somewhere in the world taking down criminals who would be only too happy to kill the man she loved.

"Did Nash tell you he's the first investor in my company for bulletproof clothes?" Piper asked, drawing Sophie from her thoughts.

"No, he didn't. I thought I was the first investor," Sophie joked.

"He beat you by two hours. Speaking of Nash, have you had any word from him?" Piper asked as she picked up a paintbrush and began to paint the trim of the new window.

"Not yet," Sophie sighed.

"It's hard, isn't it?" Layne commiserated. "Lots of the veterans I see for physical therapy say leaving your loved one is the hardest part of being in the military."

"Strange how as soon as Nash left there's been no more panty dropping," Reagan ribbed as she handed another can of pale yellow paint to the people outside. A new purple door was being attached in front of the Blossom Café while other people painted the walls pale yellow with ivory trim.

"Nash has caused my panties to drop numerous times, but I am not the public panty dropper," Sophie protested.

"Riiiiight," Riley teased as the women dissolved into laughter.

Nash was so close to going home he could smell it. He was in Prague. It was his last raid before he could return to Keeneston and to Sophie. For seven days, he'd conducted raids and worked with elite soldiers from foreign governments across the globe. The American D-Troop, along with a troop from Canada, helped on the western front as they worked eastward. Nash had started in Taiwan and worked westward. Today, he and the Americans were meeting up for this final takedown.

Nash sat in the Rahmi embassy looking over satellite photos when he heard boot steps coming toward him from the hall. The Americans had arrived. Nash stood with his team as the door opened.

Not many things took Nash by surprise, but seeing Cade Davies walk in followed by Miles, Marshall, and Cy was a complete shock.

"No Pierce?" Nash finally asked after the shock wore off.

"He's by the pool, taking pictures to make it look like we went on a brothers' trip," Miles responded.

"Before we let you in on the family secret, I'm

guessing you want to talk to me, right?" Cade asked.

"Um, sure," Nash said, pulling up a map. "I can show you where the point of entry should be."

The brothers snickered as Cade shook his head. "No, I mean, isn't there something you want to ask me?" Cade pulled out a knife and slid the flat side of the blade against his hand and smiled.

"Where did you get the knife?" Nash asked, feeling very unsure of what Cade wanted.

Cy had to turn around and Nash saw his shoulders shaking as he smothered his laughter. Marshall lost his battle and broke out laughing as Cade threw his hands up in the air. "Come on! Cy and Marshall got to do it, and Sophie's the only chance I have to do it. I've been planning it since she was born."

"Wait a second," Nash said as realization dawned. "You want me to ask for your permission to marry Sophie while we're planning a military operation of which you shouldn't be a part of since your wives think you're at some resort?"

"Yeah," Cade nodded. "You were going to propose, right? Mo told me he saw you shopping for a ring in Rahmi."

"I'm going to when I get back to Keeneston, but I want to make sure I'll still be alive first," Nash answered as he heard his men snickering along with Cade's brothers.

"Well, you're alive now," Cade said smugly as he crossed his arms over his chest and stared Nash down.

"Okay," Nash took a deep breath. "Mr. Davies, I'd like your permission to marry your daughter."

Cade pulled the knife out again and pointed it at Nash. "No. Sophie is her own woman and doesn't need my permission."

Nash must have looked confused because Miles was gripping Marshall's shoulder as he tried to contain his laughter.

"I will say, I think you're the one man good enough for my daughter," Cade said before moving so quickly it caught Nash off guard, as the blade of his knife pressed against his throat. "But if you hurt her, I will bring down a rain of pain unlike anything you've ever imagined. Got it?"

"Yes, sir," Nash said.

"Rain of pain? Oh my God, I'm dying," Miles finally broke as he slapped his thigh and laughed harder than Nash had ever seen.

Cade spun on him. "Thanks a lot. I worked hard on that. See if I help you when Layne gets married."

"I don't need to worry about that. She's never getting married," Miles said, causing everyone in the room to laugh in disbelief.

"Well, now that we got that straightened out, should we fill my future son-in-law in on our brother getaways?" Cade asked, bringing them back to the task at hand.

"Yeah, go ahead," Cy told him.

"See, we still do favors for the government—just one or two a year to keep fresh. Now you're part of it, and being part of it means you can't tell our wives. That includes your future one. Deal?"

Nash held out his hand. "Deal."

"Welcome to the family. Now, let's take out some bad guys." Cade and his brother moved to the table and the last takedown was underway.

Annie shoved her boot against the man's neck. "Move and she shoots you," Annie said, drawing the man's attention to Bridget standing with her gun pointed at him.

"Did you get it?" Annie asked.

"Yup," Bridget said as Robyn barked happily at the wall at the far end of the room.

"Make sure before we call it in," Annie said.

Bridget moved to the wall and easily put a foot through the drywall. She ripped away some of it and looked in. "Got it." Bridget pulled out her phone and sent a text. A couple minutes later, DEA agents swarmed the room as the men Annie and Bridget had taken down on their way to the heroin-filled stash room were taken away in cuffs.

Annie reached up and pulled off her wig. "So, Nabi and Ahmed are on another guys' trip?"

"Sure are. It's why I could join you. Where are the brothers this time?" Bridget asked as she pulled off the black wig and fake nose.

"I don't know. Sometimes they're hiking. Sometimes they're sailing. I think this time Cade said they were just going to relax at some resort and go golfing," Annie shrugged.

"I wonder if they know what we do on our girls' weekends?" Bridget chuckled.

"They have no idea," Annie laughed as she and Bridget accepted their congratulations for yet another drug bust.

Chapter Thirty-Two

N ash spent the entire flight home on the phone.
Sophie didn't know he was coming back. Since
he had Cade's blessing, he was going ahead with his
plans. The ring was in his pocket. He just needed to
get in touch with Mo and Dani.

"What's your plan?" Cade asked, taking a seat
next to him on the private jet Mo let them borrow.

"Yeah, you only get one shot at this. You have to
make it really romantic," Marshall said, moving to
the small table.

"Then you should listen to me. I rode down
Main Street on a horse," Cy joined in.

"Give it a rest," Miles smacked his brother as he
took a seat. "Now painting a water tower . . ."

"Yeah, vandalism is so romantic," Pierce shook
his head, "But proposing after helping to save
Tammy's life from a bomb. That was unforgettable."

"I think it's romantic if you ask her when no one
is around, because then you can celebrate it
immediately afterward," Marshall grinned.

Cade shook his head. "So, public proposal it is."

"Thanks for all of the advice," Nash told them.

"However, I have the perfect plan."

Nash leaned forward and laid it out just the way he laid out the military takedown of the last of Ares's men.

"Oh, that's good," Cy admitted as his brothers all nodded.

"Now I really approve of you and not just because Annie told me to," Cade smiled.

"Where is Annie?" Marshall asked.

Cade shrugged. "Girls' weekend at some spa or something. She'll be back today. Right in time for the proposal."

Nash picked up his phone and got to planning.

"Sydney, you know how I hate being a mannequin for you," Sophie complained as she stepped into a beautiful cocktail dress of Sydney's creation.

"It's perfect!" Syd clapped.

"For what?"

"There's this photographer in the ballroom at Desert Sun Farm who is shooting my new line. Can you wear this over for me?" Sydney asked, putting on her puppy dog face.

"I'm not a model," Sophie protested.

"Your face won't be in it. He may not even want to use the dress. But this dress looks better on a person than on a mannequin. Pleeeeease? I'll be over as soon as I alter this skirt."

Sophie rolled her eyes. "Fine, but only because I love you."

Syd squealed and gave Sophie a quick peck on
the cheek. Sophie left Sydney's house and was at
Desert Sun Farm within a few minutes. She got out
of her car and straightened the dress. It really was
quite beautiful. A mixture of greens and browns that
made her hazel eyes shine like the sequins on the
dress.

Sophie knocked and the door opened. "The
ballroom, miss," the Ali Rahman's butler said,
pointing up the stairs. She knew the way.

The photographer had music playing. Sophie
listened and was sure she heard violins. The doors
to the ballroom were closed, and with an annoyed
yank, she opened them and walked in, determined
to be done with it. The man listening to a string
quartet playing stood with his back to her, but even
encased in a suit and from behind she knew who it
was. "Nash!"

Nash turned and smiled at her as she ran to him
as fast as her high heels could carry her. "When did
you get back? What are you doing here?"

"I'm here to ask you to dance." Nash held out
his hand and Sophie placed hers in it a second
before he was twirling her around the dance floor.

"Do you know," Nash asked, holding her tight
against him as the song slowed, "that the first time I
saw you was in this room?"

"I do. I remember you smiled at me," Sophie
said, recalling the day clearly.

"And you smiled back." Nash twirled her and
then pulled her tight against him and stopped

moving all together. He looked into her face and Sophie's breath caught. "And it was worth every second of waiting to have you back in my arms."

Nash reached up to cup her face and Sophie turned her head, placing a kiss on the palm of his hand. "I love you, Nash," Sophie said softly before looking at him. This time she was going to lay her heart bare. "You, Nash Dagher, are the most loyal, kind, and brave man I know. You make me laugh, you make me feel safe, and you make me feel loved. With you, I'm a better me."

Nash lowered his lips to hers and kissed her as the strands of violin music floated around them. "I love you, too."

Sophie sighed when she heard the words she already knew as truth.

"I wanted to make sure I could give you forever because forever is what I want with you," Nash said as he went down on one knee. "Sophie Davies, you're my heart and soul, will you marry me?"

"Yes! Of course! I love you, Nash!" Sophie cried as she held a shaky finger out to receive his diamond ring.

The emotions running through Nash were the same ones he felt going into a gunfight, maybe more so because he didn't remember being so nervous when holding a gun compared to the dainty ring he had in his hand.

Taking a deep breath to steady himself, he slid the ring onto Sophie's finger. It wasn't just a ring, it was the promise and hope of their happily-ever-after. Once the ring was in place, Nash placed a kiss on her hand before standing up to kiss his fiancée for the first time. And did he kiss her. This was a new beginning for forever and he wanted to make it memorable.

Sophie sighed against his lips as she threaded her fingers around the back of his neck and met his tongue with hers. Nash moved his hand to hers and the other around her waist. When they finally broke their kiss, Nash held her tight as he swept her away in a dance of their life.

Nash heard them before the doors opened some time later. He and Sophie had spent the last half-hour alternating between kissing and dancing. "Get ready."

"For what?" Sophie asked dreamily as she danced with her head against his shoulder.

"For everyone. Your father, your mother, your parents, Sydney for helping me and who I'm sure told Deacon, who told Ryan, who told Sienna, who told—"

Sophie laughed, cutting him off. "I get the picture. Until tonight when we can properly celebrate." Sophie winked before turning to squeal as their friends and family burst through the door.

The musicians played on as well wishes, friendship, and love enveloped them all. That was until Nash's future father-in-law cornered him. "I'm still mad at you," Cade muttered. "You didn't even quiver when I threatened you. Cy and Marshall have all the fun."

Nash smiled and shook his head. "Would you prefer to have a son-in-law looking after your daughter to fall apart with fear with just a threat or two?"

Cade perked up. "I hadn't thought of it like that before. You're right. Annie! Our son-in-law is braver than my brothers!" Cade called, slapping Nash on the back as he hurried to talk to his wife.

"My father threatened you?" Sophie asked from behind him. When Nash turned, he saw her arms crossed over her chest.

"Yes, but not very well. I'll make sure I work on it so when our daughter gets married I make sure the man pisses himself," Nash said with pride.

"What makes you think we'll even have a daughter, and if we do, that you won't be wrapped around her little finger?"

Nash slid his arm around his future wife and looked at her, imagining their baby girl. "Oh, it's just a feeling. And I know she'll have me wrapped around her finger. Her boyfriends will not, though. I need to ask your dad about security cameras for the nursery. I have this great thing I can attach to the window. If anyone tries to open it from the outside, it'll electrocute them." Nash bent down and kissed his future wife.

Sophie just shook her head. "I love you, but let's try to get through the wedding before we start booby-trapping the house for some future daughter's future teenage boyfriends. Instead, why don't you dance with me?" Sophie took his hand and he lifted hers to his lips.

"Always," he swore before spinning her onto the dance floor.

Epilogue

This time Nash didn't punch Father Ben when he held Sophie's hand. Instead, Nash turned to face his bride. Her long veil flowed down her back and fanned out along the floor. The dress hugged her body down to her knees, then gently flared. She was stunning and Nash didn't know if he deserved her. But he was going to prove that he did by loving her every day of the rest of his life.

Father Ben placed Sophie's hand in Nash's as they turned to look at each other. She smiled and his world was complete.

"You may now kiss the bride," Father Ben said happily.

As Nash sealed his vow to love and protect his wife with a kiss, the whole congregation cheered.

"I am happy to present to you, Nash and Sophie Dagher," Father Ben called out over the clapping and happy sniffles.

The warm early summer night breeze blew in through the open ballroom doors at Mo and Dani's.

The ballroom was filled with brilliant flowers and colorful gowns. Sophie danced in her husband's arms. The wedding had been beautiful. She almost started crying when the doors opened and she saw her husband waiting for her at the altar. Nash had stood tall and proud, looking sinfully handsome in his tuxedo, waiting for her. He had smiled and she had almost burst into happy tears. She didn't know how she'd gotten so lucky. Everything about that night had been magical and they hadn't even had their wedding night yet.

"What are you thinking about?" Nash asked with a glint in his eyes that told her he knew exactly what she was thinking about. Sophie rose up on her toes and whispered exactly what she was thinking into his ear and felt his silent response with the rapidly growing erection pressing against her as they danced.

"Why, Mrs. Dagher, I'm shocked." Nash grinned before kissing her. "And something I'll be happy to partake in."

Sophie tossed her head back and laughed as they danced off into the night.

Annie watched her daughter laughing and raised her champagne glass to her friends. "We did it," Annie toasted. "Another one married. And by the way they are looking at each other, I'll have a grandbaby before all y'all!"

Kenna shook her head. "First, my daughter has been married the longest. It's only natural that

Sienna and Ryan will announce any day that they're pregnant."

"I completely agree," Paige said, tapping her glass to Kenna's.

"Zain and Mila will be first," Dani said confidently. "For once I didn't have to hint at it. The king was rather insistent."

"Yeah, because having a king tell you to have a baby really sets the mood," Katelyn scoffed. "Nope, I'll be the first grandmother. Sydney has that look in her eye. She and Deacon can't keep their hands off each other."

"At least we can toast to another happy marriage for our children," Gemma told the group as they all raised their glasses and silently saluted Nash and Sophie. "Even if I'm going to be the first grandmother."

Dani shook her head as she pulled out the old notebook handed down to her by the Rose sisters. "And we have another name for the book," she said, writing down Nash's and Sophie's names. "Years in the making!"

"I thought you were supposed to help set them up, not just take credit for it and write their names down later," Morgan said, ribbing the group.

"Any marriage is a win," Kenna defended.

"Who's next?" Tammy asked. "Piper needs to get out of the lab and meet someone."

"Layne needs to meet someone, too. I just need to send Miles away on an extended *guys'* trip," Morgan said with a roll of her eyes. "He always gets in the way of Layne's love life."

"I could use another girls' weekend," Bridget sighed. "And as much as I would love to see Abby settled down, she's still making her way in the world. I could talk to my dad and see if we can arrange an extended guys' trip for our husbands."

Annie chuckled. "Do you think they have any idea we know what they do when they leave?"

Tammy giggled. "No way. Pierce always sends the worst mocked-up photos."

"Just let them have it," Katelyn said. "How they thought we wouldn't know is a mystery."

"A wife always knows," Morgan said as everyone nodded.

"And I kind of enjoy the cover stories they come up with — like the resort one when they were helping Nash. Tammy, you're right. The pictures Pierce came up with were priceless."

"Well, what this wife knows is that my husband will lose it if Gabe doesn't settle down," Dani sighed. "If he's on the front of one more gossip magazine with some bimbo on his arm, I'm afraid Mo is going to kill him. The headline last week was *Playboy Prince* with a picture of Gabe at some wild party with barely dressed women all around him."

"Hmm," Paige muttered, taking the book from Dani and writing down Gabe's name. "I think Dani might have a point. While we plot an extended trip for Miles and figure out a way to get Piper out of the lab more, we'll find the perfect girl for Gabe."

"To Gabe," they toasted.

Sienna, Sydney, Mila, and Riley had absconded with
Sophie to a table in the back of the room for a
celebratory toast. Sophie kicked off her shoes under
the table as everyone set their small purses on the
table.

"We certainly didn't think you'd be the next to
join our little group of newlyweds," Sienna teased.

"But we're so happy you were," Sydney smiled.

"Welcome to married life," Mila toasted.

"And we're here for you when you want to stab
your husband or shoot your parents," Riley added.

The women at the table laughed, and Sophie
enjoyed the break from circulating. When she
glanced around the dance floor, she was filled with
warmth at all the love she saw. Her parents had just
stepped onto the dance floor along with all her aunts
and uncles. The Rose sisters and their husbands
were swaying side to side near their table. Abby was
dancing with Nolan, her old boyfriend from high
school, along with all of Sophie's other cousins and
friends. And then there was one man in a polar bear
tie.

"Would you look at Lucas and Poppy?" Sophie
laughed.

"Bless his heart, that man can't dance," Sienna
said in amazement as Lucas busted a move.

"He sure commits, though," Mila added, trying
not to laugh.

"But look how happy Poppy is," Sydney
pointed out.

"And Zinnia. That man makes her look like a

tiny doll," Riley said.

"Talon Bainbridge," Sophie said fondly as she watched the large man move rather gracefully along the dance floor.

"It's nice that Jackson has been bringing them to Keeneston whenever he comes home," Mila said.

"It is. Lucas is from a tiny town in northern Alaska so it's hard for him to go home for short weekends off. And from what Jackson told me, Bainbridge doesn't have much family left and considers the FBI his family," Sophie told them.

"Ah, our break is over, ladies," Sydney sighed as she spotted their husbands heading their way.

"But what a sight." Mila sighed in a completely different way, and Sophie couldn't agree more.

As the women opened their purses and quickly reapplied their lipstick, Sophie watched the tuxedo-clad men head their way. They were lucky for sure, her most of all. Nash caught her eye and held it as he walked toward her. She felt like the most cherished woman in the world as her husband stopped before her and held out his hand.

"I believe this dance is mine," he said, his voice devastatingly sexy.

"Always."

Miss Lily and her sisters sent their husbands to fetch them a drink as they watched this new crop of husbands claim their wives. She ignored her spouse sneaking an extra piece of cake even though she knew it would delay her breaking him to find out how he knew so much. Lily wasn't too worried. This week John would discover that the muffins at the B&B were now off the table to him.

"Ah, I remember when it was Will, Mo, and Cole at that age with their new brides," Miss Lily told her sisters as they turned to watch the young men escort their wives to the dance floor.

"Face it, Lil, we're getting old," Daisy sighed.

"I say phooey to that," Violet said, pulling out a brochure from her purse. "We've been skydiving, now what do you think about bungee jumping? If we do it over the Kentucky River, we can touch the water with our fingertips."

"I thought about hang-gliding," Daisy suggested.

"Either way, we'll be strapped to sexy young men. I say it's a win-win," Violet laughed.

Lily chuckled and silently agreed. She looked at the newlyweds dancing and sent a wink to her husband waiting in line to bring her back a drink. She might not be young and she might not be agile, but she was loved.

Lily turned to take a seat when something on the floor caught her eye. "Oh, one of the girls dropped something," Lily said, walking over to the nearby table where Sophie, Mila, Sydney, Riley, and Sienna were sitting. She stooped down to pick it up and gasped.

"What is it, Lily?" Daisy asked as Lily turned wide-eyed at her approaching sisters.

"Are you having a heart attack?" Violet asked as

they came to her.

"No. A baby!" Lily exclaimed.

"Lily, do we need to explain the birds and bees to you?" Daisy asked. "Or are you having an aneurysm? At our age, anything can happen."

"Look!" Lily shoved the object she found on the floor at her sisters. "It's a positive pregnancy test."

The three sisters looked at each other and then at the dance floor as the couples danced.

"But who?" Violet asked what they were all wondering.

"Well, one thing is for sure — we will find out," Miss Lily vowed.

The End

Other Books by Kathleen Brooks

The Forever Bluegrass Series is off to a great start and will continue for many more books. I will start a new series later in 2016, so stay connected with me for more information. If you haven't signed up for new release notification, then now is the time to do it:

www.kathleen-brooks.com/new-release-notifications

If you are new to the writings of Kathleen Brooks, then you will want to try her Bluegrass Series set in the wonderful fictitious town of Keeneston, KY. Here is a list of links to the Bluegrass and Bluegrass Brothers books in order, as well as the separate New York Times Bestselling Women of Power series:

<u>Bluegrass Series</u>
Bluegrass State of Mind
Risky Shot
Dead Heat

Bluegrass Brothers Series
Bluegrass Undercover
Rising Storm
Secret Santa, A Bluegrass Novella
Acquiring Trouble
Relentless Pursuit
Secrets Collide
Final Vow

Bluegrass Singles
All Hung Up
Bluegrass Dawn
The Perfect Gift
The Keeneston Roses

Forever Bluegrass Series
Forever Entangled
Forever Hidden
Forever Betrayed
Forever Driven
Forever Secret

Web of Lies Series
Whispered Lies
Rogue Lies – coming mid-2017

Women of Power Series
Chosen for Power
Built for Power
Fashioned for Power
Destined for Power

About the Author

Kathleen Brooks is a New York Times, Wall Street Journal, and USA Today bestselling author. Kathleen's stories are romantic suspense featuring strong female heroines, humor, and happily-ever-afters. Her Bluegrass Series and follow-up Bluegrass Brothers Series feature small town charm with quirky characters that have captured the hearts of readers around the world.

Kathleen is an animal lover who supports rescue organizations and other non-profit organizations such as Friends and Vets Helping Pets whose goals are to protect and save our four-legged family members.

Email Notice of New Releases:
www.kathleen-brooks.com/new-release-notifications

Kathleen's Website:
www.kathleen-brooks.com

Facebook Page:
facebook.com/KathleenBrooksAuthor

Twitter:
twitter.com/BluegrassBrooks

Goodreads:
goodreads.com/author/show/5101707.Kathleen_Brooks

60134453R00222

Made in the USA
Lexington, KY
27 January 2017